CAROLINE HOGG

WEAVE YOUR MAGIC

The Molland Sisters series: Book 1

For Sarah Millar, whose friendship is pure magic.

Contents

About the author

Caroline Hogg is a writer of magical romcoms who lives in Buckinghamshire with her husband and two children. When she's not reading or writing (which is most of the time, as she also works as an editor) she loves to sew, knit and attempt to lift heavy-ish weights. *Weave Your Magic* is inspired by her love of fabric, South Devon and *Practical Magic*.

Note

I have not used generative AI technology at any stage of the writing process.
And I never will.

1

Chapter 1

Hiding her magic was tricky enough for Temperance Molland, without having to wake up every morning and see a great big hooked nose. Warts and all.

A crack of sunlight through her curtains and the creak from The Witch's Nose wooden sign woke Temperance at 7am on the dot every morning. Whoever painted that sign for the pub was not a feminist: you could practically see the cartoony crone from the beach.

If Temperance didn't already know that her family's powers were less about casting magic and more about receiving and interpreting it, she would think her mum had somehow charmed that sign to creak when it did.

Her own little oak alarm clock.

Living next to a pub meant sleep was hard to come by on big, boozy Saturday nights – the least the old girl could do was let Temperance have a lie-in.

Not that Temperance herself had been out on a massive bender night before. Or for quite a few months, when it came down to it. The kind of hangover she was suffering with this morning was more of an emotional one, caused by a very crappy evening with a very crappy date. There'd been so many flirty messages, so much potential . . . But now, only sour disappointment rolled around the lining of her stomach. Temperance put her pillow over her face and let out a rage-induced scream.

'Is that you up?' her younger sister called across the landing.

Susie nudged the bedroom door open with her bum, dislodging some flaky sky-blue paint from its surface. She was holding two mugs and blowing her droopy, red fringe out of her eyes. 'Look: it's your darling sister – some would say *personal maid* – bringing you a hot cup of tea first thing in the morning!'

'Hmmm.' Temperance took the mug and her fingertips danced on the ceramic surface as the heat reached out to meet her skin. 'I know what this is.'

Susie fluttered her almost translucent lashes. '*What?*'

In some ways, Temperance and Susie were as half as half-sisters could be: Temperance with her dark hair, olive skin and a tendency to overthink and overreact, all of which meant she stuck out like a sore thumb in their tiny Devon village. Whereas Susie was pale skinned, found it easy to charm anyone into laughter and could enter and leave a room without causing even a hint of a fuss. Like one of the Devon fairy folk, but at five feet eight inches.

Despite their differences, there was so much more that united the Molland sisters: their love of vintage fashion, their kindness and compassion, their limitless appetite for doughnuts, that they would fight for the other to the death, and their deep sense of belonging in East Prawle – just like The Witch's Nose, they were pretty much a part of the landscape.

'You want to distract me with tea so you can get a read on my clothes from last night. Admit it.'

Susie feigned shock. 'Me? Never!' She laid down her mug on top of Temperance's most recent paperback and slipped her hands into the back pockets of her jeans. 'But seeing as we're on the subject . . .'

Temperance let out a long sigh. 'Go on then. On the chair.' Temperance nodded at where she'd slung her deep green velvet wrap top the night before.

Susie barely drew breath before lunging towards it, holding out her hand. Temperance watched as one velvet sleeve rose into the air to meet Susie's touch. 'Suse!'

'What? You're literally the only person I'm allowed to do that in front of! What is the point of a power if you keep it switched off all the time? It's like Blackpool Illuminations left unplugged.'

Half-sisters they may be, but Temperance and Susie had both fully inherited their mother's gift; the gift of the Molland line. They were intrinsically attuned to the deeper energies of the world, energies most people didn't realise were swirling about them every day. Just like all matter exists as atoms – atoms that break down and reform, time and again – all emotions are made up of energy that doesn't just evaporate once a feeling has been felt. An emotion radiates from a person and it can either slip back into the big invisible network of living energy, or it can accidentally cling to something nearby, a memory of its former self. The Molland women could read the emotions, the memories that clung onto fabrics. None of them knew exactly why clothes had this property: maybe it was the weave of their fibres that held feelings close, maybe it was the body heat that gave them extra life, or maybe it

3

was because clothes are like a second skin, like our armour to the outside world and always closest to our hearts. But it seemed to the Molland women that the clothes you wore were almost like a butterfly net, gently scooping up the fluttering, beating, delicate feelings of a soul. It was their job to set those butterflies free again.

If someone was overwhelmed by a huge feeling, that emotion would live on in the clothes they'd been wearing. Temperance could pick up a donated wedding dress and tell you if the bride had serious doubts on the morning of her big day. Susie could root through a donation box and pick out the polka dot skirt that had been worn to an excellent karaoke night, next to the silk Bond Street tie that someone had worn snuggly around their neck when they lost a job. Nobody was quite sure how far back through the generations this gift went, their mum not really being on great speaking terms with her own parents, but it only ever presented itself in the women. The memories remained vivid and overpowering even years or decades later, almost as if the previous owner had spilt a whole bottle of their signature scent on the garment before donating it to Try Again, their vintage clothing store.

And because these emotions were their own form of energy, and the Molland women were like lightning rods to receive them, it was as if there was something in the very fibres of fabrics that physically seemed drawn to Temperance and Susie. With a little mental concentration, the sisters could pull a garment into their hands like a magnet lifting dressmakers' pins. No more than one at a time, and not all that far – it was hardly Luke Skywalker using the Force to shift an entire spaceship – but still, being able to lift an inanimate object half a foot into the air was an impressive feat. Just one that they couldn't show anyone else in the outside world. The powers of being a witch came part and parcel with all the fears and worry of being judged as one, so the Mollands kept that party trick within their four walls. Susie somewhat begrudgingly, as Temperance knew she'd been working on being able to tuck a napkin into her T-shirt with her hands held behind her back. If given full reign, she'd be displaying that trick at the pub for all comers.

'Lazy arse. Just grab it and get it over with,' Temperance said, her voice flat.

Susie plonked herself down on the corner of the bed, the top spread out over her knees. She closed her eyes, letting her fingers wave side to side over the velvet pile, turning it by increments, lighter then darker. The familiar tingling sensation started in her fingertips, travelling to her palms as she opened herself up to the memories in the fabric.

Susie could see snatches of a misty scene in her mind's eyes.

A pub table, two chairs.

The rest of the picture was blank.

A tall man, early thirties, sat opposite her. Carefully managed stubble. He's talking, on and on, and soundbites pop through the mist:

'You just think you don't like wine: let me school your palette.'

'But surely you don't want to work in a second-hand shop all your life?'

'Service here is shocking, you know. I'm not sure I will tip this time.'

The irritation and disappointment were so clear they were making Susie's nose wrinkle.

Her eyes pinged open. 'Oh, mate.'

Temperance slurped back some tea. 'Right? I mean, am I Bill

Murray? Is this *Groundhog Day*? Because I am stuck forever in a loop of bad first dates.'

Susie's delicate eyebrows dropped right down. 'I can't believe it. We vetted this guy like crazy! I even scoured his Amazon wish list for red flags. No fungal foot creams, a solid reading list. And *secondhand?!* We're talking the very finest vintage here!' Susie's voice went into a high-pitched squeal and the pub sign creaked again as if in chorus.

'Well, exactly. On paper he seemed . . . decent.'

Susie flopped backwards onto the unmade bed. 'And you didn't read anything from his jacket?'

'Sadly not, and I held his arm for a good five minutes when I got there. Either he's as emotionally blank as he seemed, or it was a very new jacket. Believe me, if I'd picked up that he was an arrogant arsehole in the first two minutes, I wouldn't have wasted an evening of my life being patronised by him. I would have sprinted for the door without looking back.'

'Why didn't you come and find me last night? When I didn't see you at the pub, I assumed it was going really well. Not that you'd slunk back in for a mope.'

'I didn't mope. I did a face pack and a hair mask: some sensible self-care. I thought I would perk myself up by waking up in the morning all glowing and ready to laugh about it. But I'm not. I'm really not.' Her bottom lip turned out, involuntarily.

Susie stood and grabbed her big sister by the arms, shocked by the burst of actual raw emotion from someone who'd often said that they could make it through *Sleepless in Seattle* with two fully dry eyes. 'You're not heartbroken over this idiot, are you?! He sounds like a plonker. A plonker that you met once, not like when Abe—'

6

A stony look from Temperance cut across Susie's last word, and her lip was caught between her teeth and held in place for a minute. They could tell each other anything: the ins and outs of a crap date, the bath bombs that gave them thrush, the gossip they'd picked up by touching someone's shoulder on the bus. But the one thing they did not talk about was Abel Gulliver: they boy who broke Temperance's heart. Well, not so much broke as incinerated into a million tiny particles.

'No! No way. I'm not bothered about him. But I'm fed up of *all* the shitty dates, Suse. There have been so many. Like, *so many*! The last time I met anyone half decent was that summer I interned on Carnaby Street. And London to Devon is not a workable long-distance situation. I'm not leaving the village anytime soon, so the man I love has to be local. But I've Bumbled all the half-decent ones on the South Devon coast and . . . I'm in my bed at 10.30pm on a Saturday night.' She shrugged.

Susie put her hands back on her hips. 'That's why you should have come to the pub! There were some quite cute backpackers in from the campsite. They were funny.'

'I'm not looking for just funny – I'm looking for everything, for The One. Besides, I bet they were all nineteen. Please tell me you didn't?'

Her little sister studied the warped beams of the ceiling. 'Um . . .'

'Susie! That's cradle-robbing!'

'Twenty-four is not *that* much older than nineteen, come on!' Susie's peachy cheeks turned a little strawberry. 'And they might have been older, anyway. Why do you have to worry about The One? You're twenty-nine, not exactly on the brink of death, babe. Can't you just have a bit of fun?'

7

Temperance stood up and grabbed her dressing gown from the back of the door. 'By the time Mum was twenty-nine she'd had us both and had set up the shop: she knew what her life was about. I just, I just,' she shook her head, 'have this feeling that somewhere out there is a love story for me, waiting to start. But I can't get it started on my own.'

Susie raised one eyebrow. 'You just haven't borrowed the right books from my spicy shelf. I can make you a shortlist, if you like?'

Temperance couldn't help but snort a laugh. 'Seriously! Don't you ever get that . . . pull? Like the other half of your heart is out there, walking around all handsome and nonchalant, and if you could just find him then together you'd make this incredible, perfect equation. Bigger than the sum of your parts. You know?'

Susie put her tongue in her cheek. 'Not really. I don't really like long-term jobs, Temps, let alone long-term relationships.'

Without the energy for an eye roll, Temperance turned on her heels and headed to the bathroom. She was due to open the shop in twenty minutes and she hoped that a shower would wash some of her grumpiness away.

Temperance wasn't sure what felt worse: the sad flatness that followed another bad date or the lingering ache in her chest, nagging at her to find The One. Whichever it was, Temperance couldn't keep going on like this.

Something had to change.

Chapter 2

Temperance's go-to outfit on a bad morning was always the same: her mum's denim miniskirt from her student days, with an acid house smiley-face patch sewn on the back pocket, and a Grateful Dead tour T-shirt that she'd mended years ago, turning the ragged hem into a tie-up option instead. When she pulled on the skirt she could always feel a young Lee and her bright, shiny optimism at going away to Bristol Uni – the tour T-shirt vibrated with nothing but good times and hedonism.

Temperance was hoping she could hide in other people's positivity today, until, by osmosis, she felt just a tiny fleck of her own. Clothes still holding onto happy memories could put a spring in your step, just as clothes cloaked in misery could leave you dragging your feet. She had a great big pile of new stock that needed to be assessed and sorted. Temperance could hide in work, at least. Even if her heart was a dry husk of a thing, she had other people's stories to distract her.

As she stomped over the green, around The Piglet Café and to their lean-to shop next door, Temperance's head was already calculating how many garments the two massive cardboard boxes were likely to turn up, and how on earth they were going to find room on the rails for it all. Stock hadn't been moving as quickly as usual this year. It was true that the summer was only just beginning and so their busiest months were yet to come, but they'd normally have a steadier balance between the old coming in and the still-old-but-lovingly-restored going out. It was starting to worry Temperance in the sleepless hours, when she'd exhausted the topic of being alone forever, her withered corpse being picked over by seagulls and it not even making the *Prawle Reporter*.

She let herself into the shop, expertly chucking her keys across the room and into an upturned top hat behind the till.

'Steady!'

'Christ, Mum, you scared me!' Temperance felt her heartbeat in her ears. 'What are you doing here? I'm pretty sure I'm opening up today.'

Lee stood up from the barstool by the sales desk and brushed off her black jeans. 'It is, but I wanted to bring you this and tidy up a few bits of paperwork.' She pushed a Piglet takeaway cup towards her daughter.

'Hang on,' Temperance looked down at the cup and the paper bag next to it. 'A coffee and a bacon bap that isn't from home? When you always say Matt's prices are a rip-off only fit for the grockles?'

'Sshh!' Lee's steely grey eyebrows lowered. She'd gone fully grey at twenty-five, the same week she discovered she was pregnant with Temperance, and had never thought to dye her hair. Instead, she embraced the layered tones of silver, slate and white that now ran through her long hair, and it offset her grungy dress sense perfectly. 'You know these walls are basically cardboard – he'll hear you! Can't I treat you every now and then?'

It seemed to Temperance that her mother was about as skilled at hiding her ulterior motives as her sister was. Twice in one morning she'd been showered with gifts of hot drinks (though, luckily, not literally) and she'd put good money that this piping hot flat white was just an obvious a bribe as Susie's tea had been.

She spoke in just above a whisper: 'You could just as easily have made me this in our kitchen and walked it over. What gives?'

Lee folded her arms over her black-and-white striped T-shirt. 'Nope. You are wearing your classic "Help me, I'm doomed!" outfit, so you tell me first: what's up with you? You can't claim they're *just clothes*, Temp, we both know that's never true. Tell me: I can help.'

Temperance powered up the till. 'Honestly, it's no big deal. Just a bad date. *Another* bad date. Life goes on, right?' She gulped down some coffee and tried not to wince as it scorched her throat.

'Oh, my little water parsnip, I'm sorry. Do you want to talk about it?'

'Only if our family powers can also exorcise bad memories from your head, rather than just your jeans.'

Lee came around and hugged her daughter. 'Sorry, no. Just threads. But I can give what you were wearing the once-over, if you like? At least then a good cardi isn't wasted on a disappointing man. Too many have been, in my experience.'

Temperance tidied the pens into their pot and checked the till roll. 'Already put it in for a soak. Soon there will be no more bad date energy. I'm over it.' She gave a flat kind of smile. 'So that's my news winkled out of me. Do I have to get a chip fork to extract yours?'

Lee drummed her short, bright red nails on the glass counter. Underneath the glass were things she had rescued from pockets over the years: a bus ticket from 1973, half a handwritten best man's speech (luckily any filthy jokes had been lost with the top half), a Hello Kitty scrunchie, one sage green knitted baby bootie and coins from every corner of the globe. Lee had started this mini museum to the lost and found, and over the years her daughters had slipped in seashells they liked or 'Good Effort' stickers from school. Nothing had been edited or removed: it was life in a snapshot. Small, messy, important.

'I do have a bit of news, as it goes. Something good for me. And good for you, too.'

But Temperance could see her mum's face wasn't exactly beaming at this double bubble of goodness. If anything, she had a slight grey shadow under each eye and had forgotten her trademark lipstick this morning.

'Ohh-kay,' she said tentatively.

'The film contract I was offered. That was supposed to start in October? They've brought it forward,' Lee said, calmly. The offer to help kit out a movie's wardrobe with genuine sixties and seventies pieces had been too good to turn down, even if it meant working abroad – in Germany – for six months.

'To when?'

Lee went on as if she hadn't heard Temperance question. 'You and Susie can run this place without me, easy. Standing on your heads. And I've, um, found you some help for the summer.'

Before the words 'help for the summer' had fully entered Temperance's brain, the chime above the shop door gave its sweet little tinkle as a short, sunny girl with a bleached blonde pixie cut strolled in.

'Am I too early?' she asked in an American accent. 'I know you said 10:15 but I just couldn't wait!'

'No, you're right on time. Temperance, this is Stevie. Stevie – Temperance, my daughter. Welcome to Try Again!'

The young woman let out a squeal and jumped up and down on the spot. 'I can't believe it! I'm in total heaven right now!' She rushed up to the counter and planted her hands on the glass, leaving delicate but steamy prints. 'I love vintage. I *breathe* vintage. I wish I was vintage!' she laughed at her own joke, but even Temperance had to admit it was pretty charming.

Lee looked between the two women like they were two dogs meeting in the park and she wasn't sure which one would misbehave first, either through overexcitement or bad temper. 'As my timeline changed and I knew we'd need another pair of hands, I put a message out with my old art school society. Stevie is doing a sandwich year at Bristol and she came down here the next day for the interview. I could hardly stop her!'

'Um, right. When was this interview?'

'Last night. At the pub!' Stevie jumped in. 'God, I love it there. Do you know they have this whole basket of knitting that you can just pick up and carry on with?'

Temperance nodded. 'I've lived next door to that pub my whole life. I started some of that knitting at my tenth birthday party, I think.'

Stevie hooted with laughter, as if Temperance had just told an adorable joke when, in fact, her tenth birthday was attended by two school friends and half of the local WI, who pronounced her a natural knitting talent. A woolly progeny. She didn't know then that a gift with threads and fibres went way beyond

13

anything normal in her. Temperance would find that out on her seventeenth birthday. Still in the pub, of course.

'We're pretty remote here,' Temperance went on, guardedly. 'Off the beaten track. There's not much in the way of cutting-edge fashion for a design student.'

The American pressed her tiny hands to her heart. 'It's been my dream to have a real English adventure. My mom was English, you see. I'm kind of digging into my roots this year, getting to know the places she knew. She passed when I was ten, so partly I'm doing this for her.'

'God, I'm so sorry,' Temperance rushed out, as Lee rubbed the young woman's arm gently.

'Ah, it's OK. It was a long time ago and also it was yesterday, you know? But she loved clothes and she loved the English coast. So here I am. And I'm about as in love with that ocean view as I am the clothes you've got. So it couldn't be more perfect. The way you've styled that Laura Ashley maxi dress with a biker jacket in the window. Ooof,' she rolled her eyes like she'd just dived into a pool of chocolate fondant. 'Perfection.'

Temperance felt the tips of her ears glow. 'Thank you. I did that one. I liked the clash of traditionally feminine and masculine.'

'That's exactly it! And I'm not a design student, by the way: I study history. Specifically, the cultural history of fashion. These things are so my . . . my cup of tea.' She beamed.

Temperance felt her hackles drop in the glow of Stevie's smile. But there was a very solid reason why she was wary of anyone new coming behind the desk at Try Again: this wasn't just a vintage store, this was a vintage store where she and her family used their unique Molland magic on a daily basis. If a piece had only positive memories attached to it, the women mostly let it be, but would mend any tears or replace missing buttons so it was back to a saleable standard. But if they held a garment that gave them flashes of rage or heartbreak or jealousy, it would need a very different sort of repair. A sort that no outsider would understand. Because if those negative energies were left to fester, they would then influence the next person to wear them, keeping a perpetual whirl of misery and pain spinning through their life.

Temperance had grown up seeing how people laughed at modern-day 'witches', how they mucked about with tarot cards in her sixth form common room, falling about with hysterical laughter. And she knew enough about English history to realise that sometimes jokes and jibes turned cruel, vindictive. Poisonous. No matter the age you lived in, a woman with power was always a target.

Lee had been very clear with each of her daughters when they turned seventeen and their talents came to the surface: 'We keep our family secret *in the family*. No one else will understand. It's our gift and we need to treasure it, to nurture it.'

What went on in the back room of Try Again, stayed in the back room of Try Again.

And now her mother was inviting an outsider in?! To poke about in their work room, to snoop on their secrets?

As if she could sense Temperance's heart rate starting to vibrate like a hummingbird's, Lee added, 'Stevie's role will mostly be out on the shopfloor here, keeping it tidy and well stocked. And maybe if she comes across anything particularly unique, she could list it online for us? We've been talking about an eBay shop for ages, so she could take that on.'

'Buying and selling vintage for a profit helped me buy my plane ticket out here,' Stevie shrugged sheepishly.

Lee sighed with a smile. 'I think you two are going to have a great summer. You'll hardly miss me at all.' She squeezed her daughter's hand. 'And I'm always on the end of the phone, of course. But right *now*, I'd better get packing.'

'Wait, what? What – wait . . . when are you going?'

Lee briefly bit her lip. 'Tonight.'

Stevie's gaze flicked from Temperance to Lee and back again like it was the Ladies' Final at Wimbledon. 'I'll, uh, take a slow tour of your denims, give you some privacy.'

Once she was twelve feet away at the front of the shop, Lee turned to her daughter, 'I know it's sudden, Temps, but I'm hardly *Home Alone*-ing you. I *know* you're capable of this. Haven't you ever imagined running the shop yourself one day? Without me?'

Temperance had always seen her future with her feet planted where they were right now: her Birkenstocks nestled into the slight groove in the lino that had been worn down by her mum's DMs and the shoes of Matt's dad before them, the original proprietor of Bob's Baits, as it was then. She definitely wanted to run this place one day, but her visions of that future always had Lee somewhere just out of sight in the background. Not bouncing in a Berlin electro nightclub and swanking about with movie people.

'I suppose.'

Lee pushed a slip of paper across the desk to her daughter. 'Take this. It's the email for someone *in the know,* for any magical emergencies that crop up and you can't get hold of me. I don't know how much travelling I'll be doing. But just for real emergencies, mind?'

Temperance picked up the paper like it was a holy relic – she'd never heard her mum reference anyone else with the same magical know-how as them before. Lee had never spoken badly about her family over the years, but Temperance and Susie had been told enough to know that there'd been a big, unrepairable rift just before Temperance was born. This was the closest Temperance had ever come to having a clue to her mum's past. She put it carefully in the till drawer.

'But I doubt you'll need it,' Lee went on. 'I'm only a few hours away by plane. It's good for the shop that I can build some new contacts. Who knows, I might find us some great new sources for stock there.'

'Maybe,' Temperance forced herself to see the shop half-full with her as the manager, rather than half-empty without her mum. 'It might be interesting to wash away a German heartbreak for a change. I just hope I can understand those ones.'

Lee shook her head gently. 'Heartbreak doesn't have a language, my darling. It's universal.'

3

Chapter 3

'It feels like Stevie is going to be like a grown-up version of our summer friends, you know?' Susie pulled on a pair of chunky gardening gloves before she started rummaging through one of the new stock boxes. The gloves were essential kit when you have the Molland powers. Sticking your hands into a box full of old clothes when you could absorb all of the emotions tumbled in there was a risky business, a Russian roulette.

Temperance still had a battered ballerina music box some-where in her room that was full to the brim of friendship bracelets from their summer friends back in the day. She and Susie would make a long line of best friends over their childhood summers, with the kids staying at the campsite or in the holiday rentals. And although those friendships could only span two weeks or so before the children left with their families, each was like a little bubble of happiness and freedom. If Temperance put on one of those old bracelets now and pinged the elastic against her wrist, she'd feel warm, wind-whipped skin, hysterical laughter around a campfire and the taste of a '99 against her tongue. Even the thinnest threads could wrap around an emotion if it was potent enough.

'She has to come to FairyFest, get to know everyone. It's only a few nights away, though. I doubt she's got a Kraken costume wedged in her holdall.'

Susie shook her head. 'She never a Kraken. She's a sprite. Maybe a little pixie. There might something in all this lot that she could wear.'

'Mum said this was from a really good estate sale. Should get some gems.'

Susie ripped back the brown packing tape. 'I still can't believe she's going tonight. I mean, it's great for her – she should live a little. I bet she'll love Berlin, the music there and . . . Woah!' Her tone suddenly went from low and flat to squeaky and slightly out of breath.

The arch of a back. Words whispered urgently against her neck. Something red and silky tied to the headboard. Shadows moving, hearts racing, oh—

'What is it?' Temperance stood up just as Susie flopped back down into her chair, panting, the back of her gloved hand pressed against her forehead as her skin came alive with an all-consuming energy.

'Something . . . deeply . . . so . . . *filthy*.'

Temperance winced. 'Ew. I hate it when things haven't been at least through a washing machine. I'll get the tongs and the black bag—'

'No,' Susie was still trying to recover her breathing as her chest heaved up and down. 'Not filthy like it has old food stains. Like *good filthy*. Like *spicy filthy*. I must have . . . phew . . . only caught it on my forearm, but,' she fanned herself, 'I felt an erotic thunderbolt like Pedro Pascal had just cracked his whip around me or something. I saw some moves. Holy shit! I need another go.' She got slowly to her feet.

'Suse!' her big sister admonished.

'What?!'

'That's somebody else's private memory – you can't go and gawp on it like a magical peep show!'

'You don't mind when it's someone else's happiness left behind, or pride, or confidence. What's the difference?'

'People show off their new baby in a pram, or their new fancy suit and they *invite* you to admire them. People have sex behind closed doors because it's *private*. There is a massive difference.' She twisted the ring on her little finger. 'Was it really that good?'

Susie nodded slowly. 'Like all the actors who've ever played Mr Darcy at once. *That* good.'

'Oh.'

'I didn't see a face or anything. No identifying features so . . .'

Temperance held fast. 'No. No. It's still wrong. But we do need to work out what's carrying that memory so we can clean it. You're going to have to stick a bare hand in again and find it.'

Susie waggled her eyebrows. 'Avert your eyes, babe.'

After a few minutes of swashing her arm about in corduroy, chiffon and the odd tablecloth, Susie closed her eyes and gave a low, guttural groan. 'Oh, that's the spot. Oh yeahhhh.'

'Just pull it out, quick!'

'That's what they all say!' her little sister cackled, dragging out a slippery satin kimono-style dressing gown. It was short and red and looked like the kind of garment designed for anything but practical reasons. Skimpy, tactile, sexy. Temperance guessed that if she were to put it on it wouldn't even cover most of her bum. Not that she was going to put it on. She wasn't even going to touch it. Because it wasn't right. Definitely . . . not.

Susie held out her palm and floated the robe over to her desk. 'I have no idea what kind of herb mixture this one will need. If we really do need to wash it off?' she muttered hopefully, only getting a hooded look in response.

'I don't know either. People usually have their sauciest memories with no clothes on. I haven't actually come across this before. And it's not like I can Google it. I could ask Mum before she goes.'

Susie leapt back to the box. 'Fingers crossed the same person had something else saucy in here . . .' she started to move her hands through the contents, purposefully leaning so far in that her elbows were touching all the fabrics. 'No, nope. Ew, no. This is . . . ahhh!'

With both hands she started to pull out a dress that Temperance could hear before she could really see. It was rustling and crinkling like mad: a huge white ballgown of Shantung silk, with a huge, voluminous skirt and small but poofy sleeves. No, not a ballgown: a wedding dress.

'Maybe the red gown is from the honeymoon?' Susie said, holding the dress up to herself. 'I can check.' She went to pull her right glove off with her teeth, but Temperance swooped in quickly.

'Let me check this one. I don't want you fully swooning while we've still got work to do tonight.'

'A likely story,' she replied sardonically.

As the older sister put her hands to the almost-spherical sleeves, her vision was flooded with royal blue, like the most concentrated firework ever had exploded just a few feet from her eyes. She felt warmed by the colour, strengthened. Every muscle, every tendon in her body woke up and reminded her she was lucky to be alive. Energy floated through the dress like it was a new cosmic river diverting a flood of emotion onto Temperance , all of it bright and strong and electrifying. Temperance felt like she could climb a mountain, paint a masterpiece, sing an opera. But it wasn't just confidence in this dress, there was curiosity and playfulness and loyalty and excitement and . . .

'Love,' she said, holding the dress against her chest. 'It's actual, pure love.'

There was a buzzing tingle in her fingers as she closed her eyes again and saw a carousel of memories play in her mind: *a man opening a fancy car door for her, one white shoe emerging from under the rustling skirt to step onto the churchyard gravel. The scraping of pews as an organ played and she stepped into the aisle. A beaming smile from the altar, bouncing back her own. Glittering eyes. Champagne, paper confetti, her heart swelling beyond any rational size. The start of an adventure.*

'No way,' Susie breathed, reading the look of awe on Temperance's face.

'I've never felt anything like it. Not even on our baby clothes. That love was just as strong, but the colours were all different, the energy was very different.'

Susie pulled off a glove, reached out and gently put one finger to the waves of the layered skirt. Her eyes closed slowly and her head dipped. 'Oh blimey. I see what you mean. That is crazy strong.' She pulled her hand back and let out a long breath. 'If it's the same woman as the satin number then she lived a *good life*. Well done her.'

Temperance begrudgingly laid the dress down on the desk,

covering the robe. She laced her fingers behind her neck, as if resting them from the intense load of emotion they'd just carried. She could still see the odd spark of blue behind her eyes.

'You know the awful part?'

'What could possibly be awful about true love, Tee?'

Temperance ran her hand along the scalloped hem, another burst of deep blue taking up her senses with the most deeply comforting tingle. It was a giant meringue of a dress, the kind of heavy thing that needed all the bridesmaids lifting from their knees to manoeuvre. Puffy sleeves; corseted bodice of damask silk with tiny rose buds sewn on the neckline; about seven layers of swooshy skirting.

'It's an eighties wedding dress. We'll never sell it. It's like a pure love genie trapped in a bottle wrapped in barbed wire.'

Susie groaned. 'Oh, that's so sad. We could have given some bride out there the happiest wedding day known to man. Not to mention the happiest wedding *night*.'

Temperance nodded. But she wasn't thinking of some bride out there. She was thinking of how ironic it was that she had the magic to read the echoes of true love some forty years on, but not the practical skills to track down her own for even five minutes.

4

Chapter 4

The Fairy Festival of East Prawle was a huge deal. Not just for the kids – both local and holidaying – who got treats and games for the full day, but also for the grown-ups who could enjoy the fancy dress party on the same night. The pub had a huge gig space out the back, a converted hay barn with a good sound system and a permanently sticky floor, perfect for a boozy rave. Temperance had fallen into a slight rut of going as a crystal-ball-reading kind of fairground witch the last few years, all layered skirts and a belt with shiny little medallions, silk scarfs tied in her hair. It was easy to throw on, but Temperance also got a perverse thrill from hiding in plain sight amongst all her friends and neighbours.

Plus, it was great for business at Try Again. Stevie had sold a particularly gorgeous seventies tan suede jacket with fringing down the arms that one lucky teen planned to wear as a Space Cowboy. Temperance's homemade fairy wings (made from old tights and wire coat-hangers) had been snapped up by a gang of Scottish blokes who argued over who got to be the green fairy.

The till was full, the 'Closed' sign had been flipped around and now Temperance, Stevie and Susie were enjoying a few beers and a well-earned wind-down on the shop floor.

Susie nipped into the back and returned with their last four beers and a dusty bottle of Malibu. 'It's not exactly top drawer stuff but after a busy day we deserve something with some backbone, so this will have to do.'

Stevie twisted open the bottle and took a sniff. 'That stuff smells like . . . lip gloss?'

'Mmmm delicious, boozy lip gloss!' Susie laughed.

Temperance cracked opened a can. 'Malibu makes people do stupid things. I'll stick to beer while it's going. Did I see you get the lime green fairy's Snapchat, Suse?'

'Wasn't it Magenta I was talking to? Ah well, we'll sort it all out on the dance floor tomorrow.' She raised one eyebrow. 'Where *you* will be dominating in the sexy little costume we're going to find you . . .'

'Magical,' Stevie said, and the sisters' heads whipped round to her on the same beat. 'Or mythical, right?'

'Um, yes. Right,' Susie went on. 'A mythical creature, but hot. Easy.'

'And I'm guessing just throwing on a pointy hat wouldn't cut it, right?'

'Uh, no,' Temperance laughed nervously.

'Not to nerd out in my first week with you guys, but I actually did an entire paper on pointy hats in my history of fashion class. The whole 'witch' ensemble: black clothes, warty nose, ugly shoes. When you look at it through a feminist lens, it's really telling about how that image was used make women fear being perceived as ugly or cruel or powerful, how that would lead to societal rejection. Be pretty and sweet or it's into the ducking pond with you!'

Susie shivered.

'OK. I have taken this to a weird place. Sorry.' Stevie's eyes flicked between the Molland sisters anxiously and she tried to rally. 'Maybe I should just pay for my outfit before I'm fired.' She dug into the very far corner of a full-length rack at the back of the shop, and pulled out a hot pink lame catsuit. 'Sorry that I hid it, but I knew it MUST BE MINE.' She belted her last words out like a pantomime villain.

'Frederica!' Temperance breathed, the beers loosening up her inner monologue.

'Huh?' Stevie held the stretchy metallic number to herself. 'Whoever Frederica is, I'll fight her for it.'

Temperance shook her head. 'No, *that's* Frederica. Some-times we get a piece in that's so special that we have to give it a name. Especially when Frederica came with memories of falling in love with a backing dancer in the eighties.'

Stevie squinted. Suddenly her eyes seemed to sober up ahead of the rest of her. 'How do you know so much about it?'

Temperance's hands stilled on the glass counter. Susie paused, her beer an inch from her lips.

'The thing . . . the thing is . . .' Temperance cursed her own brain for floating about stupidly in so much alcohol.

'The previous owner told us herself. Didn't she, Temps? She was an *oversharer*, if you remember?'

'Oh yes. Yes, that's it. And of course you should have it! Employee discount included. You and Frederica will be very happy together.' Temperance let go of a deep breath.

Stevie's eyes flicked back and forth between the sisters before she shook her head and smiled once again. 'Thanks! I was going to spray paint an ice cream cone for my head, pop on some ears and go as a Uni-kitty. Frederica, it's nice to meet you.' Stevie shook one of the empty sleeves. 'Let's get you stashed away out the back, my pretty.' She bounced into the office.

'You're not off the hook,' Susie sing-songed after the beer sloshed down her throat. 'You need a jaws-on-the-floor look. A look to start the love affair of the century, as that's what you always say you're after. Maybe a stranger walks through the door, your eyes will meet across the crowded dance floor and your bodies will talk the language of lurve.' She shimmied her shoulders and rolled her hips.

'Or I get all dressed up, cram my vital organs into some Spanx, and spend the night being breathed on by all the usual suspects.'

'I promise you, there are some really nice guys camping here at the minute. You could like them if you *gave them a chance*.' Susie looked down her nose at Temperance and straight into her soul. The way only a sister could.

'But what about the next day? All our neighbours seeing me . . . like that. I care about what they think, even if you don't.'

'I care. But I just don't think it's the worst thing in the world for them to know I have a heartbeat. And genitals.'

'Sarah!' Stevie screamed from the other side of the wall.

'No: Susie, but close.'

Stevie's faced popped around the doorframe, her cheeks flamingo pink. 'I've found Sarah!' With an almighty rustle, she held the wedding dress up to her chin. *The* wedding dress that had the sisters seeing deep purpley-blue blasts of all-consuming love.

'Why on Earth is that a Sarah?'

'Sarahhhhhhh,' Stevie put on a gravelly monster voice.

'Sarahhhhh!' Her eyebrows shot to her hairline and she waddled towards them with the dress pressed to her front, about as easy to shift as a dead body in a carpet. '*Labyrinth.* The movie?! David Bowie. Awakening pre-teen sexual desires everywhere?! And the big hairy monster dude that's really sweet? *Sarahhhhh.* Come on, you gotta see it!' She thrust the layers of crunchy silk forwards.

'Oh!' Susie fumbled for her phone. 'I do see it! The dreamy ballroom bit, in the bubble, and suddenly she's waltzing about in this big, massive . . . *this!*' Susie puffed up one of the layers of skirts. Luckily, Stevie didn't pick up on the fact that she swooned for about thirty seconds before recovering and starting to type on her phone. 'See?' She held up the results to Temperance, showing countless stills of Jennifer Connelly in the classic movie.

'If I scrunch up my eyes, I kind of . . . get the gist.'

Susie grinned. 'It just needs some fake pearls swagged along just so. Tease up the hair. And I think it would fit her perfectly.'

'Wait – fit who?!' Temperance blinked.

'Stevie, would you grab my sewing kit, please, doll?'

Stevie gave a salute and disappeared again, leaving the dress half-standing on its own on the polished wood floor.

'I can't *wear* that,' Temperance whispered. 'I'll be high as a kite the whole time!'

'Oh how awful,' Susie deadpanned, 'you'll be full of pure love at a party.' Her lips pursed. 'Besides, have a little fairy fest mead beforehand and you're good – you know alcohol dulls our magic. Yet another reason to get into the party spirit and let go for once.'

Temp's eyes flicked down to her sister's phone screen. 'You think I could pull it off?'

Susie grabbed her by the shoulder. 'You would be the ultimate fairy princess bewitched by the Goblin King. The only way if it could be more perfect if is an actual Goblin King in tight jodhpurs rocked up after you, but one thing at a time, hey.'

Temperance snorted through her nose. 'That would be on brand for me and my sucky dating life. I'll finally find The One and he'll turn out to be a dodgy underworld despot. Who snatches random babies and randomly bursts into song.'

Susie lowered one eyebrow. 'But Bowie – you would, right?'

'Oh every *day* I would.'

When Stevie and Susie finished glue-gunning on a ton of extra lace, pearl trimming and looping floaty pastel scarves through Temperance's hair, Stevie dotted some glitter on her cheekbones for the final touch.

By now, Temperance had finished her beers and begrudgingly moved onto the Malibu, swigging it while she played mannequin. The hug of true love sneaking past her alcohol-numbed power had given her a goofy kind of daze, enjoying the moment too much to think about the consequences.

Susie looked at her watch. 'Shit. It's almost tomorrow!'

'Midnight! The witching hour!' Stevie cackled drunkenly. 'You're going to think I'm nuts, but where I'm from – Massachusetts – we are kind of witch-obsessed. I must have seen *The Craft* more times than is healthy. That's why I think I keep trying to work them into my history studies.' Temperance flopped down onto the changing room stool, the magical energy of the dress rushing to her head and making her feel briefly dizzy. She pressed her hand to the silk bodice tightly, as if she could push the little roses and lace trims into her own being and carry them with her forever.

Her palm glowed like she was holding a hot water bottle. 'I don't want to take this off now. It'll be eight hours until I can put it on again and . . . I'll miss it. The *feeling*. Like, now I know what being in love must be like. And I don't want it to end.' Unconsciously, her bottom lip stuck out.

Susie's eyes went wide as she looked from Temperance to Stevie, shocked that Temperance had said so much – too much – about their powers.

Stevie gasped. 'You love the dress! Of course you do: it's like it was made for you, babe. You shouldn't take it off. Like, ever. Oh my god – let's go and do the enchantment scene! When she finally tells the Goblin King that he has no power over her. It'll be . . . like . . . you're living the movie!'

Susie smiled slyly. 'There's bound to be someone on the beach having a cheeky bonfire that we could dance around.'

'Yes!'

'Yes.' Temperance's voice came out strong and assured before she really thought about what she was agreeing to. It was like the dress was speaking for her, as if it was longing to have one more dance, one more adventure. As if it was dying to twirl around in all its poofy glory with its true love again.

'But it's chilly, so bring something warm.'

She grabbed the purple emergency beanie that always lived on the shop's hat stand – the one her mum had knitted her years ago – and pulled it down over fluffed-up curls.

The almost-midnight air was cold, sending their breath out before them like a huddle of squiffy dragons as Susie lit the way with the shop torch and Stevie brought up the rear behind Temperance, carrying the train of the dress in the dead of night like the most dutiful, deranged bridesmaid ever.

'You'll love the beach in the dark, Stevie. It knocks California into a cocked hat.'

'Sure,' she replied gently. 'But . . . I don't want to know how a hat gets cocked, OK? It's been a long day.'

Soon the footpath was taking them down, on sandy, jagged stones clumped together with sea grass, towards the beach. A light drizzle started to fall.

Susie squeaked. 'A fire just on its last embers! We can stoke it back up again.'

They dashed to the edges of the beach to grab some dry wood. Well, the others dashed. Temperance sort of ungainly slouched there as the heavy silk got stuck in the sand.

Frustrated, and buzzed by so much cheap rum and pure love that she mostly forgot herself, Temperance held out both her hands, palms down, at her waist. The top two layers of the skirt floated up to meet her touch and with some of the mighty weight lifted, Temperance managed to stagger another few metres forwards. She flopped down by the fire pit and watched the flames lick back to life as the others fed it.

The night air was sweet and crisp. Unadulterated. The waves washed themselves against the beach, soft and rhythmic and slow. Playing their music even if there was hardly anyone around to hear it.

Temperance shut her eyes. She loved being here with her sister and her very new friend, but a big part of heart was crying out that this was precisely the kind of moment you wanted the Love of Your Life for. The wool of her beanie itched at her head, and she pulled it down lower to keep her ears warm.

Temperance put her hands to her middle, pushing the fabric in where it gaped slightly, drinking in the warmth and the

31

charge of a real love, even if it was borrowed and second-hand.

'Hmm, just as I suspected.' Stevie's hands were behind her before she even realised what was happening, looping something under her arms and pulling it tight. 'It will need a belt for the party. But this was all I could find at the store.'

Temperance saw a flash of red as she glanced down and then a feverish heat ran up the back of her neck and down her front, ending up between her legs. Her breath caught in her lungs. She was aware of every inch of her skin that was kissed by the cool night air.

Wrists clasped by a strong hand. The delicious building pressure. The anticipation as he . . .

'Oh my god!' Temperance lurched to one side.

It was the red dressing gown cord.

Susie clocked what was happening and fell into the sand, laughing her arse off.

'What?' Stevie asked, a little worried.

'Um, nothing, don't worry.' Temperance fanned herself. 'Chuck me more rum! Quick!' Temperance swallowed three mouthfuls, closing a door in her mind to the R-rated scene still playing there. For now.

'Let's begin.' Stevie's eyes glittered.

Temperance struggled to stand, swamped as she was by tulle and silk. She drew a line in the air with one flick of her wrist and the bottom of the skirt shook itself free.

Stevie blinked. Then blinked again. 'This English beer is strong stuff, right?'

Susie only giggled nervously and tried to eyeball Temperance across the campfire. 'So, erm, how does it go, Stevie?'

Stevie cleared her throat and started to speak, low and controlled: '*Give me the child. Through dangers untold and .*

.. hardships unnumbered, I have fought my way here to the castle, the castle . . . beyond the Goblin City. For my will is as strong as yours, and my kingdom is as great. You have no power over me!'

'Wahey!' Susie applauded from her prone position on the sand.

'Very cool.'

Stevie looked down at them both. 'Come on, join in. We've got a much better shot at banishing the Goblin King if we do it together. Girl power! Hold hands,' she ushered them with her fingertips. 'Now repeat after me . . .'

They stood in a circle, clutching each other's booze-clammy hands, squeezing tight and somehow keeping their balance as they started to walk around and around the fire. They soon fell into a sort of a chant, but Temperance's voice drifted away as she let her mind wander back into the dress's memories of its wedding day. In fact, she sought them out – so delicious and moreish were these snapshots of a happy life, suffused with bright and beautiful love.

A four-piece band playing Rat Pack classics in one corner of the hotel ballroom, a giant fruitcake impeccably iced in another. Temperance in the bride's shoes, being twirled on the spot until she was dizzy. A small pageboy tries to cut in but a low voice says very firmly, 'Not today, Tim. I'll think you'll find she's all mine today.' They are holding hands under the table as telegrams are read, they are standing hip to hip as they cut into the cake with a sword, of all things. Cheering, laughing. Happy tears.

Temperance felt the biting current of magic, starting in the very tips of her fingers and then travelling up into her shoulders and down her spine. She started to rearrange the memory in her head. To redesign it. It wasn't something she'd ever done with a real memory before, but now, more than anything, she wanted this memory to be *hers*, as she would have it. As if the dream of her future had already come true. She squeezed her eyes and painted a scene in vibrant technicolour behind them.

It's not a hotel ballroom – it's the barn at the back of the Witch's Nose. Gold and silver streamers everywhere. A DJ in the corner, playing 'Get Lucky'. A huge tower of profiteroles and French Fancies. Because who actually likes fruit cake? Susie and I are dancing like crazy, the sequins from her mini dress almost blinding me. Until a hand finds my waist, snaking around, drawing me to him. He smells like something familiar, like being outdoors maybe. Shells and pine needles. 'I can't believe you're mine,' he says. We hold hands as funny speeches are made, we bump into each other as we jostle to smush a French Fancy into the other's face first. We're so happy, we could burst.

Temperance saw herself in all of those moments, embroidering her own hopes into the story of the dress, mingling with its echoes of eternal love. She blinked up at the starry sky, clearing the tears in her eyes, pulling herself back to reality. Where were they again? Oh yes, the Goblin King. Totally normal.

As she tuned back into Stevie's chant, Temperance found herself making her own version of the words in her head, born of the sort of honest desperation only a midnight beach and too much Malibu can bring out in a person.

Give me The One. Through long lonely nights I have found myself here, at the beach holding all of nature's wonder. For my will is as strong as yours, and my magic as great. Love can have all power over me, if it brings The One to me. I swear.

5

Chapter 5

Temperance had never been chucked out of a pub before. It wasn't the kind of thing that happened to her, and she'd never dreamed it would happen because she smelled so bad.

'You're green around the gills, Temperance Molland, and you smell like pond water to boot. Clear off out of here and help outside,' Margie, landlady at The Witch's Nose, had told her this morning. Margie has been like an official granny to Temperance her whole life, but the kind of gran who told you when your skirt was too short as she fed you a massive Sunday roast. You didn't mess with Margie.

So Temperance had given up stringing up FairyFest decorations over the bar, echoes of synthetic coconut coming back to her even though she'd scrubbed her tongue like she was removing barnacles from the bottom of a ship, and she stumbled outside to set up the kids' treasure hunt.

Temperance itched at her scalp. She'd not fallen asleep on the beach since she was nineteen, maybe. She didn't remember bringing so much of it back home with her in her hair or her knickers last time. That meringue of a wedding dress was like a tent in itself, though, and she'd slept so deeply next to Stevie and Susie by the firepit. Even those mad dreams didn't shake her awake. Dreams like she'd never had before.

Thunderclouds so dark they were purple, rolling towards the village like a herd of wild horses, spooked and seething.

A hand trailing through knee-high wildflowers, but everywhere the fingers dance, the blooms turn instantly to fire. Burning like sparklers right down to their roots, leaving only ash on the wind.

The mottled glass of Try Again splintering and fracturing right through the middle as the door slams shut.

Temperance had sat in the sticky doom of a hangover before: the roll of her stomach, the sweaty sense of guilt that she'd said *something* to *someone* she shouldn't, the painful thump of dehydration behind her eyeballs. But this doom was different. This doom went deeper, into the marrow of her bones, it pulled at the roots of her hair like it was making her stand to attention, as if her whole body was trying to say: *danger is coming. Get ready.*

She told herself for the seventeenth time this morning that it was just hangxiety talking and tomorrow this would all be a silly memory. There were no curses here. No horror-movie storms or wildfires on the cliff paths. The shop was perfectly intact. Not that she'd checked this morning but . . . it was all fine. Fine. The lead lining her stomach would melt away just as soon as the alcohol evaporated from her system. Totally fine.

The festival volunteers had put together some tiny organza bags filled with marshmallow mushrooms for the children's toadstool hunt around the village green. Temperance had the task of hiding them in clever but accessible spots for children aged three and up, a job which at least involved lots of salty fresh air to help bring her back to life.

She sucked in a lungful as she stood looking out over the grass. It was 9am and the village was still mostly asleep. Dew sparkled on the ground and a swallow swooped low to snap up a tasty insect. Hugh and Praveen from the committee were the only other people around: timidly using a rubber-ended mallet to knock in a fairy circle of tent pegs with papier-mâché 'stones' glued on top in the middle of the green. Temperance suddenly marvelled at how much of her life had taken place on this green. She had learned to walk here, to ride a bike. Temperance could so clearly remember the exact moment she did a perfect cartwheel here aged twelve and then instantly knew it was a totally babyish thing to do, and so not cool. She used to share sandwiches with Abel in the bus shelter when she'd had enough of Susie and just wanted to vent to her best friend. They met there at least once a week. Until things between them changed, and felt altogether different. And then, the night after Temperance turned seventeen, when she was fizzing with a magical knowledge only she and her mum shared, she went to find Abel at the bus shelter with a slice of birthday cake especially for him. He was gone. Only a note on his hoodie waited for Temperance on the bowed wooden bench. The closest thing she got to a goodbye.

She felt her feet moving her towards the shelter now, scattering a few sweet bags in the potted plants and behind parking bollards. Still waiting for the heavy haze of doom to lift around her heart, Temperance went to sit down. But as her hand reached out for the well-worn wood, the doom only seemed to find an extra gravitational pull within her, pushing her heart down directly on top of her stomach.

The purple clouds.

Burning flowers.

Cracks in glass.

Why couldn't she shake this dream? How badly fermented was that old bottle of Malibu?!

As much as her rational brain reminded Temperance that her body was out of whack after too much alcohol and a short night's sleep out in the wild, another part of her kept whispering: *danger, danger!* The part of her that knew magic existed, that weird things were woven just underneath the fabric of the 'real' world, out of sight but still pulling the strings. That everything in this universe of beautiful chaos was linked by energy, recycled over and over again, and that one tiny push of a domino on one day could bring down a skyscraper the next.

She gripped the sleeve of her sky blue cardigan tightly. No new feelings there. Could the wedding dress have left a strange kind of nightmarish imprint on her, perhaps? It didn't feel possible: that dress had only stirred up the very best, most glorious feelings. Temperance was sure it couldn't cause one wince of pain to anyone.

Something *else* swirled around her heart, cinching it in like Stevie had cinched her waist last night. It was like watching a beautiful, priceless vase on the edge of a high shelf teetering back and forth, back and forth: the terrible dread that a smash was coming, you just didn't know exactly when. Someone was in trouble, someone close by. Someone important.

Susie.

Temperance quickly stashed the remaining ten bags of sweets under the bench – sod the kids, they wanted easy wins anyway, didn't they? And she whipped her head round to face The Witch's Nose again, and seek out her baby sister.

But there.

Standing in the fairy stone circle.

A very rumpled, slightly irritated – twelve years older but unmistakeably – Abel Gulliver.

The belt around Temperance's heart loosened by one notch.

6

Chapter 6

Of all the things Temperance had ever imagined saying to Abel if she ever saw him again, 'You're in the fairy ring,' was not at the top of the list. She'd rehearsed angry things, cutting things, flirty things and faux-nonchalance, but never sounding like a deranged children's TV presenter.

'Oh, what?' He took a huge step to the left, as if she'd pointed out he was about to tread on a rattlesnake. 'That's . . . that's new.' He nudged a toadstool with the toe of his boot. The hollow paper shape wilted to one side.

'Well, don't knock it over,' she tutted and bent down to straighten it, congratulating herself on morphing seamlessly into a *nagging* children's TV presenter. She stood up again and became very aware of her hands just hanging there, obvious and awkward. She shouldn't hug him. Should she? Did you hug your ex-best friend and one-that-got-away after they deserted you? Was that a thing?

'Sorry. Sorry.' He shoved his hands into the pockets of his grey jeans.

Temperance didn't want to care about how he looked, but

she'd already memorised his entire outfit: authentically worn-in jeans, workmen's boots, a cobalt blue checked flannel shirt over a grey T-shirt. He looked really good. She was suddenly really aware of how stretched out the neckline on her favourite Blondie T-shirt was, but she'd only been able to think of very strong builder's tea and toast this morning, not looking casually yet effortlessly hot.

And Temperance wasn't just taking in the detail of what he wore, she was greedily noting how his eyebrows had filled out, now he was a proper grown-up; the pattern of his stubble, a little patchy at the hollow of his cheeks; the way his mouth now held itself entirely flat, whereas all her memories of him were smiling, talking, always in motion.

She realised she'd been holding her breath. She still didn't know what to do with her hands.

Even though she was full-on staring at Abel, he wouldn't make even the most fleeting eye-contact. His eyes darted over the green, to her fluffed-up bedhead, over to the pub then down at her baggy grey joggers. It was as if the state of her was too much to bear, but too gross not to goggle at, all at the same time. Eventually he ran his hands over his mouth and chin, and spoke.

'Hi, Temperance.'

'Hi.' Somehow she dragged the one syllable into three nervous gasps of sound. And still her hands dangled there in confusion.

'I um—'

'What are you—-?'

She laughed as they spoke over each other, expecting that the old Abel she'd known would laugh too.

Abel let out a sigh. 'Strange to be back here.' He looked over

41

her shoulder at the pub again. As if Temperance was hardly even there.

'Twelve years.'

He nodded. 'I know.'

Temperance tried to steady her breathing, somehow giving herself a bubble of heartburn, which she swallowed painfully. 'So what *are* you doing here?'

His brow furrowed. 'This . . . is going to sound weird. Pretty weird.' He shuffled his feet on the spot. 'I had a dream last night. This massive storm wrecking the village, and I sort of *knew* there was trouble coming. I woke up thinking— worrying maybe something had happened to Gran? She didn't answer her phone this morning, so I jumped in my car and came straight here. I just parked up two minutes ago.' He pointed his thumb to the right and a dented white van on the thin strip of gravel by the green. 'I know it sounds insane.'

You have no idea.

Temperance pushed down the stickiness in her throat. 'Margie is fine – I've been with her this morning. She probably didn't hear the phone, what with all the festival stuff going on at the pub.'

Abel closed his eyes for a beat. 'Thank Christ. Wait, what festival?'

'The Fairy Festival. It's become quite a big deal over the last few years. I'm surprised Margie hasn't chewed your ear off about it.'

He looked away, studying the broken roof tiles on one of the holiday cottages. 'She knows that I don't really need to hear village news anymore.' Once again, the Abel Temperance had expected was overtaken by this strait-laced, sombre, *buzzkill* of a man. There was a stinging behind her ribs.

42

'Right.' Temperance stretched out her T-shirt an inch further. Of course he didn't care. He left this place so long ago. The old Abel would have cared: the teenage Abel that Temperance had once known inside out. The boy who used to give her his last Dorito from the bag and always helped Susie with her Brownie badges. But that boy overnight became the kind of man who just disappears on his friends, never to be heard of again. So why expect anything more?

In one of her many rehearsed scenarios, Temperance played this cool: barely making eye contact, perhaps casually sipping a Negroni with impeccable coral lipstick. But Abel was so laid back, so unruffled, that he seemed to suck all the cool out of the air, leaving Temperance a twitchy, awkward and strangely sweaty mess. And far from barely making eye contact, she found her gaze glued to this very adult version of Abel. She could have been studying an impressionist painting in a gallery: searching for clarity, for meaning, for the secret. That patchy but golden stubble. A new tiny scar under his left eye. His skin was no longer that impossibly soft, peachy perfection of teenage youth: it had texture, it had a story.

A story Temperance wasn't part of.

'So, you're . . . still here?' he asked flatly, not really dredging up enough polite energy to make it sound like genuine curiosity.

Another nail in the coffin for the old sunny, silly and open teenaged Abel. This grumpy sod had risen from his grave.

Her pride stiffened. Her defence mechanisms coiled back on their springs, ready to pounce. She was used to her college friends and bad dates laughing at the fact that she'd never left her tiny, cutesy village, and had no aspirations to, but she didn't expect that kind of snobbery to come from one of

43

their own. Well, someone who had once been one of their own, anyway. She winched up her best cheesy smile. 'Absolutely! There's no place like home. I'd say you've got to be dead inside to want to walk away from this place.'

As if on cue, a loud roaring crash of the waves on the beach reached their ears. Like the East Prawle tourist board were listening in and wanted to play their part.

'Hmm,' he started to walk away before he'd even finished talking, 'well, I'd best just check on Gran, to be safe. See you.'

Temperance watched the retreating back of Abel Gulliver, taller and broader these days than she'd imagined. *See you?! Twelve years vanished off the face of the earth and 'see you' is all he's got to say?!* In her daydreams of a time when Abel might saunter across the green again, she'd imagined shouting and insults and fireworks, but she'd never imagined a dull whimper like this. Even if it wasn't rosy, she thought she might get some answers.

Why did you go, Abel? Why did you leave us?

She watched his back walking further away as the words echoed in her head.

Temperance knew she should feel relieved, that the awkward reunion was finally over: she never had to do that again. Maybe she should feel angry, that he clearly gave zero fucks about seeing her and even sneered about the fact that she still lived in the village. Or maybe some stirring of old love or lust or even nostalgia should be whirring around inside her heart?

No.

Her heart said something else as her eyes were trained on that cobalt shirt, looking bobbled in places but still invitingly soft.

Her heart said *doom.* Very loudly, it said *doom.*

44

Already panting, Temperance burst in the front door and took the stairs two at a time. 'Get out of the bathroom if you're in there, Susie!'

'I'm not,' came a reply muffled by toast crumbs.

'Good!' Temperance slammed the wonky bathroom door and threw her clothes off her body and onto the floor as she started the shower.

Susie crept up the stairs, munching on her sourdough and honey. She plonked herself down on the top step. 'What's going on? You weren't sick on yourself, were you?'

'Ugh,' Temperance thought for a beat as she stepped under the steaming water, 'worse.'

'Oh sis! Like . . . a code brown?!' Susie swiftly put down her plate.

'No! Imagine the most embarrassing thing that could ever happen when your hair is a sandy greaseball and you smell like stale rum.' She scrubbed the shampoo bar deep into her roots.

Susie picked up her breakfast again. 'You bump into some-one you fancy.'

'Or?'

'An ex. But you don't have any exes round here.'

'No, but what about one that we assumed was *far* away, never to return.'

'No!'

'Yes.'

'NO! *Abel*?! *Here*?'

Temperance finished rinsing her hair and let the hot water run over her shoulders for a minute. 'Right here. On the green. Just now.' She could feel each hair on her arms rise as she thought about Abel standing there, like a vision plonked down directly from her daydreams.

45

'Wha . . . How . . . What did he look like?'

Temperance closed her eyes. Taller than six foot, cropped blonde hair and a stubbled jaw. She was suddenly extra aware of how naked she was. 'Good,' she said wistfully.

'Hence the rush to clean yourself up, right.'

'No! It's not that,' she stepped out of the shower and wrapped a big towel around herself. Temperance pulled open the door, a puff of steam unfurling behind her onto the landing. 'I had this dream last night. And I think it was about Abel.'

Susie crunched down on the crispy toast, her eyes wide. 'And it was so filthy you needed a shower.'

'What?! Suse, I'm trying to tell you something *real* here. I had a dream – a really bad dream. One of those nightmares that feels so real that you have tears on your face when you wake up.'

Susie wiped her crumby hands on her leggings. 'OK, sorry. Tell me. Tell me everything.'

'There was,' Temperance's hands wheeled around, grasping for the right words, 'danger coming to the village – a storm, wildfires. Something going seriously wrong at the shop. And this big, heavy veil of *doom* in the dream. It's stuck with me all morning. Then when I saw Abel . . . my heart . . .'

Susie worked very hard to keep her eyebrows in their natural place. 'Your heart?'

'My heart was telling me that it's him. The danger is coming for him. It feels like magic somehow, only not the usual Molland magic. There's something . . . big going on here. Like a spell was cast.' She let out a long, shuddery breath, leaning back against the landing wall and trying to ground herself in the thick, moss-green carpet.

Susie frowned. 'But we can't cast. Right?'

'The Mollands *don't* cast,' Temperance's mum had told her on the night of her seventeenth birthday, in the Witch's Nose, as Lee told her all about the powers she'd just inherited and they both pretended the rosé wine Temperance was sipping was her first ever alcoholic drink. Lee's voice was uncharacteristically steely as she said it for a second time. 'Mollands don't cast. It's something other witches can do but our family don't lean into that side of our abilities. But that doesn't mean we're not powerful witches. To me, it's like we're holding the reins to these big powerful, beautiful horses that are racing away in different directions. We can feel which way they've been running and we can steer them gently onto a new path if we need to. It takes skill, you have to be an incredible listener and be able to hold your nerve.'

'So we can't, like, put spells on people?' Temperance had asked through her thick fringe, her hands making the wine glass go warm and sweaty.

'No. That's not within our powers. And I understand that you'll want to find out more about this world and you might start to research Wiccan customs. But *do not* try to cast, Temps. It's not for us. It can be . . . extremely dangerous, OK?'

Temperance nodded, her head woozy. 'Is it dangerous to . . . is it *illegal* to be a witch?'

Lee had smiled sadly. 'No, babe. Not anymore. But I can't pretend that you wouldn't get a load of weird looks and sniggers and even,' she smoothed a hand over her hair, playing with the ends, 'insults, if you wore that part of your identity on your sleeve. That's why I've always kept it to myself. But it's your decision to make – just yours.'

Temperance stared into her pink drink. 'Ah huh.' She and her mates from school were into roller derby and scribbling

Lady Gaga lyrics on their backpacks and finding somewhere in Devon that served Bubble Tea. She couldn't really imagine how they'd react if they knew she could feel their deepest, darkest fears just by grabbing their cardigans. Just like her crush on Mr Soames, the young physics teacher with prepattern baldness, her magic was best kept secret.

Lee licked her lips, dislodging a little of her cherry-red lipstick. 'You know how you used to ask about your name? Why you were the only Temperance at school? Possibly the whole of Devon, to be honest . . .' Her mum had looked intently into her eyes. 'Well, when I was first told about my own powers, at seventeen,' her eyes glazed over, 'I wanted to know everything about where this magic came from, who'd gone before me, who were the first witches even? And I'm talking pre-internet here, so I went to the library. And what I read scared me, to be really honest, love.'

Temperance felt her heartbeat thump in her throat. *Oh no. Oh god. Am I going to turn into a hag at eighteen? A dragon at twenty-one? Will the house burn down if I sneeze?!*

'Hundreds of years ago, being a witch *was* illegal. In fact, it was punishable by . . . death. Now,' she grabbed Temperance's hand, 'that's not going to happen here and now. But it did happen, to all kinds of women. Women that, for whatever reason, others saw as a problem. A problem they wanted gone. They made up wild lies about them hexing or cursing others, making crops fail, and they held these sham trials to prove their case. Women died on the basis of gossip, of jealously. The last women to ever be executed for witchcraft lived in Devon, in fact.'

Lee squeezed her daughter's hand more tightly. 'When I read that, I vowed I would never use magic, and I would never

48

tell a soul what I was. I started wearing gloves everywhere just so I wouldn't feel anything. Luckily for me, this was 1985 and the neon glove thing was big. For months and months I tried to push it down, deny it all.'

'What happened?' Temperance didn't like how pale her mum's face had turned or how gravelly her voice was.

'I made myself sick, for a while. I bottled up my powers, I bottled up my worries. I think I . . . hated who I was, without knowing it. All I would do is pour over history books about the witch trials, terrorise myself with it.'

'But you don't feel like that now.'

Colour came back into Lee's cheeks. 'No! Not at all. I am so glad I am who I am, so glad. Two things really helped me see the light. While I was obsessing over the history, I took about twelve million buses one Saturday to go to Rougemont Castle. Do you remember I took you guys a few summers back? In Exeter. But this first time I was still about seventeen. There's a plaque there that commemorates the last women to lose their lives in the trials As there was no one else around, I kept my gloves in my pocket. I touched the plaque. And even though it's metal – and I've never felt this before or since with any other kind of solid thing – I could feel the memory in it. Love, pain, strength. Definitely the traces of other magic too, from other witches who'd been there to pay their respects. I wasn't alone in feeling the heartbreaking cruelty of what had gone on back then. It gave me hope. Hope about people. Hope about the best version of people.'

Lee shifted up closer to her daughter on the creaking padded bench. 'The second thing that changed it all for me was looking down into a pair of the deepest brown eyes I'd even seen. The midwife told me that she'd never seen a pair so dark, like midnight on the perfect summer's evening.' She smiled and wiped a threatening tear from the corner of her eye. 'And all this big, fierce love in me said I wasn't going to let anyone tell you to live in fear, to hide who you were, to step back from your power. And so I named you Temperance, and your sister Susie, after two of the last women to be lost to those trials. Because we're reclaiming that stolen power and no one is taking it from us.'

'Woah.' By now, Temperance had drained her glass.

'Yup. Happy birthday, kid.'

Teenage temperance had kept her word not to share the truth about their powers with Susie until it was her own time, and she'd also kept the truth from friends over the years. The only person she might have come close to sharing it with was Abel. But when he took off without explanation the next day, never to be seen again, that took the decision out of her hands. And when Susie did come of age, their shared abilities only brought them closer as sisters.

Sat next to each other on Temperance's bed in the here and now, Temperance and Susie stared out of the tiny window as The Witch's Nose sign squeaked back and forth in the breeze. Temperance was still in her towel – feeling too stuck in what she was trying to say to be able to think about what to wear. What's the perfect outfit when you need to warn the boy that broke your heart that he's in some kind of mortal danger?

'Now don't leap in until I'm finished, OK?' Susie turned to her big sister. 'Let me pose you a hypothetical, like we're seeing this from the outside, yeah? Then when I've finished, you tell me how it seems.' She cleared her throat. 'I have a friend. Let's call her . . . Chastity. She had a big First

Love. A real *Dawson's Creek* of a situation, if you will. But her Pacey upped and left before all these teenage longings could be satisfied.'

'Who's the Dawson in this thing?'

'There's no Dawson here. It was never about Dawson and you know it. Anyway, Pacey runs away. Chastity-slash-Joey never knows why, despite dropping all the hints around Pacey's Gran for, like, twelve years. Chastity's little sister even once, long ago, busted her improvising a bonkers little spell to locate him, featuring about forty candles and a road map of the British Isles. Luckily only one sofa cushion was singed that day.'

Temperance's cheeks flushed hot pink.

'Chastity has lived her life, had some other boyfriends, but no one ever comes that close. She's looking for true love. She's *very* vocal about that. One day she finds a wedding dress absolutely stuffed with the purest love ever. Which she can feel, because she's a witch. Should have led with that.' Susie paused to tip her fingers in a salute to the pub sign. 'She drinks too much one night. Has a bad dream while sleeping on the beach and tanked up on expired rum. But because on a normal day she can feel the magic in some things, she is *maybe*,' Susie scrunched up her eyes, 'seeing the magic in things that are in fact just ordinary. Ordinary worries. Storms and fires are bad, they're scary. Seeing your ex with yesterday's mascara on your cheekbones is cringe. But does it necessarily mean any of it is linked? Or in any way magic? Maybe Chastity is still,' she pinched her fingers together, 'this much drunk?'

Temperance folded her arms. 'I know the difference, Suse. I can *feel* it. The difference between putting on a nice warm coat and enjoying it because it's made from really good wool, beautifully stitched. And putting on a lovely coat that warms you from the inside because it remembers friendship and trust in its fibres. The way you can listen in to the magic, the memory, by opening yourself to it, being still and tuning in. This feeling I have, about this danger – there's no stillness. I'm not tuning into this one: it's blaring right in my ears, whether I want to listen or not. it's like a Stevie Nicks song on concert speakers. It's loud. It's deep. It's taking no prisoners. It's not like having a perfectly good dance around to some Ariana Grande and then switching the radio off. I *can't* turn this off, it is shouting in my heart all the time. And I felt it *before* I saw Abel on the green. I'm not making it fit around him. I'm not even that bothered about him at all!'

Susie kept her hands firmly wrapped around her mug and her tongue in her cheek.

'But I can feel he's in trouble. Big trouble. So I can't . . . as a good human being, just let him toddle off into the jaws of some awful tragedy. I mean, if for nothing else than for poor Margie. She's like a surrogate gran to us, right?'

Her little sister nodded, waving her right hand over the duvet cover to tuck it more tightly around them both.

'And as much as Abel has apparently lost his sense of humour and become a moody douchebag in the last twelve years, he's technically still one of us. We can't let him come to harm, can we?'

'No. But . . . saying you're right about this magical danger . . . which for the record I'm not . . . what do we actually do about it?'

Temperance bit her bottom lip for a moment. 'You're on shift in a bit, aren't you?'

'In three minutes, to be precise.'

'OK. You get to the pub, and do not let him out of your sight,

Suse. Seriously I'll try and come up with some sort of plan.'
She gulped. 'Abel's not going anywhere until I work out what's
happening here. Even if this village is beneath him. He's
staying whether he likes it or not.'

Chapter 7

'Well, if it isn't Mr Miagi,' Susie drawled, bringing out her old nickname for a boy she'd once loved like a brother. The summer Susie turned nine, she decided she wanted to learn to surf and that fifteen-year-old Abel would be her teacher. It hadn't really gone so well, but he'd been patient and kind through it all.

Abel looked up from behind the bar, polishing optics with a tea towel. A smile cracked its way into his cheek on one side. 'Wipe Out?! Christ, you're so . . . grown up!' He lifted the polished wood hatch and strode out to pick her up into a hug.

Susie blinked. This certainly didn't seem like an Abel with a stick up his butt, the way Temperance had just described. Much more like the boy who used to play stuck in the mud with her on the green long after all the other older kids lost interest. 'Oof! Good to see you, too. Growing up is a thing that tends to happen. I wasn't going to stay in tie-dye leggings and a Polly Pocket T-shirt for twelve years.'

He put her down, his smile washing away into something wistful. 'I remember that T-shirt.'

Susie laughed 'Tee had to turn it into a pillow for me, just so I'd agree to stop wearing the raggedy thing.'

'Gran said you work here now. That's awesome.'

'Yeah, amongst other things, here and there. I've done a bit of seasonal stuff along the coast too. But you can't beat The Witch's Nose for the tastiest local gossip. It'll be buzzing with the news that you're back. The prodigal grandson.'

'Yeah, I mean . . . the thing is, I'll probably get going soon.'

Margie came through the swing doors from the kitchen carrying a tray of IPA cans. 'Not until you've helped me with the delivery, you won't. Let a little old lady cart all this about like a Shire horse on its way to the knacker's yard? Pfft.' She shook her head, making the collection of gold chains and charms around her neck tinkle.

Susie bit back her smile. Margie was little but she packed a sinewy punch when she wanted to, from so many years of changing barrels. She was clearly working an angle with her grandson and Susie was only too happy to oblige, especially as she'd stepped into the pub with the same mission: keep Abel in sight, make him stay.

'It's the big city in him now, Marge. Only out for himself, no sense of community,' she teased. 'Where have you come from, anyway?'

'Bath,' Abel replied, quietly.

'Bath?!' Susie guffawed. 'All this time Temps and I thought you were in Melbourne or Texas or . . . Casablanca, and you were only in Bath.' Her tone cooled suddenly. 'Bath isn't that far away. Close enough to come back for visits. Easily.'

Margie gave him stony look. 'Well, he's here now. Come on, lad.'

Abel shrugged off his checked shirt and left it on the bar,

55

following Margie back through the swing doors.

For a moment, Susie's hands twitched to reach out and pull a reading from Abel's shirt. Temperance wasn't the only one who'd been heartbroken the day he left East Prawle: Susie had lost the closest thing she'd ever had to a brother. Would she find a reason behind it all, if she just drew out a memory from the soft blue flannel?

Her fingers flexed, magic sparking in her palms. But she balled them up again. Somehow, it felt like an invasion of privacy, like reading the diary of your best friend. When Abel was ready, he'd tell them, she was sure. This was the good-hearted guy who never made her feel like an annoying little kid, who helped her tie her shoelaces when everyone else had already run off for an ice cream. He had to be in there somewhere.

Susie remembered Temperance's urgent command: *'Don't let him out of your sight, Suse. Seriously.'* Well, taking in a delivery might not be her favourite thing to do at work but at least it would keep Abel busy under her watch for the next few hours.

'I'll give you a hand!' she yelled through the doors. Susie slipped her phone from her back pocket and shot out a text to her big sister:

I think Margie is on our side. Come to back of pub and help xxx

'This is a lot of booze, Gran.'

Margie clutched her chest in mock-horror. 'Oh deary me, whatever will I do with booze in my knitting shop?!' She rolled her eyes. 'The fancy dress party is a big one, Abe, bigger than New Year's almost. Come tomorrow you'll be sweating over all the empties on the green.'

Abel cleared his throat. 'I can't stay, Gran, you know that. I've got . . . things to get back to. Work.'

Margie rolled a small barrel over to the door, putting her hand to her lower back and wincing as she straightened up again. Susie thought it was a masterful touch – light yet effective. 'Your mum can cope without you for a few days and keep the business ticking over. Honestly, you turning up here, it's like you heard my deepest wishes or something.'

'It is?'

'Oh yes. I love this weekend, but it's a hard one. And I'm not getting any younger.' She put her hands to her cheeks, covering up the perfectly placed blusher and pushing her cheeks up, introducing a few exaggerated wrinkles. 'Having you around will save me some serious aches and pains come Monday.'

'Right.' Abel kept his eyes on the boxes he was hauling from the car park tarmac, but Susie could tell the cogs were whirring. She needed to help seal the deal, if she could.

'And now you're here, you've got to see the party. You've got to *dress up* for the party!' Susie said excitedly.

He winced. 'I don't do fancy dress. And I didn't bring anything with me, literally just jumped in the car like this.' He plucked his grey T-shirt between his fingers.

'Good thing we have a whole shop of clothes at our disposal, then!' she chirruped back, not letting his downer of a mood reach her. 'I remember you being pretty inventive back in the day. And even if it's just a mask and some glitter spray, you'll still be getting in the spirit. Gary had the Scouts make some paper-mâché ones. I mean, they smell a bit of damp old newspapers but they do the job.'

'How can I resist?' Abel muttered under his breath.

'Hmm?' Margie's beady eyes were on him in a heartbeat.

'OK, I'm in,' he said more loudly. 'Just for one night, though. Just that.'

Margie put her hands under a cardboard tray of little lemonade bottles and then proceeded to stumble on what Susie could clearly see was perfectly flat ground. 'Oooh!'

'Gran!' Abel rushed forward and caught her by the arm. 'Are you OK?' He took the clanking bottles from her and set them down. 'You don't need to do any more today: Wipeout and I will finish it. You go and have a cuppa.'

Margie held the back of her hand to her forehead for a moment and Susie buried her laughter in her shoulder. 'Maybe that's a good idea, lad. It's just, when I heard you say you won't be staying for my birthday party next weekend, I came over all funny, you know?'

Abel shut his eyes. 'Your seventieth. I'd forgotten.'

Margie's voice went reed thin and wavery. 'Of course, it's easy to forget about your old Gran when you're off out and about, living your life. I understand. It's just a simple barbeque on the green for the people I hold closest to my heart. To raise a glass to the fact I'm still here. For now, anyway. You'll be there, won't you, Susie love?'

Margie had never before called Susie anything remotely like 'Susie love'. Affectionate nicknames in Margie's worldview were 'bugalugs', 'harpy' and 'silly knickers', but nothing so sappy as 'love'.

'I wouldn't miss it, Marge. You know, Temps and I were just saying this morning how you're the closest thing *we* ever had to a gran and you mean *so much* to us. Helping out with the cooking and serving is the least we can do.'

Abel growled. 'I didn't pack a bag, Gran. How can I stay a week and miss that much work? And you know I can't—'

Margie held up her hands, her signet rings catching the sunlight. 'I've got you pants and pjs, all that stuff. No bother. I keep a little drawer of essentials ready for you, in case you ever come back.'

Susie's heart lurched. This bit wasn't a trick. She could see the vulnerability in Margie's eyes all of a sudden. Even though Susie and Temperance had long ago accepted that Abel was long gone, never to return, Margie must have been leaving the door open just a crack all this time.

'Oh, Gran,' he put his arm around the small but mighty woman's shoulders. After a sigh, he went on, 'I haven't taken a week off in . . . a long time. Maybe years. So I'm overdue. I'll move some things around, OK? But *just* a week. And I'll work here at the pub so I'm,' his eyes flicked to Susie briefly, 'kept out of trouble.'

'. . . and it turned out the woman was making all the cat ornaments in her shop from *real* cat fur! *Bleurgh.* So I gave my notice in after my lunchbreak and never went back. I'm more of a dog person anyway.' Susie stacked a box of beer bottles just inside the back door and wiped her hands on her jeans.

Abel shook his head, laughing.

Temperance couldn't believe the sight she was taking in. Abel: relaxed, smiling, not bolting in the opposite direction to someone from his past. She couldn't deny that her ribs were squeezing her heart in a confusing way. One part of her was happy deep down inside that Abel and Susie were catching up like no time had lapsed at all. But another much more shallow part was stung that something about Susie made it easy for

Abel to chat and laugh, whereas he'd had a total of about six syllables for Temperance earlier on the green.

What was so irritating about this particular Molland sister? Her inner critic piped up with an answer: *Because Susie never threw herself at him back in the day, not like you did.* *So embarrassing.* Temperance squeezed her eyes shut for a minute, silencing her saboteur and the roll of nerves in her stomach.

'Oh, hello there, Tee!' Susie said in a big, panto-like voice. 'If you're not up to much there's this huge delivery to get inside.'

'Um, sure. I can help.'

Abel's face went from wide open to shutters down in a split second as he took in Temperance walking towards them over the car park tarmac. 'We're covered, but thanks.'

'Seriously, I can—'

'It's probably an insurance thing,' he cut in. 'If you're not an employee then you're not covered for an accident from carrying heavy stuff.'

Susie frowned. 'Well, *you're* not an employee, for starters. And when have you ever known Margie to be bothered about health and safety? Temps is fine, come on. She can stick to the tiny mixer bottles if you're really worried about her.'

His mouth opened as if to protest again, before he clamped it shut and took a deep breath. Temperance would never know if it was her involvement or the idea that Abel could be worried about her that he objected to.

'Whatever you like. Let's just crack on.' His shoulders hunched almost up to his ears, he turned on the spot and stalked into the pub.

Whoever had dug out the cellar to The Witch's Nose hundreds of years ago had been a lot shorter and a lot narrower than Abel Gulliver. As the three of them trooped up and down the well-worn steps, he was having to stoop to get through the passageways and occasionally Temperance would hear his whispered curses as he shoulder-barged yet another doorframe painfully.

They carried the boxes in awkward silence, like those funny little penguins that click-clack up the toy mountain to race down the other side and back up again in an endless manic loop. Once Susie had stacked a box, she would patiently wait to one side for Abel to come down into the storage room to stack his, before she slipped upstairs again when the coast was clear. But Abel had no time to give Temperance the same grace and he would head back up the narrow staircase while she was still halfway down, forcing them into a tussle for what little space was available. She would have to duck her head under his chin, the stubble on his neck within a whisper of touching her forehead for one spit-second. Abel would lean so heavily back on the white-washed walls behind him in those moments that Temperance fully expected him to merge into the rough plaster and disappear. At one stage she thought it best to move the box of tiny orange juice bottles she was carrying out of his way, but she mistimed the move and winded him in the stomach instead.

'Oh! Sorry! It's so . . . cramped in here.'

'S'fine, yeah,' he spluttered, taking the steps now two at a time in a bid to escape.

Temperance's cheeks burned in the dim lighting as she went on her way. She added her box to the pile and took a minute to count her breaths in and out. Going from twelve years of silence to only millimetres of distance between them was a lot.

61

It was too much. Her hands felt clammy but her mouth was dry.

'Get a hold of yourself, Temperance,' she chided herself quietly, her sharp tone echoing around the stone walls. 'You're not seventeen anymore. You don't go weak at the knees.' But being that close to Abel on the stairs, just for a heartbeat, feeling the warmth of his breath, watching his tongue lick his bottom lip . . . Temperance's thoughts had not been the sensible, twenty-nine-year-old kind. They were embarrassingly adolescent.

How was it going to go, having Abel Gulliver suddenly back in East Prawle? Could she strike up a conversation in the bakery queue, all nonchalant? Could she casually chat to him at the bar, like he didn't just vanish all those years ago with no explanation? OK, he left a note and his hoodie, but that hadn't really explained things at all. And when she'd touched that hoody twelve years ago . . .

Temperance shuddered in the cool of the cellar at the memory of what she'd felt in its fibres. It was only the first day of her powers waking up inside her – her seventeenth birthday – and this was the very first strong emotion she'd ever read. The tingle in her fingers still felt overwhelming and uncomfortable that day, like driving a car before you feel ready and worrying you'll veer off the road and cause a fireball of damage. Being told she was a witch had sent Temperance into a spin, to say the least: she was looking for the reassurance of Abel to ground her again. Rain or shine, he was the one she could depend on and she had raced to their usual meeting spot to find him. But there was only his hoodie. And even without any magical experience behind her then, she didn't have any trouble interpreting the feelings thread through the sky-blue material.

Stomach-churning disgust. Deep regret. Panic. Temperance saw herself and Abel, their lips millimetres apart, closing the gap in agonising slow motion. His eyelashes, his hand on her wrist. But as their kiss connected, the vision went black and cloudy. Her skin crawled, her heart screwed into a knot. She felt everything Abel felt: and he was sick to his stomach that they had done it. He wanted to run away. The next thing she saw was him throwing things into a bag, his mum standing behind him, her face drawn and anxious. They were talking, it was emotional, but something about the memory made the words distort and bleed, so Temperance couldn't make out a thing they were saying. She could only pick up the anguished tone that wrapped around everything they said.

Temperance's fingertips had brushed the hoodie sleeve that day before her hand shot back, as if it had been scalded. She could still feel the memory coursing through her veins, even after she'd broken contact.

In the years that followed, Temperance rarely found a lingering emotion that had the same effect: like a riptide that could pull you under and deep, deep down. The intensity of what she'd read told her in one heartbeat that everything she thought she knew about Abel was no longer true. It made her question whether it ever had been.

Having a week with Abel Gulliver now meant a week to save him. But it also meant seven days full of reminders that he'd once been so horrified by Temperance's major crush on him that he'd packed up and left East Prawle forever. He'd abandoned a lifelong friendship without so much as a backward glance. That kind of wounding rejection had crushed her for years: she didn't need to keep feeling echoes of it in the pub, on the green, or at the beach, or even just glimpsing out of her bedroom window. Especially not when she had the shop to run in her mum's absence.

Her heart squeezed as she realised she wished her mum was there – just then – with a cup of tea and some sage advice.

She was jolted out of her reverie by Susie calling down the stairs, 'That's the last of the drinks. Just kitchen supplies to do now. I'll put the kettle on!'

As Temperance left the cellar room and put her foot on the first stair, she looked up and saw the tall shadow of Abel filling the doorway at the top, the strip-light behind him drawing a sharp outline of his head bent uncomfortably under the low ceiling. Why was he just standing there like that? Like the Hunchback had been evicted from Notre Dame. At the sound of her trainers hitting the stone steps, he suddenly moved off and into the light.

Temperance entered the pub kitchen a few minutes later and found Abel fiddling with the electronic kitchen roll dispenser and Susie stacking what seemed like a hundred spare blue rolls of paper in the walk-in cupboard.

'This fiddly bast—what's wrong with just a roll on a stick? Why has it got to be automatic and hands-free? This isn't a bloody spaceship. It's a pub,' he muttered, wrestling to get the front of the dispenser off.

Susie came out of the cupboard with her hands on her hips. 'You try getting some paper off the roll while you have an exploded bottle of sweet chilli sauce all over your hands and halloumi burning in the deep-fat fryer and Margie bellowing for service. A busy pub *does* need a fancy paper towel thing so just treat my baby gently, OK?'

Abel, suitably admonished, went back to jiggling the container less violently.

'What shall I do?' Temperance ventured.

'Tea, *please*,' Susie spoke from behind a rack of lightbulbs, tea towels and ash trays.

'Coming up.'

Temperance tried to be normal as she made the tea, standing right next to Abel. She tried to stand normally, move her hands normally, drop the tea bags in normally. But every now and then she would realise she'd been holding her breath, watching him in her peripheral vision, and all the air would come stuttering out of her mouth like an avalanche. Something about being in his orbit made her forget the most basic things. It was just so fascinating to see how he'd changed and how he hadn't: he had a good few inches of extra height, but still the same silver slice of a scar behind his right ear. Temperance bet that if she ran her fingers over it, it would feel the same, and her hand even lifted briefly in the air before she snatched it back.

Abel had never pressed his mouth into such a rigid straight line in the old days and his lips were maybe a little fuller now too, but that easy laugh Temperance had seen him give Susie earlier was classic Abel – his eyes closed in happiness, his head shaking twice, and the way each burst of laughter seemed to charge through his body and make his whole being lighter, warmer.

But studying this new version of Abel was like looking at a museum exhibit behind glass: Temperance would never get close enough to really understand him. And mooning over a boy was not going to solve any magical doom riddles. Temperance needed to distract herself from the way his strong hands were gripping at the dispenser, rattling it, the swear words he was murmuring under his breath that sent a strangely delicious shiver along her spine. So she took up a mental checklist of all the boring little things she'd need to run Stevie through in the shop: how the till got rebooted, where the receipts were stored, the accounts software. Plus, all the things she'd need to hide from her: their ancient cauldron, the drawers full of dried herbs, the fact that sometimes she went—

A sharp flash of bright purple preceded a short but loud pop and Abel jumped backwards. 'Fuck!'

Before she knew what she was doing, Temperance had moved towards him, taken him by the wrists and blurted out, 'Are you OK?'

Abel looked too stunned to be able to register that she was now right in the middle of his personal space, even closer than they had been on the stairs. 'The damn thing shocked me! How do you get a static shock off plastic and paper?'

He blinked and set the paper roll he'd been holding down on the work surface, next to the big industrial hob. 'Any chance that tea is ready? I could do with eight sugars in mine.' He blew out an exaggerated sigh and smiled.

But the minute he lifted his eyes to Temperance's, almost hidden under a frown of concern, it was like a director had called 'Action!' and Abel switched back into his grumpy old sod performance. He yanked his arms away from her touch and Temperance fought hard not to flinch.

There was a deep tingling in her fingers: the same sensation she had when reading magic, but right now her hands were only held in mid-air, her fingers still shaped around the dimensions of Abel's wrists as if refusing to believe they were no longer making physical contact.

'What's going on?' Susie emerged from the stock cupboard, her cheeks pale, and Temperance could tell by the way her little sister was flexing her hands that she too had the same strange sensation.

'Honestly, nothing. I'm just . . . ready for a break. That mine?' He pointed at one of the teacups and Temperance nodded dumbly.

Susie's eyes bore into Temperance but she could only give the tiniest, mystified shrug. She'd felt the wave of magic in the air, but she had no explanation for it.

Abel sniffed. 'Is it Earl Grey, this? Something smells floral in here. Or like lavender?'

'Argh!' Susie lunged forward and threw a tea towel over Abel's abandoned paper roll, which now had a column of flames licking up one side. She went to switch off the hob burner, but all the dials were set to zero. 'What the . . .? How?'

'It smells like wildflowers,' Temperance said, almost to herself. 'But burnt.'

8

Chapter 8

Susie and Temperance walked in numb silence over the green, past Stevie on the cash desk at Try Again, and then slumped into their desks in the office.

'Believe me now?' Temperance asked, her fingers fiddling with a tape measure. 'I know you felt that weird magic surge too. And the fire smelled like *wildflowers*, Suse. Just like I dreamt. This isn't some boozy nightmare. This is . . . well, I don't know what it is. But it can't be good.'

The loved-up wedding gown was lying over Temperance's desk and she scrunched her fist into the silk skirts, grounding herself with an echo of second-hand joy and devotion.

'Right. Shit.' Susie's eyebrows were up around her hairline. 'So some sort of magical . . .'

'Doom,' Temperance provided.

Susie nodded. 'Some sort of magical doom is coming for Abel, but we don't know what and we don't know why. We just have to stop it. You see, this is where it would help to have a big *Buffy*-style library full of magic books.' She kicked her legs up on her desk.

'Let's just keep Abel in the village, for starters. Once FairyFest is over we'll have a bit more head space to work it out. Somehow.' Temperance winced at the paper-thin substance of her own plan.

'OK. That makes sense.' A small smiled warmed up Susie's features. 'Do you know what Abel said to me this morning, in the pub?'

Temperance's head shot up. 'What?'

'He called me Wipeout. I'd completely forgotten that nickname! From my old surfing phase.'

Temperance couldn't help but snort a laugh through her nose. 'I don't think you can call two weekends a phase. Especially not when you mostly tasted seawater and threw tantrums about it.'

'I was passionate, you have to give me that. Just not gifted with the right kind of balance, unfortunately. Paddle boarding is much more my thing. Much more chill. Oh, do you remember that last surfing lesson with Abel, where I swore I was on the verge of a breakthrough so you had to come and watch?'

'Maybe.'

'You must do! I was absolutely soaked, seaweed hanging off my ears, furious and crying. I came over and plonked myself in your lap to hug it out, getting you wet too? Abel wrapped us up in his towel, insisting his wetsuit was enough. But his lips were fully blue by the time we got to the pub.'

The memory glowed through Temperance but then turned into a singe of bitterness. When Abel left East Prawle he left her out in the cold without a second thought. And this older, meaner Abel wouldn't wrap her up in a towel, not even if she was on fire.

Susie looked across on the wedding dress. 'Are you still

wearing that tonight?'

Temperance looked up. 'Yes. Why?'

'No reason. I'm glad. You look amazing in it. And if anyone should have the night off to twirl about like a Fairy Princess, it's you. And what better way for you to get back on your True Love mission, right.' She winked. 'In *this* dress, after all. No Goblin King with eyes in his head could resist you. It's just a shame that it now smells faintly like BO and seaweed.'

Stevie appeared at the doorway. 'Isn't that why you have all the herbs? You've got time to give it a quick rinse and let it dry for tonight.'

'NO!' the sisters both yelled in unison, making Stevie take a step back.

'Okayyyy.' She edged away, her eyebrows drawn together.

'Um, no, sorry Stevie. It's just . . .' Temperance searched for an explanation, 'there's no point in cleaning it, only to get it mucky again tonight. The old barn smells like hops and sweat anyway and I'll probably come home with a tide mark of cider on it.'

Temperance had already caught Stevie admiring their old walnut bureau at the back of the office on her first visit and had speedily fudged an explanation that the dried flowers and herbs inside were there to keep the vintage clothes smelling fresh, and to act as organic deodorisers when they needed to wash the odd garment.

The wildflowers that the Molland women gathered from their own cliffs in East Prawle helped amplify their magic: lavender to counteract memories of anger or fear, to soothe a raging heart and bring balance to the mind; rosemary to treat lingering guilt or shame, to let go of the past and take only the lessons of it into the future; cedar to banish self-doubt and self-loathing, encouraging that void to be filled with confidence and strength one day. Lee kept a fresh pot of basil growing on the windowsill for any stubborn negative emotions that wouldn't shift on the first try. Strongest of all, and used most sparingly, was rue. When Temperance picked up a piece of clothing and saw only jagged weeping in an endless night, felt the twist behind her ribs of loneliness and hurt, the echoes of betrayal, she knew that rue was the herb to exorcise memories of a broken heart.

It was a unique skill passed through their female family line to be able to feel the emotions that lingered on clothing but Temperance's mother had also taught her that even when ordinary people weren't conscious of the memories attached to their clothes, they could still be affected by them. They thought it was superstitious or sentimental to hold onto a T-shirt they'd raced their first ever 5k in, never knowing that the joy and confidence it carried emanated out when they pulled it back on for their first marathon, keeping their heart full even as their energy depleted. Or the sting or disappointment that hid in the folds or a daringly loud shirtdress which an old friend had told them was 'brave for *you* to wear' and how that would work its way into the back of their mind every time they went to pull it from the wardrobe, only to falter and shove it back. The negative energy that had its hooks in a piece of clothing would sit next to the new owner's skin, leaching into their system, whispering doubts and frustrations and bitterness into their subconscious, distorting how they saw themselves and others. Like any sort of parasite, these negative feelings wanted to set up home under the surface and would only be forced to leave once witches like Temperance and her family could do their thing.

The Molland women at Try Again didn't just love vintage clothes for the love of clothes. That was there, of course: marvelling over a Pucci print, discovering a hand-tailored suit in a battered old suitcase or whispering in awe at a Hermès silk scarf. They loved clothes the way a vet loved animals: to pet them on good days and save them on bad ones. With some care and attention, they could tease out the bad memories that had been woven years, even generations, before and send a garment off with a new owner who would really treasure it and perhaps embroider it with their own happy moments. Temperance knew that Stevie's love of vintage passion was just as pure, if not a lot more straightforward. She'd somehow have to try to hide the extra element to their work at Try Again, without dimming the intern's enthusiasm.

'How about I grab you when I'm doing my next batch of refreshing and I can . . . walk you through it?'

'Sure,' Stevie replied, distracted as she watched Temperance tenderly move the dress onto her lap, like it was a delicate little newborn kitten.

'Come over to ours at six and get ready with us,' Susie offered, keen to change the subject from one veering too close to their secret magical ways. 'We could do you some fancy whiskers with face paint. And then it can get smeared all over the face of one of the hot backpackers.' She grinned.

Temperance lowered her eyebrows. 'Not everyone is looking to pull every night, sis.'

'And not everyone is obsessing over a One True Love like you, sis.' She stuck out her tongue.

'Romance isn't really the top of my list,' Stevie chipped in, her eyes still on the heavy embroidered bodice Temperance was holding up to herself with one hand. As if it weighed nothing. But Stevie knew for a fact that it weighed the same as a small pony. 'I'm just getting a feel for the place, that's all.'

9

Chapter 9

'You, kid, are a bloody wind-up merchant.' A mask covered in glossy black paint spoke to Susie as she was unstacking chairs in the barn. Dance music was warming up the speakers around her. An hour to go before the night kicked off properly, but the buzz was already palpable.

'Huh?'

Abel lifted the mask to the top of his head. It was a half-mask with a long beak-like nose. Clearly Gary had been getting the Scouts to study Venetian tradition. 'Where's your costume then? If I'm wearing this musty thing all night, you've got to put in some effort.'

Susie turned fully on the spot. 'Uh, excuse me? I've put hours of work into this.'

Abel looked her up and down quickly, disbelief still making his eyes wide. 'Into what?!'

She sighed. 'I'm a sixties pixie. Get it? Micro mini, flower power, pointy ears, even a pixie *cut*, although this thing is getting itchy already.' In turn, she pointed to her miniskirt in a psychedelic print, the Day-Glo flowers Stevie had painted on her cheeks, pointy pixie ears, and a cropped blonde wig she'd found in the shop. 'It's vintage fashion, dahling, look it up. Besides, Margie has a prize for originality, so any old goblin won't cut it. What are you then?' She scrutinised his black T-shirt and jeans.

'I am wearing the only clean T-shirt my gran had for me and one of the Scouts' masks like you said. So let's say I'm a mask thingy, yeah?'

'No medal for you then, Miagi.'

'Only for the biggest chump, maybe. Getting roped in to work for free all week. I've just seen Gran lift a whole bench by herself and carry it out to the green. She certainly chooses her moments to be frail and helpless.'

Susie smiled. 'One of those things that comes and goes.'

He pulled his mask back down and took a deep breath before speaking again. 'Is Temperance coming tonight?'

'Of course. But you must have seen her just now, on the green?'

'No.'

Susie rolled her eyes. 'Bloody men. She's literally impossible to miss. She's finishing up the fairy picnic so the little ones can be put to bed before the real fun starts.'

The mask looked down at Abel's trainers. 'Right. Well, I'll give you a hand, shall I?'

A light came on behind Susie's eyes. 'No, Stevie's coming over in a minute to help me. But the sooner Temps gets those kids back off to bed the better. I'm sure she'd appreciate you chipping in.'

'Ah. Well . . .' His head turned around the space, looking but not finding any other kind of necessary job. 'I'll do that then.'

Abel walked back through the cavernous little rooms of the

pub, ducking his down under the low timber doorways, just as he'd had to ever since he hit a growth spurt at fourteen, and leaving his mask on the bar. He could navigate this place with his eyes closed, even after all this time. The smells, the textures, the hum of the fridges and air vents: it was all so familiar. He and his mum had had a tiny flat above the bakery when they still lived in East Prawle. Waking up to the smell of doughnuts frying was no bad thing, but the pub always felt like his true home. Abel felt like he'd left a part of himself in the village when he went that night, at eighteen, and if you could sweep a soul detector over East Prawle to find where the missing fragment of Abel Gulliver lay, it would probably give a tinny ping somewhere behind the bar, maybe next to the glass dish of lemon slices.

But life wasn't as simple as staying in your hometown all your life, he reminded himself, stepping onto the wide stone porchway. Thousands of feet over hundreds of years had worn a dip in the flagstones: visitors had a great time at The Witch's Nose and then they moved on. Maybe ten minutes down the road, maybe a hundred miles. You couldn't always stay in one place.

Even if you wanted to.

Some cheery accordion music wheezed its way over the grass as he took in the busy scene, still as bright and buzzing at 6.30pm as it had been earlier this afternoon when Abel had carried trays of drinks out to the benches and seen snippets of the toadstool hunt, games of fairy Simon Says and What's the Time Mr Werewolf? But Abel couldn't see Temperance anywhere, just a few sets of parents lounging on the grass as their children played with one of those party princesses.

Just then, the princess broke the ring-a-roses circle to tuck her hair behind her ears, and in that gesture he suddenly saw her. She used to tuck her hair behind her ear like that before a recorder recital, or when they were tackling maths homework together in the pub, or nervously awaiting her GCSE results. Swallowed up by that massive dress almost, a far cry from the denim shorts and T-shirts she used to wear when they were kids. And her hair was . . . fancy, in massive tumbling curls and something in it making it sparkle. It was no wonder the little kids looking up at her were totally smitten, gooey with admiration for what seemed like a real-life fairy princess in their midst.

Abel wandered over the road to the green, hands in pockets. He got close enough to hear what Temperance was saying but not close enough to interrupt.

'Okidokey, we've done the summoning dance to send the fairies to bed. They're all tucked up in their walnut shells with their little moss blankets. Lovely. Now, very soon it will be ice pop time – but only for every child who can put their chip wrappers in the bin. And whoever is first back can choose their favouritest colour! Go go go!'

There was an instant rush and Abel stood back to let the stampede pass, catching Temperance's eye as he did so. She gave an awkward wave. He waved back and moved closer, even though his head told him not to.

'Anything I can help you—' But before he could finish the question, he was verbally rugby-tackled by twenty or so small kids.

'Who are YOU?'

'What is that costume?'

'Are you her DAD?'

Abel let out a throaty laugh. 'I'm not her dad! I'm her friend.'

The word felt odd to say, somehow, and it didn't seem to satisfy the four-foot crowd.

Temperance's eyes met his for just a second, before she busied herself packing away balls and skittles.

'Like a fairy friend?' asked one little girl at the back, her eyes blazing with belief.

He winced just slightly. 'Yes?'

A boy at the front poked Abel's knee. 'You look like a bad fairy. You have NO sparkles. Bad fairy.'

A tense hush fell over the group. Temperance raised her eyebrows and swished her skirt side to side. It was a crunchy, almost hypnotic sound that filled his head and it didn't exactly help Abel to think of what to say next.

The girl with the wings started to blink rapidly and her bottom lip turned over.

'But uh, um . . . I *used* to be bad and then, then,' he looked to Temperance, hoping he could somehow communicate 'SOS' in her direction.

'Then . . . he was lucky enough to find a magical fairy ring of fairy apprentices on this special fairy day. And they told him if he promised to stop being bad,' Temperance put one hand to her hip and waved her wand in front of his face, 'to stop being so grumpy and monosyllabic, to remember the good fairy he once was, then they could cure him with an enchanted ice pop . . .'

Abel's shoulders relaxed.

'. . . *after* we perform the sacred fairy dance one more time.'

He groaned.

'Let's hold hands.' Temperance ushered the kids into a circle. Without really looking or thinking, Abel lifted his hand at his side out to her. Temperance stared at his palm, before grabbing him by the shoulders and shoving him into the middle of the ring. He could feel how tightly her finger tips dug into his shoulder blades for just a second. 'You stand there, Bad Fairy.'

The children giggled and trapped Abel in their ring-o-roses.

'And now we chant: *You're a good fairy, you're a good fairy, you're a good fairy!*' Her minions quickly joined in, voices sweet but commanding.

'And now *you* say,' she locked her eyes onto his with intensity, her forehead furrowed. It was clear that complying was his only option. 'I'm a good fairy, I'm a . . .?'

'Good fairy,' Abel breathed.

'Bit louder.' Her voice was firm, but with a lilt of teasing to it.

'Good fairy.' He wanted the paper-mâché toad stool ring to spontaneously burst into flame and take him down with it.

'Can't quite hear you.'

'*I'm a good fairy!*' Some of the parents looked over, one barely hiding their laughter behind a newspaper.

Temperance clapped, bouncing on the spot. Abel found himself watching the way it made the thick curls in her hair bounce too. 'That should do it. An ice pop is the final magical ingredient and then he's cured. Hooray!' The mini fairies all cheered. 'Now . . . hang on, I've left the cold box in my . . . er, fairy freezer.' She squinted for a minute. 'You all line up behind Bad—Good Fairy, wait here and I'll be back in a jiff. A magical jiff.'

A scrambled queue came together in no time and Temperance was heading off to the porch before Abel could say anything to stop her. Ten pairs of beady eyes turned on him.

It was slow-moving, carrying out the cold box full of ice

lollies, which would have been heavy on a good day. But today Temperance was also wearing a dress that weighed the same as a small pony. It took her a good fifteen minutes to get from the kitchen back to The Witch's Nose porch, even when she was subtly using her powers to pick up a little of the heavy petticoats when she was sure she couldn't be seen. She was doubly glad she'd asked Stevie to take off the red satin belt earlier – that was not complication she needed in Mary Poppins mode. Stevie had made Temperance swear to put it back on before the party started though, because it would be an 'affront to accessories everywhere' if she didn't perfect her look.

The pillowy comfort of the love wrapped up in the dress had Temperance feeling so confident and centred that entertaining a rabble of sugar-fuelled kids had been a breeze today. And she'd only had a slight wobble when she saw Abel coming to join them.

It's lucky I don't care what I look like in front of him, Temperance thought to herself. *Because my face is probably beetroot right now and my eyeliner is possibly somewhere near my ears. But I don't care. So that's handy.*

As she nudged open the heavy pub door with her bum and swung the box around through it, her breath caught in her throat. Abel lay on the green, spread-eagle, face down. The kids were all stood around the edge of the grass, as if terrified to go near him. They just stared, silently. None of the parents relaxing nearby were moving either.

Oh my god. It's happened. The doom. It found him – I'm too late.

Temperance could feel her heart beat in her ears. She let the cold box drop to the floor with an almighty thud, hauled up her skirts as best as she could and sprinted towards the green.

No, no! I didn't get a chance . . . I was going to fix this . . . I can't lose him again!

Her brain was tumbling through what she knew of CPR, if there might be a doctor on holiday nearby, if you could call 999 and say 'I think some magic has taken out my first love – help!'

It can't end like this. It can't.

As she raced back past one of the kids, she heard a squeaky voice say, 'Not fair! He didn't say go yet!'

'WHO disturbs my SLUMBER?!' Abel raised his head and yelled, jumping up to his feet with unbelievable agility for someone so tall and who Temperance could have sworn was dead three seconds ago. She stopped in her tracks, treading on the hem of the dress and nearly losing her balance. Abel held out his finger, pointing at the boy who'd complained as Temperance rushed in front of him.

'The dragon will eat this one first! Then the rest! Arrgggghhhhh!'

There was a chorus of happy squealing as the children starting running in all directions, back and forth over the grass. Abel flapped his long arms and took chase after them. When he caught Temperance's eye his cheeks coloured and he hesitated for a moment. But she shrugged and waved her hand at her outfit, as if to say there was no shame in being ridiculous for a tiny audience, so off he roared. Slowly, her heart rate dropped to something like normal and she tried to discreetly rub away the sweat that had gathered between her cleavage, under the dress's tight corset.

Once all the kids had been caught with a soft tag to the top of the head and had had their chance to do a noisy, over-the-top death scene, Temperance shouted, 'Time for a snack. Any zombies here that like ice pops?'

She opened up the cool box to a pile of almost-neon coloured frozen treats.

'I know you'll have lime,' Temperance said to an out-of-breath Abel, passing up the tube of frozen green slush, the memory of his favourite flavour so deeply ingrained in her that she wasn't even conscious she'd accessed it. It was simply a fact of nature: the tides came and went, the sun sometime shone and Abel Gulliver loved lime. 'Martha, what would you like, lovely?'

'Strawberry, please, Princess.'

Standing next to her as she crouched down to kid-level, Abel could see Temperance's neck flush red just a little. He could also see the way, from where he stood, that dress was forcing her figure into an even more accentuated hourglass and he tore his eyes away to study the grass, the kerb, the bus stop. Anything else.

'Can you open it? No? These things are always such a blood—such a fiddle, I should have got some scissors from the pub.'

'Let me.' Abel raised his eyebrows, glad of a distraction, and gently took the ice pop from Martha and snapped it in two. 'There you go.'

Martha's eyes went wide, as if she'd witnessed some real fairy magic that she shouldn't have.

Temperance laughed. 'How did I not know that? God, the hours of my life I must have wasted trying to tear my way into them and I could have just . . .' she picked up a cola-flavoured one and cracked it open, 'boom! Do you like cola, Tristan? Here you go. Strawberry, Jenny?' She snapped another and passed it over. 'Oh my god, so satisfying. I feel like Lara Croft running a Mr Whippy.'

Abel burst out into a heavy, deep laugh. Temperance couldn't help but drink in the noise – the first time she'd heard her old best friend properly laugh in a very, very long time. It caught her so off guard that she laughed too and then rushed to change the subject. 'Parents! We're ready to say goodbye to our fairy apprentices if you'd like to come and get them.'

The children were collected, their water bottles and abandoned cardigans scooped up, and the little mayhem makers were reluctantly led off to their beds.

Somehow, standing on the now empty green with Abel felt a lot stranger than being with him and a bunch of five-year-olds.

Temperance looked at him, but his eyes were on the horizon, his jaw clenched. It was on the tip of her tongue just to blurt out, 'Why did you go? Why couldn't you have at least talked to me first?' And her heart seemed to be rallying with confidence, like the dress was nudging her to do it, to get answers, to get some long-overdue closure. Maybe the tense Abel that turned up yesterday had just been in a bad mood, weighed down with worry for Margie? Maybe he was coming back to himself, here at home, with people that really knew him?

Abel's head dipped, then he turned to her. 'Tee, I . . .' He held his bottom lip between his teeth. 'Being on the green like this, like when we were . . .' he frowned, his words tailing off.

'Yes?' Temperance's heart was screaming at her now to take charge. *Ask him! This is the old Abel, can't you see? Ask him, quick!*

His eyes held hers, those green eyes flecked with grey that she would know anywhere. Abel seemed to almost frown in concentration for a moment. 'I sometimes think . . . I mean, if I could . . .'

Temperance nodded frantically. A sudden breeze passed over her bare shoulders. But she wasn't aware of the goosepimples on her arms, of how ridiculous she looked in a full wedding gown in the middle of East Prawle. She didn't even know she was holding her breath: all she could focus on were the words coming out of Abel's mouth. *He was going to explain it all: the sudden vanishing act, the hostile moods. He had to.*

'The green,' he cleared his throat suddenly, 'is for everyone. We shouldn't leave it a mess. I'll help you with this stuff.' He nodded over to the rainbow parachute the kids had been using earlier, still unfurled and draped over a bench.

Her mouth opened and closed uselessly as it felt like a stone was weighing her heart down to the pit of her stomach. She shook her head and found some sort of shred of composure. 'Right. Sure.'

Temperance felt dizzy from such a U-turn between them and numbly picked up one edge of the parachute, rolling it along the grass as Abel did the same from the opposite edge. It had *really* felt like something was opening up between them, just then. But clearly, yesterday wasn't a blip. Clearly, he was someone totally different now. Someone who lectured others on being a public nuisance. Who had no lasting affection for the places or people that had made up his childhood. It was like Abel was photoshopping himself out of all her memories, leaving just a sad, blank smudge in Temperance's heart where the thought of him should have been.

Temperance kept her head down, scrunching up the canvas under her fingers, concentrating on this thankfully soulless fabric and not all the tangled threads between her and Abel.

Maybe, sometimes things were just too messy. Sometimes you never get back to the knot at the heart of it all.

Her knuckles brushed against Abel's as they reached the middle together. His skin was warm, his hands broader than she remembered. She heard him draw in a breath.

'Sorry.' He pulled back, standing up tall and checking his watch.

Temperance knew for certain that she had to say goodbye to the playful Abel of the olden days. He'd vanished into the air again like a popped bubble. 'I should see if Gran needs me. Not long till kick off. You're done here, yeah?'

She nodded her throat too constricted with sadness to say anything at any rate.

So much for the good fairy.

10

Chapter 10

Stevie put her hands nervously to the tops of her thighs. 'It felt like this catsuit had a bit more "suit" to it, in the store. It's pretty . . . clingy,' she said just over the music in the beer garden.

Margie was taking a breather after three hours of hurriedly serving drinks and advising two amorous mermaids in one of the booths to go somewhere more private before one of them lost a clamshell. Her feet were up on the rim of a plant pot full of begonias and she was sipping a large G&T. She winked at Stevie. 'As my mum used to say, I can see what you had for breakfast in that. But – my darling – you are young and beautiful and free, why not show off what you've got? And with all those sparkles, you're like an extra glitter ball on the dance floor. You should be charging me a fee.'

Stevie smiled and fixed the placement of her cat ears. 'Thank you.'

'Though you're wasting it out here. Susie will be due her break any minute. You two can tear it up with my full support. Life is for living. And speaking of which . . .'

Abel hurried past them on his way inside, his mask on top of his head, a round tray of empty glasses balanced on each hand.

'Are you taking a break any time soon, lad?' Margie called.

Abel looked over his shoulder then down at the trays. 'What do you expect me to do with this lot? The limbo?'

Margie cackled. 'So much of your grandfather in you.'

Stevie noticed that Abel didn't exactly seem pleased to hear this. In fact, by the way his jaw was moving it was like he was grinding his teeth. 'When things are quieter, I'll take my ten,' he said finally, and quietly, disappearing inside.

'Oh, I bet. Ten minutes is more than enough time to chat up my customers!' She winked.

'Gran,' Abel said flatly, 'I'm not interested in anyone in this village. You know that.'

Margie rolled her eyes. 'Whatever you say, my boy.'

'I'll, um, see how Suse is doing.' Stevie set off a few paces behind Abel, still very conscious of how tight her outfit was and cursing the unusually flattering mirrors in Try Again.

The pub was full to the brim and crackling with chatter and laughter: minotaurs squeezing past warlocks on their way to the loos, a leprechaun spilling the dregs of a Guinness on his curly green shoes. There was not an inch of free space available at the bar. The queue was at least three people deep. But at the centre of it, an elbow leant on the polished wood and her false, jet-black lashes batting languidly, was Susie, who looked like she had all the time in the world to focus on just one customer.

Stevie had spotted him on her first night in The Witch's Nose. It was hard not to. He might not have been the tallest or broadest man in the room, but he was certainly the best dressed. In her line of study, she could spot a pair of Italian handmade boots a mile off. This guy wore well-tailored clothes with confidence. Nothing about him screamed 'Look at me!' and somehow it made him all the more magnetic.

Tonight, he had made a small nod to the fancy dress theme: he'd gelled the curly chestnut hair at his temples into two horns and put kohl around his eyes. Some kind of devil. And the grin to match as he flirted with Susie at the bar.

'Any chance of a pint?!' a local yelled from the other end of the room and Susie rolled her eyes, walking slowly away to take some orders.

'Keep a lid on it, you rabid crew,' Margie hollered as she emerged from the kitchen doors and the whole place cheered. In a flash she was passing out drinks and clearing a little of the backlog. Stevie saw her beckon to Susie, whisper something in her ear with a roll of the eyes and then point in the direction of the barn. Susie tried to look chastened, but her happy yelp escaped her all the same. She found Stevie in the crowd as she ducked under the bar's flap opening and pushed her way over.

'I'm free for half an hour. Dance?!'

'Yes, totally! What about your friend, though?'

'Hm?'

'The guy at the bar. The *devil incarnate*?'

Susie bit down a smile at one corner of her mouth. 'Oh, Mark. He's staying in the campsite. We've been chatting the last couple of nights.'

'*He's* staying at the campsite? Really?'

'Yeah. Why?'

Stevie snuck a casual glance back in his direction, at the crisp claret shirt he wore with an impeccable collar, and his very clean shave. 'He doesn't look like he's just stumbled out of a tent, to me.'

Susie grabbed Stevie's arm. 'Wait, can you hear that?! They're playing our anthem!' She dragged her new friend through the jam-packed crowd. It was like trying to pull a whippet through a colander.

'Hey! Ouch. Wait up!'

As they finally emerged into the more spacious but just as sweaty dance hall, Stevie had a chance to tune in to what was playing. 'Is that Kate Bush?'

At the centre of the dance floor, right under the glitter ball, they found Temperance, and Susie instantly mirrored her sister's body language: grinning madly, flopping their arms back and forth in the air like willow trees in a hurricane. About five or so other women were part of the waving act, bursting into song all around her. Dry ice rolled around them in huge waves, making Stevie panic for a minute that she'd lose her new friends all together.

'HeeeaaaaathCLIFF!'

'It's ME! Cathy! I've come home now!'

Temperance clocked Stevie and squealed. 'Stevie, don't you love this song?! It's our absolute classic. We used to do the dance on the green when we were little and charge people to watch,' she yelled over the speakers.

'What dance?' the intern yelled back in total innocence.

She might as well have said she'd never tasted ice cream or never dipped her toes in the sea. 'WE HAVE TO TEACH YOU!' Temperance pretty much shouted in her face. Her eyes were glossy but focused as she pulled Stevie to stand right next to her. 'It's an essential part of English culture! And you did say you wanted the full English experience this year, right? Now wait for the chorus to start again and then follow me. Or just move your hands past your face like this, like you're clearing

89

a really fogged up mirror. OK?'

'I think!'

Susie nodded. 'You'll get it in no time! It's so fun, seriously.'

The chorus started again and the women fell into a rough and tumble synchronicity of howling the lyrics while they wove around the space, all wild hair and limbs and massive smiles. Stevie agreed – this was serious fun.

All too soon the song had finished and half of their Cathy gang retreated to find a drink. The next song started, a little quieter, slower and even more intense, and Nina Simone starting singing deliciously about spells and romance. 'Oooh, this a good song for tonight.'

'Always a good song in my view, right Tee?' Susie grinned wolfishly. 'But a bit of a couple's dance though.'

'Ugh, I'm fed up waiting for the perfect man to come along. I don't need one to have a good time!' Temperance replied, starting to move to the hypnotic tempo.

Susie gave a dirty laugh. 'That dress is really getting to you. And that belt . . .'

'Huh?' Stevie asked. 'How is the dress *getting to her*?'

'Nothing. I'm just glad she's going for it tonight. I hope this feisty fairy princess is here to stay.'

'She is!' Temperance yelled. 'No overthinking. No so much as a slight frown. *Because you're miiiiine*.' She closed her eyes as she sang.

Susie's eyes flicked to the doorway and back again. 'You know, dancing is a pretty good first step to falling in love. Body contact. Chemistry. All that.'

'But you're forgetting I've already been out with all the available men in South Devon. I did not want their bodies anywhere near me and the chemistry didn't so much as set off a Bunsen burner.' She wonkily shook her head.

'So try something . . . new.'

'Show me someone new and I will!'

'Deal.' Susie sloped off and Temperance went back to closing her eyes and dancing without thinking. It was a relief to push away the worries about the *doom*, even just for a few hours. Whatever was going on – with the dreams, the fact that Abel had experienced the exact same one and the swirling feelings in her head and heart – it could wait until tomorrow. He'd agreed to stay for a week, so that gave her time. Tonight, she *needed* to have fun.

Even through her boozy fog, the glow of love wrapping around Temperance was having an effect. She felt freer in her body, twirling on the spot, letting her hands trail out as she closed her eyes and gave in to the music. Occasionally her fingertips would accidentally graze a costume and pulses of other people's happiness hit her lungs, making her dance more, sing more, smile more. Nothing about nudging someone else on the dance floor and laughing was weird, not on FairyFest night, and Temperance felt an illicit thrill of letting her powers off the leash, subtly sampling the emotions in the room. The magic woke up in her as she opened herself up fully to it without a worry about being caught or judged. Energy danced along every hair on her arms, the pins and needles feeling not just in her fingers but at the tips of her ears, behind her neck, down her thighs. Temperance sat happily in the knowledge of what she was: a witch.

'Here's someone to dance with,' Susie suddenly breathed in her ear, spinning Temperance around to find a blushing Scout who only reached her shoulders.

'Oh, hi, Dexter. You don't have to dance with me really:

Susie's just being . . . well, her usual dickish self. Don't let her embarrass you.'

'No, I want to,' his voice squeaked. And he took her right hand and waist like it was a waltz.

'Oh right! OK.' Temperance tried to spare his feelings as he marched them around in a boxy step, but after three minutes she couldn't hold back the laughter much longer. Nina came to her rescue and wound the song up. 'Ahh, it's finished. Thanks for the dance.' He nodded once, gave her a Scouts' salute and then legged it out of the barn.

'See?' Susie appeared again, her eyes twinkling. 'Someone new.'

'But I was thinking more like someone who can vote. And has gone through puberty. I'm picky like that.' Twangy guitar chords bounced out of the speakers and around the barn as 'Wicked Game' started to play. The DJ was leaning hard into his slow dance section.

Temperance gathered up her skirts and started to turn away.

'Wait! Give me one more chance. Someone with GCSEs, got it. Just stay there.'

Temperance closed her eyes and let the sway of the music fill up her senses.

A whistle made her turn to the back of the room. Susie was standing with her arm around Roy, the old milkman, who, as he'd moved further into his eighties, had slid further down the height chart too. Susie mouthed, 'Fancy it?'

Temperance laughed and flicked her sister the Vs, spinning back to the speakers and letting the low notes of the song radiate through her.

A moment later, something big and solid bumped into her back. She turned around to see a tall figure half-hidden behind

92

a haze of dry ice, one of the Scout masks looming down at her.

Susie's third attempt, then. A smile crept up Temperance's face. *At least he seems roughly the right age.*

'Sure. Why not?' Without time for a second thought, Temperance looped her hands behind the guy's neck and started dancing with the random. She'd take Susie's approach – the backpackers only stayed a week, so why worry about the fallout? It was just a dance.

She moved half a step closer, the crinkly white silk of her dress flowing around his legs, almost taking him prisoner. He hesitated at first, but then fell into the same rhythm of swaying, side to side. Their shoulders synced, their hips too.

'What a wicked thing to do . . .'

Suddenly, Temperance couldn't feel the weight of the dress pulling her down anymore. It was like it was holding her up now, guiding her steps, keeping her locked in a daydream. The dress was all of a sudden the choreographer, not just the costume. It rustled between them, like a static charge about to explode. Temperance gave in to the moment, losing herself in the hypnotic melody of the song and the magnetic pull that seemed to draw her closer, closer, to her dance partner.

Heat chased through her torso. A current of something bright flashed behind her eyes. She was aware of the soft skin of her forearm pressed against his neck, the hard cord of muscle there, the rough prickle of his short hair. Green-grey eyes blinked behind the mask but didn't look at anything but her. Teeth holding his bottom lip. Temperance couldn't pull away. Wouldn't. Neither did he. She moved in closer. Her breathing sped up, her hips nudged forwards until she could feel the strength in his chest crush against hers.

As aware as she was of her own hands, every tiny goosebump

along her collarbone standing to attention, Temperance suddenly felt his hands move: running over her hips, around her waist until they rested at the very small of her back. A firm hold, one that anticipated her movements and led her through them.

She sank into that touch. And now her dance partner was the force holding them up, together, now he was calling the shots. Inching closer, swaying deeper. The corset seemed to clutch more tightly around Temperance's ribs: her breath felt light and shallow.

Was it the disco lights or was everything suddenly tinged with in deep blue? Temperance blinked her eyes hard to try to clear her vision, the wooziness of the hot, thin air and the dress and the song making her dizzy. But tonight was not the night for sensible thoughts, for overthinking. Or even thinking. Or even under-thinking. She was just *doing*, she was just *being*.

As the two moved as one, it really did feel like a wicked game: they were daring each other to move even nearer, press even closer. It was a test to see who would lose their nerve first and Temperance swore to herself she wouldn't wuss out now. She kept her eyes locked onto his as his head dipped, his shoulders rounded and he leant down towards her. Temperance could feel each breath rasp in her throat, her pulse rattling in her veins. Somehow, through all the layers of this dress, she could feel the pressure of his fingertips.

His forehead, albeit underneath the black mask, came to rest on hers. The heat of his breath fell on her upper lip.

The sway. The song. Those eyes. She was hypnotised. And she was giving in to it, completely.

They could have been the only two people on the whole dance floor.

But the song petered out. The dry ice drifted away. 'Backstreet's Back' kicked in around them, making it impossible to keep up a slow dance. Reluctantly, Temperance broke contact and felt those strong hands drop down from her back.

The man pushed away a step, lifting the mask from his face.

'Abel.' She barely spoke the word out loud.

He didn't seem aware of the hoard of dancers pouring in around them, bouncing on the spot and throwing monster moves. Abel still held her gaze, his eyes liquid, his jaw held tight, and if the speakers had lost power she felt sure she'd be able to hear the crackle in the air between them.

She put her hand out towards his arm. Her fingers closed around the crisp cotton of his shirt, could feel the reassuring strength of his forearms under her touch. Abel reached forward and brushed a curl away from her brow, to get a better look at her eyes, as if searching for something he knew was there but was just out of reach. But then his mouth drew into a hard line. 'I'm sorry. This will never happen.'

11

Chapter 11

'Subtle' was not for Susie Molland. In her world view, being subtle was just taking a long, boring detour when a sprint would get you there five times as fast, even if you did bash your ankles on the way. She was a big believer in saying yes – to a new adventure, a new gig, an unplanned night out. If it all went wrong, she knew that home was always there. But even if she could sometimes be impulsive and impatient, she also liked to think her more positive qualities were just as unsubtle but in a good way – she loved without ever holding back, she dropped compliments as big as buses, and she would open her heart to a new friend in a heartbeat. Sometimes to someone *more* than a friend.

'Pretty handy, aren't you?' Susie sat on the edge of one of the bar tables, her legs dangling and a jay cloth in hand. She'd given the ancient wood a hardcore wiping down already – there was no way she was trusting her vintage miniskirt to its usual sticky state, and definitely not after an eight-hour boozing extravaganza like FairyFest.

Mark was carrying in the pub chairs that had been sneakily

taken out to the green as the night had worn on and splinter groups of friends had left to drink and laugh under the stars. Margie didn't really mind, as long as she didn't have to ferry them back herself after one of her biggest nights of the year. When she'd seen Mark still chatting to Susie after 1am last orders, she'd swiftly bowled over, pinched him on the upper arm and said, 'If you've got time to flirt, you've got time to work. Go get my furniture back, boy.'

Rather than grump or grimace, Mark in fact seemed to light up after being chided, and hopped to it. He was now tucking his sixth chair away in the snug and dusting his hands together in the international gesture for 'a job well done'.

'I like to try,' Mark said, smiling. 'And Margie is a not a woman you say no to.'

'Watch it,' Susie lowered one eyebrow, 'I might get jealous.'

'Don't worry, I've plenty of room in my life to be bossed about by several women at any one time.'

Susie nodded. 'I can work with that. Bacon sandwich?'

'Sorry?'

She slipped down from the table and subtly checked her knickers weren't showing as a result. 'Festival tradition. If you've made it until the very end of the night – either as punter or staff – we open the kitchen back up and do a round of bacon sandwiches. 'The most rewarding food on the planet, Margie always says.' She bit her bottom lip. 'Unless you're veggie?'

'No, I er . . .' Mark checked his watch. It was an under-stated, simple face ringed with gold, with a black leather strap. Definitely vintage. Susie bet it had some history to it and her fingers itched to gently reach out and touch the material around his wrist. But that would be ever so slightly creepy as a come on, she knew. 'It's half one, though. Isn't it a bit late?

Or,' he scrunched his eyes up for a moment, 'a bit early?'

She shrugged. 'We're probably an hour's drive from the nearest kebab shop here, even if they were still open at two-thirty, so this is as good as late-night snacks get. And Margie's got the *good* bacon in from the butchers in Salcombe. It's so thick and it goes so crunchy under the grill that my sister once chipped a tooth on it. You have to try it!'

'OK, I will.' Mark obediently followed her through the back of the pub and into the kitchen.

'Apron for you,' Susie looped the blue and white cotton apron over his head, moving in close to tie it up behind his back.

His smile went wolfish. 'You take your hygiene regs pretty seriously then?'

'Oh yes,' she pulled the last loop of a bow tightly and dropped her voice just by his ear, 'except when I'm feeling dirty.'

Mark's laughter exploded and bounced around the stainless steel worktops. 'You, Susie Molland, are incredible. Can I kiss you now or after the bacon sandwiches?'

'Let's do both and compare notes,' she muttered against his lips, most definitely in his personal space now.

His lips moved against hers as his hand smoothed its way along her collarbone and behind her neck, resting there and gently pulling Susie even closer to him.

Susie's hands were clutching at the cool, crisp cotton of his shirt at his shoulders and she was entirely too swept up in their kiss to be thinking about tuning into what she might be able to read from him in that moment. Using the full strength of her magic involved focus and composure. You needed a clear head to be able to absorb someone else's feelings and memories. All she had space for in her head was the sensation of how Mark's tongue moved against hers, how the subconscious little murmured growl of pleasure that he gave shot a bolt of electricity through her. It may have been true that Susie had enjoyed some cheeky moments with campsite guys over the last few years, and had even run to a six-week relationship with a fellow paddleboard instructor in Woolacombe last summer, but this kiss was banishing all that to a dim and distant memory. This kiss rewrote the rules. Susie *suddenly* understood what 'Like a Virgin' was all about.

She sunk even further into the moment, letting her hips budge right up against his and earning another guttural growl. Mark smoothly manoeuvred Susie back a few paces until she was up against the big stainless steel fridge: the cold metal against the back of her thighs contrasted deliciously with the heat she felt between their bodies. She risked a gentle bite of his bottom lip and it definitely hit the spot.

'Susie,' he half-whispered, pulling back for just one second, 'how has it taken me my whole life to find you?'

It was a while before anyone got their bacon.

'Fucking phenomenal,' Mark said through a mouthful, his hand casually stroking back and forth along Susie's shins. She had kicked her legs up onto his lap when they took their plates to sit in the snug and they'd been comfortably chatting and chomping there for twenty minutes, neither of them wanting to eat too fast and bring this moment to a close. The snug was Susie's most favourite place in the whole pub, if not the whole world. A tiny cave-like area with thick walls painted in a deep green, it felt like you had crawled into the perfect thicket as a kid and made a secret den surrounded by undergrowth. Susie should want to be anywhere but the pub after a long, crazy shift, but she always felt like she could while away all the hours in a day here. Especially with such good company.

'Tell me again about the smugglers.' He squeezed her leg gently.

'You've asked me about my favourite sandwich fillings, about my short-lived career as a hand model and my top five beaches in the South West, and now you're after a bedtime story?'

'No, I'm after keeping you here with me for as long as I can, before Margie kicks us out and I have to say goodnight.'

Susie smiled. Mark was proving an enjoyable riddle so far. He kissed like a goddamn animal, had plenty of flirty talk, but he also asked her lots of questions – about all the different jobs she'd had, how she grew up in the village, everyone she works with at the pub – he was interesting and told her about the places he'd been travelling. But he wasn't pushing his luck. She'd already mentioned she lived just next door and left that little opening about a bedtime story, but he was obviously enough of a gentleman not to see that as an invitation. Susie was impressed. And a little disappointed.

She let out a long breath. 'The Witch's Nose is over three hundred years old, and it's had a lot of different lives in that time. But to start with, it was a smuggler's inn. If there was a shipwreck along the coast, the smugglers would pick over the wreckage, carry off the booty and hide it here. Margie swears on her life that she's still got some fire pokers that belonged to the King of Spain, but I'm not totally convinced.'

Mark licked his index finger and picked up the last crumbs on his plate. 'You'd argue with Margie and a red hot poker? You're even more of a badass than I thought.'

Susie bit down the smile creeping up into her cheeks. 'I mean, I wouldn't say it to her *face*. But yeah, we like to think the pub is still a hub for the village and anyone coming on their holidays here. They might not be stowing nicked barrels of rum anymore, but people get drawn here, sometimes accidentally – they took the wrong lane and they're too knackered to go on. But however they find us, they never forget us.'

Mark's eyes pinned her to the spot. 'That's exactly it.' His hand stopped moving along her legs, now above her knees. 'And East Prawle is in the Domesday Book, right? It's that old?'

Susie felt a little breathless. 'Super old,' she managed.

Getting to know Mark was great; they'd clicked over the beaches they loved, the cities they wanted to visit, the best local beers. But, God, she was longing for him to talk less and act more, push his hand right up along her thigh, under her skirt and kick off a chemical reaction that she just knew would be deliciously explosive. If that twenty-minute snogging session was anything to go by.

Unconsciously, her bottom wriggled side to side by just an inch and his eyebrows raised in response. Mark's fingers moved imperceptibly up, and up.

Susie could feel every tiny follicle on her skin come to life and she held her breath.

His hand – warm and smooth – was gliding now, up her thigh, to the hem of her short miniskirt.

But just as Susie went to say something, even just to give half a gasp, the lights went off.

'You don't have to go home . . .' Margie's voice yelled from somewhere in the back.

'But we can't stay here,' Susie chimed back, reluctantly. 'Night, boss!'

There was just enough of a glow from the fairy lights strung around the bar and the doorways for Susie to lead Mark behind her to the front door. His hand held hers tightly.

Just as they walked past the bar, Mark stopped suddenly. 'Hear that?'

Susie froze. 'No. What?'

He waited a beat before replying. 'Silence. I think Margie is upstairs.' He tugged on Susie's hand to spin her around. 'You look glorious in the fairy lights. Like a real Devon sprite.' Mark moved closer towards her. 'Please don't say I'll wake up tomorrow and this was all some sort of magical dream.'

Susie could barely see him, just his outline as he closed the last centimetres between them and she felt the warmth of his lips on her neck.

'Promise me you won't disappear into the mist for a hundred years?' he murmured against her skin.

'Mmhm. But that's . . . Scotland,' she sighed.

Mark trailed his kisses up her jaw, to the outline of her lips. It was so late that yesterday's clean shave was starting to prickle with new stubble, and she could feel it on the delicate skin of her bottom lip. 'Just don't go anywhere, Susie Molland. I need you right here in East Prawle. Always.'

Before Susie could reply again, his lips had covered hers and their tongues met in perfect synchronicity. It could have been their hundredth kiss, not their second.

The scrape of a chair against the floorboards upstairs broke the spell and Susie pulled away, swallowing a happy laugh. Men did not usually make her go this ditzy, but there was something about Mark. Something different.

They walked through the porchway and out into the crisp, jet black night. After being so close, Susie now felt the empty space all around her body – and resented it.

Mark blew a gust of breath up above his head, watching as it turned into a faint mist. Dragon's breath, she and Temperance called it when they were kids. 'This place is unbelievably beautiful,' he said, almost to himself. 'I just can't believe hardly anyone knows it's here.'

'We do all right, given our size. Only dust bunnies left in Margie's cellar tonight. That crowd drank the place dry.'

'Of course. I meant . . . this place is so brilliant. I want *everyone* and their milkman to know it. It's a rare gem. It's like you've opened an oyster shell and there's a pearl. Priceless.' He shook his head, as if waking up from a daydream.

An unfamiliar tingle crept around Susie's ribcage. Despite the chill of the night, she felt full of warmth inside her bones. Mark felt just the same way she did about her village: it had a breathtaking beauty all of its own but beyond that the people, the community, made it one in a million. You could stroll between a beach, a pub, a café, a vintage store, saying hello to everyone you passed – what more could anyone want?!

'Sometimes, when I'm away , the other people I meet are trying to leave behind their hometowns. They can't stand them. But I never leave to *escape*. I go and have some mini adventures, knowing this is always here, waiting to welcome me back. That's what makes going easier, in a weird way.'

Mark reached out and curled his fingers around Susie's wrist gently. 'I wish I had about a tenth of your guts. You've gone and done the things you're curious about.'

Susie laughed nervously. She wasn't used to having such intense talks with guys that made her heart beat erratically. She felt like she was glowing under a spotlight all of a sudden. 'I'm not sure about guts. I haven't made it all that far yet.'

He shook his head, his face earnest. 'It's not about the miles:

anyone can hop on a plane and get a stamp in their passport. You've uprooted yourself, tried new jobs and ways of living. You haven't just accepted the path laid out in front of you by other people.' He frowned for a beat. 'But don't head off on another adventure too soon, right? I'm going to need to see you again. Dinner?'

Susie leant her shoulder against him, enjoying the feeling of the crisp cotton of his shirt against her skin once more. She didn't really usually 'do' dinner with the guys she saw. That all felt a bit too proper, too grown-up, too dull. With another man, Susie might have countered with clubbing or a pub crawl, or an afternoon spent on the beach. But she surprised herself with how much she wanted to sit across a table from Mark and talk until the small hours. There was so much more she wanted to know about him. 'Dinner after you've done a busboy shift doesn't feel exactly fair, but I'll take it. I'll give you my number.'

Mark patted his back pocket and his face fell. 'Oh – my jacket. I left it inside, by the fireplace, I think. Will Margie have deadbolted the place by now?'

'To be honest, she never really locks it – never has the need. Hold on.' Susie nipped back inside, aware of a pair of steely grey eyes on her as she went.

Through the door, Susie moved forwards, her fingertips outstretched into the gloomy dark, fairy lights flashing at her back as she shuffled past tables to reach the fireplace. She could just about see a solid shadow draped on the back of one chair.

She turned her palm up and the well-worn leather, buttery soft but with the occasional crack, flew into her hand. Suddenly, it was like all the floodlights came on in Susie's head.

But it wasn't Margie on the light switch this time: it was what Mark's jacket was telling her.

Her fingers stung with the strength of the emotion suffusing the leather. Her whole body flinched in response to the sensation. A blinding white burst of excitement and energy and . . . something new Susie had never read before in any clothing she'd ever felt. What was it? Not *hunger* exactly, but a craving for sure. A need, but not to fill a hole. More like the giddy satisfaction of an online shopping spree. Clicking 'checkout' times a thousand. Susie didn't want to read deeper, she was afraid to. But this startling feeling was like coming across an old landmine washed up on the beach: she couldn't just walk away from the chance it could blow up in someone else's face. With a deep breath, she closed her eyes and pushed her fingers deeper into the fabric.

A map was laid out on a table. No, not a map exactly – not like an old timey novelty up on the pub walls, all ochre yellow and smudgy lines. This looked official, clinical. It was like an architect's plan.

Susie calmed her mind, let the energy flow through her, so she could channel it and focus on the detail written in the top right: *East Prawle Development.*

Two tanned forearms leant on the table, a crisp shirt rolled up to the elbows. Curly hair and energetic eyes. Mark held a thick black marker in one hand. With bold swipes he circled one of the buildings on the plan and scrawled underneath it: Witch's Nose. Housing?! *He put down the pen, crossed his arms and leant back in his chair.*

Susie dropped the jacket and wrenched her eyes open, her breathing ragged.

What did Mark want with The Witch's Nose?

Susie gave herself a minute to catch her breath and then emerged into the night air again, holding Mark's jacket with a bar jaycloth.

He turned as he heard the heavy oak door shut behind her. The moonlight caught the devil horns still gelled into his hair.

'Hey, it's not that bad, is it?' He laughed lightly.

Mark held out his hand and Susie passed the jacket over, the cuff catching the sensitive skin of her wrist in that moment. This time she could name that powerful white buzz of energy coursing through her, and the desire she'd had not ten minutes before of talking Mark into a nightcap back at hers disappeared like dragon's breath in the air.

Ambition. Dedicated, driven, relentless. Ambition.

12

Chapter 12

'Suse? Are you OK?'

'Hm?' Susie looked up from her old laptop, one knee hugged in against her chest as she scoured the South Hams County Council website. 'Oh hey, didn't hear you come in.'

'I know. You didn't hear me offer you a cup of coffee or then tea or then a nice line of cocaine.' Temperance made her way to her desk.

'Huh?'

The big sister slumped down into her chair. 'What on earth is up with you? I haven't seen you reading anything that intently since you did drama at school and someone told you there was a swear word in the play.' Her face suddenly pulled into a serious expression. 'Did something happen last night? You can tell me anything, you know that.'

Susie slowly creaked the laptop shut and pulled her oversized denim shirt more closely around her middle. She'd felt chilly at 2am this morning and she'd stayed that way ever since. 'Well. Yes.'

'Yes?' Temperance's voice yelped nervously.

'Nothing *bad* like that. For me. But maybe bad. For all of us.' Susie shut her eyes and tugged at her long red hair, now in desperate need of a wash after being sweatily crammed under a wig last night.

'Wha . . . what?! Did you carry on drinking after I left?'

'Nope. But I wish I had. I wish I had been drunk so my senses were numb, and then I wouldn't have read it.'

Susie didn't need to elaborate that she didn't mean a text or a newspaper headline. Temperance knew exactly the kind of reading unique to their family that could turn your heart inside out and pull it through your ribs.

Temperance went to the kettle. 'You start talking. I'll start brewing.'

When they were down to the last sips of sugary builder's tea, Susie finally took a breath. 'So he wants the village. For something super *ambitious*. And I need to find out what that is. Fast.'

'OK. OK.' Temperance was staring into the bottom of her mug. 'Let me just . . . get to grips with this. You didn't feel anything from what he was wearing earlier on in the night? And when you were, you know . . .'

'Sucking his face off?' Susie replied sardonically. 'Nope, nothing then. I didn't exactly have my head in the game. So now I'm thinking maybe they were new things he bought to dress up in. I don't know. Ughhhh.' She threw her head back and smacked her palms on the desk. 'He asked me question after question about the village, about the pub, and I just cockily though "*Ooooh he's so into me!*" And all that time he was just snooping around to get some sort of advantage! How up myself could I be?!' Susie buried her head in her hands and was quickly wrapped up in a big hug.

'You're not up yourself. Not at all. He really got to you, didn't he?'

Susie felt her cheekbones burn with shame. 'It was something totally different with Mark. The hot bits were . . . incendiary. But also when we talked . . . he really got me. He listened to my plan to go to San Sebastian next year; he seemed to genuinely love the village as much as we do. But it turns out that he only loves it for its profit margins.' Her mouth screwed up into a knot.

'Before you recruit an angry mob, remember that we don't *actually* know what Mark is up to. Before we write him off as a moustache-twirling bad guy, we need some facts.'

Susie surfaced from the reassuring folds of Temperance's bright green cardi 'But I'm not going on a date with him either, until I know. Even if he does kiss like a bloody Greek God.'

'Completely fair. I wouldn't either. Don't let things get messy and tangled.' Temperance went back to her chair with a weariness Susie didn't pick up on.

'I need proof of what he's up to, but how am I going to find it? It's not like I can frisk him to see if any diabolical plans just fall out of his pocket. And if he is up to anything dodge he's not just going to spill the beans, is he?' Her hands wheeled in the air. 'I don't know what to do next. But I need to do *something*.'

'We could ask Mum?'

Susie ran her tongue along her teeth. 'Let's not bother her unless we really have to. She's probably still finding her feet with the job. Right: the second homers want an extension or a new conservatory or whatever, they have to get council planning. The council have to know if big changes are happening in the village. Who do we know on the parish council?'

'Gary! He joined last year, I think.'

'I'm on it!' Susie slipped on her trainers, grabbed her phone and legged it out the door.

Temperance found herself staring after her for ten good minutes. 'I can't say I hate the new-found focus, Suse, but I had thought we'd run the shop together today. Oh, and *my* night? Thanks for asking. I'm pretty sure I let the love and lust in my costume kickstart a really hot dance with who turned out to be Abel, who then rejected me in no uncertain terms, with the Backstreet Boys for a soundtrack. Great night. Epic. One for the record books.' She pursed her lips and went to boil the kettle again.

The queue running out of Gary's bakery and onto the gravel path was agonisingly slow today, maybe because Susie had lost all patience while the weight of the world was on her shoulders, or maybe because all of East Prawle were catastrophically hungover and in need of fresh sugary carbs.

'Hey, Suse. Thought you would have still been dead to the world this morning.'

Susie turned to see Will, one of the campsite guys she'd met alongside Mark a few nights ago. 'Oh, hey. No rest for the wicked, you know? Um, you're not with Mark, are you?'

He rubbed his chin. 'No, he headed back to Salcombe this morning.'

'Salcombe?'

'Yeah, you didn't think a posh boy like that was actually camping, did you? Not when his family have got one of those mega mansions built into the cliffside. Looks like a Bond villain's place.' Will shrugged. 'We let him kip with us a few times when it was too late for him to get his boat over the estuary.'

Susie couldn't help but roll her eyes. 'He has a boat. Of course he does.'

Will laughed nervously. 'Just a little rig. Feel like I'm stitching him up now – I honestly didn't mean to.'

'No, no. It's fine.' Susie held up her hands. 'The stinking rich can't help how much they stink, I guess.'

'Do you know, I . . . I don't think I need a sausage roll after all. So, see you later, Suse.'

'Will, wait!' she spluttered. 'What's Mark's last name, do you know? Just so I can add it to his contact on my phone – he gave me his number last night.' She jiggled her phone in its pink bunny ears case, as if some kind of proof.

'Beston, Mark Beston.'

'Thanks.'

When Susie finally got to Gary's counter she was faced with an unfortunate wince. 'Iced buns went first thing, my dear. I know they're your favourite. But you've got to be quick for those when the campsite's as full as it is. And when the Faeries' Delight was as punchy as it was last night. I feel less than delightful myself.' He chortled at his own joke.

'I'll have all the almond croissants you have then, please.' Being the last in the line, Susie didn't feel bad for clearing him out: she wanted him content and chatty, after all.

'A big night, eh? Saw your Temperance running off just after midnight, looking grey. But two of these will perk her up, anyhow.' Gary did the twisty flip on the paper bag that Susie had seen him do a million times and she took it from him. 'So that's six-fifty, love. Thank you.'

Susie cleared her throat and leant an elbow onto the counter. 'Can I ask you something non-bun related, Gaz? It's a parish council thing, actually. Just wondered if you know anything about big plans. Anything near the pub, in particular?'

Gary stood a little straighter. 'What have you heard?'

'Just a few . . . rumours going around.'

Gary's eyes moved to the shop door and back to Susie. 'I can't share confidential information. But I will say that should you look up – on the council website – a public document. It's the one that shows how the last private owner of the village left it in trust for the first fifty years after his death.'

Susie's nerves felt too raw after four hours of sleep to understand half of what he was saying. 'Huh? Privately owned? How can someone own a *village*? You make it sound like we're going back down the Victorian mines or something, Gaz.'

He folded his arms around his barrel chest. 'It's archaic, I'll grant you. But way back when, the village was part of the Cavendish estate. Old Spencer Cavendish didn't want his son breaking it off into little pieces for sale, so he wrapped it up in a trust. But in two years' time that expires. And certain *development companies*,' his mouth moved around the words as if he'd found a worm in one of his Chelsea buns, 'have already started to circle. Looking to shoehorn badly built second homes into every nook and cranny, pricing out locals too. The Parish Council have got our eyes peeled for anyone out measuring up the fields or taking fancy photos, but these firms are sneaky. They'll find a way.'

'Like staying in a campsite when they've a perfectly good villain mansion to get home to. On their *boat*,' Susie muttered.

'Sorry?'

'Beston – is that one of the development companies?'

Gary looked at Susie like she was seven again and he'd just

112

caught her minesweeping glasses of Coke from the pub tables. 'What are you wrapped up in, Susie Molland? It's not like you to get involved with village politics and what have you.'

'Well, maybe it's about time I did. Seeing as I love this place as much as the next man. More, in fact.'

'I promised your mum I'd keep an eye on you this summer, and I won't let her down. You keep away from the Bestons, you hear me? Far away.'

13

Chapter 13

'You really think I'm ready?' Stevie's slim fingers danced together at her throat.

'*So* ready.' Temperance gave her a firm squeeze on the shoulder, picking up a subtle trace of quiet pride in the cable knit cardigan. A brief vision of library stacks and coffee cups. 'This is vintage, isn't it? Your cardigan, I mean.'

'Oh, yes. It was my mom's. She knew I'd always loved it, so she told my dad to give it to me for my first year of college. She loved clothes, too, you know? All eras, all styles. I think I get it from her. You have a great eye too, Temperance. That's why I'm so nervous about closing out this evening. What if someone comes in and I let them buy a Biba original for the cost of a pasty, by mistake? What if someone shoplifts a feather boa and I don't notice?'

Temperance smiled and pulled her canvas backpack onto her shoulders. 'You're going to be fine. Better than fine. And when you run the floor, you can pick the playlist. I'm sure you want a break from Susie's deep cut of Fleetwood Mac betrayal songs. Go for something sunnier, maybe, like a funeral march.'

'I heard that!' Susie came out from the office, her face loaded with a scowl. She was wearing ripped denim shorts over black fishnets, a man's grey T-shirt tucked in at the waist.

'You said you're going for a hike, right?' Stevie asked hesitantly.

'Yup,' Temperance replied quickly. 'It's something we Devon folk love to do. A long hike along the coastal path. For fun.'

'So much fun,' Susie deadpanned.

'Yeah. We hike back at home too. But I usually break out the sweatpants and a pair of sturdy boots.' Her eyes moved briefly to Temperance's converse and away again. 'Have a good one!'

'We will,' Temperance trilled back, looping her arm through Susie's and practically dragging her out of the shop.

Ten minutes of huffing along the path towards the beach, Susie said sulkily, 'I still don't see why we couldn't have just washed this stuff back at the shop like we normally do. Instead of me carrying a laundry basket's worth of gear down to the beach and back.'

'I explained why,' Temperance tried to keep her voice upbeat, 'because Stevie is bound to start asking questions if she sees us working through an industrial quantity of potpourri each week. And it's a pain in the arse to keep clearing all our magic stuff away each night. Besides, you desperately needed to get some fresh air.'

'What?!'

'You've been glued to your laptop, making your little dossier against that company—'

'The Beston Portfolio. *Fuckers.*'

'Yup, them. I have never seen you put that much work into anything. Like, *anything.* You've not left the house except to do a surly shift at the pub, and even then you pulled a sicky after two hours.'

Susie stumbled on a loose stone and Temperance grabbed her by the arm, hauling her up again. 'I was worried that if Mark walked in I wouldn't be responsible for my actions. And Margie says blood is a right pain to get out of the carpet.'

'Has he tried calling you again?'

'Seems to have given up after four texts and three calls, thank God.'

'Persistent.'

'Clearly thought his little Casanova performance would have me bending over backwards. I'll show him.' Susie snorted through her nose and wiped her hair out of her eyes. She hated that it had taken a surprising amount of willpower not to answer Mark's calls when they flashed up on her phone. Half of her head wanted to scream obscenities down the line, but the other half was remembering that twenty minutes in the kitchen with him, how his eyes had stayed locked on her when they talked, how she'd never felt more like herself in a guy's company. How could that all be cleverly plotted crap?! He must be a master bullshitter of the highest degree.

It was an overcast late afternoon in East Prawle: muggy, still air filled with annoying pockets of tiny flies and a strange sort of grey-yellow hue to the sky. It wasn't exactly the kind of weather to take her out of her funk, but she had to admit that just taking great big angry strides along an uphill walk was at least channelling some of her rage.

They reached a natural fork in the scrubby path: one route took you to the local beaches and the other took you further uphill, along the cliffside. A heavy rustle to their left signalled someone else was nearby: usually a dog walker or family of holidaymakers with buckets and spades. But in this case a white surfboard popped out from behind the trees, followed quickly by its daydreaming owner.

'Oh, hi, Abe!' Susie called out, and as Abel clocked who he was a metre from bumping into, the distant, dreamy look in his eyes hardened into something else, something sharper, and he stopped in his tracks. 'You off down to the beach? We're . . . uh . . . taking a picnic to Swift Cove.'

Abel's head flicked between Susie, Temperance and his surfboard. 'Yeah, I'm going for a surf. After a bit of a walk, though. I'm headed up there.' He nodded up the steep path to the cliffs.

Temperance could practically hear the blood pumping in her ears as she swallowed a sticky feeling of hurt. He couldn't even bear to share the same five minute walk with her. He would rather make up a blatant lie and sweat his way up an incline for twenty minutes. Carrying a goddamn surfboard! The curl of hurt hardened into a stone of anger. 'Makes *total* sense. Enjoy your walk,' she spat.

Before she'd even finished speaking, he was headed up and away from them.

After another ten minutes of angrily marching, whacking away any stray brambles that dared get to close, Temperance burst out, '*WHO* goes walking with a surfboard?! Could he not think of a smoother way to dodge me? There's you avoiding Mark, and Abel avoiding *me*. The full spectrum of man trouble in one little village. God!' she seethed.

'What do you mean?'

Temperance ran her hands over her hair and down her thick ponytail, pulling it tight. 'You didn't buy that, surely? He just can't bear to breathe the same air as me. It's painfully obvious.

In the couple of days since the party, he's run straight to the kitchen whenever I've been in the pub, and as I came out of the café this morning I'm pretty sure he ducked behind the bus shelter to avoid me.'

Susie bit her lip. 'Maybe that wasn't him. Maybe it was . . . um.'

'It was him. He obviously regrets the dance. He found it gross that I fancied him at seventeen and he still finds the thought of me in any sort of . . . romantic way totally disgusting. Clearly. And that's fine.'

'Hey!' Susie grabbed for Temperance's hand and spun her round. 'It's not fine! No one could find you gross – you're a goddamn siren. It's not your fault he went away someone cool and came back a massive bell end. That's no reflection on *you*, Tee. Just that he's a bit of an arsehole now.'

Temperance shook her head, some stray loose hairs stuck against the back of her neck in the close weather. 'It's like I haven't grown up at all from being a lovesick teenager. He was so sweet with the kids at the fairy circle, and he's being all protective of Margie while he's here. And then on the dance floor . . .'

'What?'

'The connection I felt,' something prickled deep in her heart, like it was waking up with pins and needles after a long sleep, 'seemed so real.' She took her hand back from her sister's grip. 'But it was the costume. Putting me in a trance. Along with all the mead, ugh. Someone else's love story had me fooled that I was dancing into one of my own. I've been so obsessed with tripping over The One that I convinced myself I . . . God, I must have looked so pathetic to him. Not that I care.'

They set off walking again, in an uneasy silence.

'It's good that we don't care, about *either* of them,' Susie said flatly, the sound of waves interrupting her as they rounded the path to the top of Swift Cove. You couldn't walk around to Swift Cove from the next beach along, or land a boat there as the waves were too rough much of the time, meaning they could safely count on it being deserted.

'You get some rocks, I'll start digging.' Temperance started unpacking the tarpaulin and small plastic shovel from her backpack when they reached the sand, leaving the paper bags of herbs and flowers inside until the bath was ready.

'Roger.' Susie moved with a little more of her natural bounce towards the cave at the back of the beach, searching out some big stones that were still light enough to carry.

After about twenty minutes, the sisters had a big hole in the sand lined with tarpaulin and rocks, and had dug a small channel in from the sea so that it filled up with water.

'Perfect.' Temperance dusted the sand from her hands. 'Let's start with that really sad black silk shirt.'

'Definite funeral vibes.' Susie nodded, opening her bag and gently floating the woman's blouse away from the top of the pile using her powers. It was beautifully cut, liquid-like silk, but it also echoed with a deep sense of longing and loss as it dropped into Susie's hands. She shivered as she pressed it down into the sea water.

She could see drawn curtains, a barely touched buffet, polished black shoes, tissues scrunched nervously in a pocket.

'Plenty of rue for this one.'

Temperance passed her sister a paper bag of rue. Susie closed her eyes, dipped her hand in and felt the paper-like dried flowers tickle her palm, the familiar tingling sensation beginning.

The pain has ended. All the goodbyes have been said. We release the burden: we set it free.

She closed her fingers around a big handful of the dried flowers and then sprinkled them into the bath. Temperance was sat cross-legged now on the sand, her eyes also closed. Lee had never specifically spelt out a script of what each of them should think as they worked these rites to cleanse negative feelings: she insisted that each witch felt her own, unique way into her magic and all that mattered was that you focused, you meant what you said and you said it with a full heart. She couldn't tell what her sister was thinking exactly in this moment, but she knew that in her own way she was also showing the lingering sadness that it was time to move on, to let go.

Susie imagined herself opening the curtains to winter sunlight, putting the black shoes back in the cupboard, dusting a mantlepiece of treasured photos. She spoke to the images in her mind: These things have passed. We let go.

As her hand moved in one more complete circle, the images slowly faded to nothing like a swirl of paint from a brush disappearing into water. Susie took a steadying breath, exhaling and releasing that memory from her mind and back into the universe. She then gently lifted the shirt out. She carried it to a waiting towel and laid it down, smoothing the sleeves flat. It felt different to handle now: reassuringly blank.

'I'm ready for the next, Tee. What have you got?'

'I'll do it, you have a moment to yourself. There is a very angry but posh gilet that I want to have a go at. I think the boating crowd round here would snap it up at a chunky price.'

A thought of Mark rankled at the back of Susie's mind and her own anger flared. All that natural charm he had, his intellect, his knee-weakening kissing skills – and he chose to use them for evil. They could have had something so special if only . . . And what did it say about her, that she'd felt the deepest connection ever with a man who turned out to be a soulless corporate goon? Not that she was going to give up and let him win, oh no.

'Does it ever piss you off that we can only ever use our magic after the fact? Like, we come along and clear up the messes but we can't step in *before* the mess is made.'

Temperance pulled on a glove to root around in the bag full of clothes. She looked up and to the right. 'Sometimes. But I suppose I've just always thought it was pretty special that we are tuned into the magic at all. That we can feel things other people can't.'

Susie's shoulders hunched up. 'Me too, me too. But . . . imagine if we weren't just working around the emotions people have *already* had? What if we could influence what they're about to feel?'

Temperance frowned. 'What do you mean?'

Susie started stalking in circles, throwing little clouds of sand up with her heels. 'I'm so . . . frustrated,' she growled, 'that I can see Mark is clearly up to something, but I've just got to watch from the sidelines. I know he's burning with ambition and that ambition is potentially going to change our village forever. His family owns a property investment portfolio and the village will be on the market in two years – how much more proof do I need? So what if I could wash that ambition away right now?'

Temperance blinked, the gilet now abandoned beside her. 'How?'

'Well . . . we know that some clothing holds on to strong

emotions, and that can influence the next person that wears it. So if I could find a fisherman's sweater, say, absolutely riddled with anxiety and self-doubt and misery, then maybe it would take the wind out of Mark's sails a bit. But it could take us years to come across just the right memory in the right kind of clothing to do the job. And then he might not want to wear whatever it is. I don't know. What if . . . what if there was a way to put a feeling into something *on purpose*? Exactly the feeling we need. And fast.'

'I've never heard of anything like that before.'

'Neither have I. But maybe we could email that person mum told us about, the one that might have some emergency magical answers?'

'I'm not sure. It feels a bit dodgy, doesn't it? Like we're hypnotists tricking people into believing they're chickens or whatever. Feels morally grey, Suse. And mum always told us never to cast – this feels dangerously close.'

Susie blew out her cheeks. 'Saving our whole community is morally grey, really?! And – and if we managed that kind of magic,' she pointed at her big sister, picking up momentum in her argument, 'you could make sure Abel sticks around long enough for you to figure out this doom nightmare situation thing you've got going on. Maybe smooth out some of his animosity towards the village so he doesn't do a runner right after Margie's party. It would be useful, right? We *need* this.'

Temperance sighed. 'I'm still having the nightmares. I can't be sure Abel still is, seeing as he'd rather dive into a shrub than talk to me, but they're coming thick and fast. Every night. Sometimes when my mind drifts off in the day, too. Storms. Wildfires. Cracked glass. They feel so *real*.'

Susie threw her arms wide. 'There you go then! Extraordinary times, extraordinary measures, right? We need some new tricks, babe. And fast. I'll email tonight if you give me the address.'

Temperance took a moment to consider her sister. Twitching with nerves and worry, dull peachy shadows under her eyes from broken nights. She was hoping a trip down here might change the subject on loop in Susie's mind, but clearly not.

'No worries, I can do it. I need to ask about that sexy robe, anyway. And . . .'

'And?'

Temperance uncrossed her legs and hugged her knees under her chin, looking out at the waves crashing into rolling lines of foam. 'And I wanted to ask about the dreams too. I think . . . I think maybe I caused them, that night on the beach with you and Stevie. It's a pretty big coincidence, don't you think, that I chanted under a full moon and suddenly I'm haunted by a nightmare that won't shift? Plus, I've dragged my ex into exactly the same vision. It can't be a hangover anymore. It can't be weird timing. Maybe, what we did around the fire was . . . casting. Mum always said it wasn't something to muck about with. I think I brought Abel here, Suse, and I brought this doom hanging over us. Shit!' she gasped. 'Maybe the doom brought Mark here too!'

Susie's eyes went wide. 'Have you talked to Mum about it?'

'How can I? How can I admit to her that the second she leaves me in charge, I go on some insane Single White Female rampage and meddle with magic I don't understand? Not exactly confidence-boosting. She always made us promise, remember, that we'd never try and cast. I'm not sure I can handle her knowing I've messed up like this. So maybe I'll ask 'F' instead.'

'Mum didn't give you their name?'

'Nope, just the email: FEverything.'

'Off topic but I wish that was my email address.'

'Off topic but me too. So, I'm just going to casually drop them a line and ask about sexy satin robes, whether we can change someone's current emotions, and whether I cursed my own village by wishing for a Goblin King boyfriend,' she counted off on her fingers. 'Super chill.'

'Well, that's definitely not a WhatsApp kind of convo. And in the meantime, what do we do?'

Temperance picked up the gilet again. 'We keep going. Keep the shop open, keep avoiding Mark but watch him from a distance. Keep Abel safe and sound in the village. And try not to accidentally trigger any other waves of doom.'

She rustled around in the backpack for her lavender and basil. 'For now I'll do something positive with my Molland genes and take the frustrated male rage out of this thing.'

14

Chapter 14

From: FEverything@hotmail.com

To: TinyTempsM@yahoo.co.uk

Re: Help us please?!

Hello Temperance,

I have to say, you could have bowled me over with a duck's fart when I saw your name pop up in my inbox. You say that your mum left you my address as a sort of magic emergency contact?! Well, I'm going to choose to take that as a compliment, under the circumstances. You had a lot of questions so I won't beat around the whatsit but I hope when this is all sorted we might have more time to talk. Maybe.

Thank you for itemising your questions. I can tell you are a can-do sort of girl.

1. As disappointed as I am to hear that you don't want to keep this saucy red gown just as it is . . . if lavender isn't having an impact, you'll need to layer up the calming herbs on that horny beast. You'll need lemon balm, dill and sage. Toast the sage leaves in a dry pan first, until they start to smoulder. The lemon balm and dill are calming; the sage is there to purify all those leftover naughty thoughts. If that all sounds like too much work, just pop it in the post to me! I'm joking. Kind of.

2. Can you use your magic to influence what is still unfolding? Dear Mighty Goddess of the Heavens, what has Lee been teaching you girls?! YES YES OF COURSE YES. It's like she made sure you could read, but then locked up the library!!! You and your sister share a heritage that so few people are lucky enough to inherit. You are attuned to forces others can't feel, this much you know. The spiritual energies of the universe. But you can also listen so closely to those forces that you can learn to guide them, to direct them. Think of it like a river: we can't create the water but we can move rocks and dig rivulets to subtly change its course. You say powerful ambition is the problem here: then you need to drive it the other way. You need to dam that ambition and invert it. Luckily, the plant world gives us lots of lovely sedatives to do this. The most useful to us witches is *Atropa belladonna*. So you're going to go on a little scavenger hunt. You'll need about five bunches of the leaves (wear GLOVES, my girls) and then you'll need to boil it into a tea (in a WELL VENTILATED ROOM) and then you need to have an item of clothing that will be worn often by the person you're looking

to influence. Seep it in the tea while you meditate on the quality you're trying to quieten in them, or divert them away from. Keep that thought always in your mind. When you feel like you've nothing left to give, you're done. (Rinse and REPEAT as necessary. Maybe that didn't need to be in caps but I'm in the zone now.) Then return the item as swiftly as you can. The effect will wear off in time.

3. Now onto your midnight adventures, Temperance. The apple doesn't fall far from the tree, I see. I've no doubt the premonition you've been seeing came as a result of what you cast that night on the beach. Midnight, moonshine and the power of women united – you really didn't think that would pack a punch? You opened yourself up to nature's powers and you asked for true love to be brought to you. And so the magic saw what your mind's eye fixed on as true love and delivered it – but against the young man's will. And so: boom, you got doom. You used strong magic to go against free will and the cosmic powers that be DO NOT like that (there I go again – but deserved caps this time), so it's all gone weird and wonky and decidedly dark. I can't tell you what the burning wildflowers and the purple storm and the cracked glass mean. The premonition is speaking to you and you alone. But I do know that if you want to reverse it, you're going to have to *reverse* it. Literally. Wear everything you were wearing that night but inside out. Say the same incantation but reverse it. You'll need to be there at daybreak, not full moon. And *mean it*. You got greedy, Temperance, and now your hand has been slapped for reaching into love's cookie jar. I don't know

if that analogy has turned filthy or not. But I didn't mean it like *that*. What I'm saying is, yes, you did do this. But you didn't mean it. And we've all had magic go horribly wrong on us. Just ask your mum.

Go carefully, girls, but go with power.

Yours, truly, always,

F x

F's instructions were repeating in Temperance's head later that day as she walked along the single-track lane to Praveen's Pick Your Own field. Belladonna sounded like serious stuff, not to be treated lightly, and Temperance didn't want to risk any lingering magical poison transferring onto Try Again inventory or – God forbid – their customers, so she'd thrown on her roughest denim shorts and trainers to go and track down some disposable equipment for the witchy gathering mission.

She could have taken the car, but the sun was lighting up the sky a glorious buttercup yellow and Temperance figured an uphill walk in the blistering heat was a sure-fire way to clear her head of doom and destruction. And old flames. It was so bright that, at times, she almost walked with her eyes closed behind her sunglasses, one hand trailing in the hedgerow, her ears listening for cars but only hearing crickets. By the time she reached the rusty farm gates, she could feel the sweat gathering under her baseball cap and between her cleavage, but she couldn't have cared less. The endorphins were helping pick up her feet, and knowing she was on the right track to be able to fix some of the mess she'd unwittingly made cleared some of the fog in her head.

Seeing Praveen in the little tin hut by the strawberry field, Temperance went over and knocked gently on the corrugated metal.

'Hiya, Prav.'

'Hello, Temperance, lovely. How are you then? Gosh, didn't you look gorgeous at FairyFest. You had all the heads turning.' Praveen leant back on her chair and laced her fingers together.

'Erm, not sure about that, but thanks. It was . . . fun.' Temperance had to briefly shut her eyes to chase away the memory of how the rustling wedding dress filled her senses with love, how the cocktails dulled her inhibitions, how it felt to sway in time to the music in Abel's arms, his tall frame pressed against her . . .

Her neighbour let out the kind of incredulous sigh that married middle-aged people seem happy to give any single adults they know. 'Psshaw. You were fighting them off with a stick.'

Temperance was glad that her cheeks must already be beetroot red anyway, from her boiling hot walk. *What a wicked thing to do . . .* the song whispered from the back of her mind.

'I wouldn't even need a cocktail umbrella to fight off my admirers,' she shrugged and gave a jokey grimace.

Praveen smiled and frowned at the same time. 'Well, the field's packed today. You never know who you might meet over a strawberry plant. A natural aphrodisiac and all that.'

Temperance craned her neck around the side of the hut to the busy field beyond. The only examples of her preferred gender were sunburnt dads chasing pink-lipped toddlers through the furrows or impeccably dressed retirees at least twice her age, nervously bending down to add to their punnets, perhaps unsure that they'd make it back up again.

'Hmm. Thanks, but I'm actually after some random bits and pieces, if that's OK? Do you have any old buckets I could buy off you? I've got some . . . scruffy work to do. At the shop.'

Praveen bit the inside of her cheek. 'I do, I think. In the shed on the far side of the strawberry field. There's some old stuff stacked up at the back I haven't used in years – you're welcome to it.'

'Thanks. And any of the . . . snippy garden things? Like really hench scissors?'

'Secateurs?' Praveen laughed. 'Yes, there's a few of them hanging on the peg board in the shed. Bring them back when you're done.' She squinted at Temperance. 'I can't imagine what would be so grubby at your vintage store that you need old buckets and *hench scissors*.'

Temperance felt too sweaty to come up with a reply. 'I know, right? Thanks, Prav. See you in a bit.' Temperance wiped her forehead and then set off for the field.

It certainly was busy, with clusters of families crouching down to pick the ruby-red berries, the odd slap of a hand when too much sampling was going on. It was always a tourist hotspot on a sunny day: a wholesome activity out in the open with the very big bonus of having the toppings for your afternoon cream tea sorted at the same time. Temperance's mouth watered at the thought of a deep, crumbling scone heaped up with clotted cream and sun-warmed strawberries. She'd have to hit the bakery on the way home.

In the sea of brightly coloured summer clothes, one tall black smudge was patently obvious. Temperance's eyes were still half-closed against the sun but when the figure stood up she knew exactly who it was.

Instantly, she dodged behind the nearest tree.

'Fucking Abel.' she hissed to herself. How can you spend twelve years thinking about the one that got away and then all of a sudden he's the one you can't bloody well escape from?

Temperance was not in the mood to be disdainfully judged right now, not while she was dressed like a gym teacher and smelt like a locker room. Besides, Abel had made it undeniably obvious that he wanted nothing to do with her. *This will never happen.* Hiking with his surfboard. How much clearer could he be?

She risked a peek around the tree trunk. In a black T-shirt and shiny red shorts, he was completely incongruous amongst the khakis and chinos. Temperance had a vague memory of red shorts like that. From Year 10 netball. She looked again. He wasn't wearing his old PE shorts, was he?! Maybe that was all Margie had kept of his from back in the day. They certainly were a snug fit. If she hadn't been worried about giving away her hiding spot, she would have cackled with laughter like the witch she was.

The old shed was right at the end of the field but Temperance realised from where she standing now, she could just hop into the field's ditch and follow it all the way down. Bingo. No run ins, no more humiliation, no muttered exchange where Abel would clearly rather be slowly eaten to death by aphids over a thousand years than talk to her. This time, she would run away from *him* in a public place.

She hopped down ungainly into the ditch and started to jog along, head lowered, dodging stinging nettles and pretending she was some kind of very niche RPG character on a side quest, a goofy grin spread across her face. At the shed five minutes later, Temperance hauled herself up onto the grass, not caring that she now had dusty elbows and knees, and that sweat was running down between her shoulder blades. This wasn't a beauty pageant. This was serious magical business.

Inside the shed there was a refreshingly cool, if musty, atmosphere and Temperance flapped her vest top away from her body to feel the air reach her skin.

'Buckets,' she muttered to herself, wandering down to the corner and a big stack of cobwebbed crates and a wheelbarrow without a wheel. She found two with only small cracks and figured they'd do nicely for holding belladonna leaves. If they were just gathering dust here they might as well come home with her and get up to some magical mischief. As she turned back towards the workbench and peg board, she saw a heap of hessian sacks.

'Never read hessian before. Maybe potatoes have big feelings.' Temperance raised her eyebrows. She held out a hand over the top sack and it rose easily to meet her touch. Her fingers sparked as she gripped the rough fibres, but nothing was there. What had she been hoping for? Maybe a Lady Chatterley style agricultural love affair? Two forbidden lovers making their bed on scratchy hessian, too engulfed by lust to notice? Temperance shook her head.

Once this doom is off the books, I will start internet-dating again, no matter how painful. In fact. . .

She put the sack down and fished her phone out of her back pocket. Opening up the Devon Loves app, Temperance switched her notifications back to 'On'.

No time like the present. You've got a lot of hormones built up in you, babe. Look how you threw yourself into that insane dance with Abel – the man who quite literally wants nothing to do with you! Even if you're just kissing more frogs, it'll get you closer to The One Frog. A frog who's actually up for it.

Temperance flinched as a deep whistle reached her ears. She looked out of a crack between two wooden panels in the wall. Black T-shirt, red shorts.

'Are you kidding me?!' she muttered. Temperance scanned the shed for a hiding spot. No way was she going from seeing Abel in her best make-up and a fantasy gown to having to face him drenched in perspiration and shame.

She didn't fancy diving into the pile of loose hay. She didn't fancy her chances behind the boxes that smelt super strongly of turpentine either.

'What the fuck is my fucking life.' Temperance grabbed at the hessian sacks, hopping into one like it was a school sports day and pulling another over her head, then shuffling down, out of sight, just beside the work bench.

Abel was still whistling as he strolled into the shed. It sounded to Temperance like an old Noah and the Whale song they'd all loved back in the day. Whatever the tune, it was weirdly upbeat for his usual slapped-arse personality. Temperance strained her eyes through the loose weave of the cloth, trying to get a look at him, but all she could see were his bare calves as he walked slowly towards her.

She sucked in a tiny pocket of air, her heart hammering in her ears.

His shoes stopped. They turned on the spot. In her direction.

'What do we have here, then?' Abel murmured softly.

Temperance screwed her eyes shut.

'Phillips, Phillips. Nope. Ah, here we go. Cross-head.' There was a clank and then Abel's feet stepped back and his whistling picked up again as he headed towards the shed door.

Temperance risked a slow breath out through her nose. Her lungs complained for more oxygen.

That was too close.

'MWAH MWAH! MWAH MWAH!'

There was a buzzing and an eruption of sound from Temperance's back pocket.

Oh god, the Love Devon alert. Now I remember why I hated it.

Another round of tinny kissy noises played, another growl of vibrations against the metal work bench.

All of a sudden her vision was flooded with light: like a captive having their blindfold removed, and Temperance was about to sell all her state secrets for some sweet, sweet freedom.

'*What* the ever-loving fuck?!' Abel shouted down at her, a sack in his hand. 'Tee!'

'Hello.'

'Hello?! *Hello?* What are you doing in a sack? In a shed? Who has—'

She could see the whites of his eyes, his hands balled into fists by his side. He stared around the room, his head flicking in every direction wildly.

'It's just me,' she tried to laugh casually. 'Hiding. Uh . . . playing hide and seek. With some of the village kids.'

He let out a jagged exhale and then ran a hand over his hair. 'I didn't see any kids hiding out in the field.'

Temperance stood up awkwardly, shoving the sack down to her ankles. 'I er . . . I'm such a hide and seek ninja. They must have got bored and gone home.' She nodded with fake nonchalance, because what was more natural than an almost-thirty-year-old woman hiding in a potato sack to amuse some children? And she was not going to show weakness in front of

Abel Gulliver today, not when the memory of that dance could still burn her insides with shame.

'Right.' His body language softened slightly, just for a beat, before he folded his arms.

'MWAH MWAH.' Temperance winced and wrestled her phone out of her back pocket, silencing the notification at last.

'Someone's keen to get hold of you,' Abel said gruffly. 'Weird text sound, but whatever floats your boat.'

'I didn't choose it,' Temperance rushed out in mortification. 'It comes with the app and I don't know how to change it over. Love Devon,' she waved the screen his way. 'Local dating . . . thing.'

Abel assessed it for a split second, before holding up the screw driver in his hand. 'Well, I just came in for this. Praveen's gate is about to come off its hinges so I'm sorting that out.'

Wine tonight? Please say yes.

Temperance saw the little white message box at the bottom of the phone screen as she tucked it away. The condescending turd from the other night clearly hadn't got the message yet.

'That's good of you.'

Abel looked her up and down: dirt on her limbs, scuffed trainers, dusty shorts. 'You could help, actually. Seeing as you're dressed for it. I need someone to stand there and hold things.' He turned around and started to walk away before she had a chance to spit something out in reply.

Temperance shoved some sacks in her broken buckets and followed in his footsteps. If it had been Abel's farm she would have happily let it all fall down into a wonky heap, but it was Praveen's. And Praveen was part of their community network, so Temperance was never going to turn down the chance to help her. Even if it meant being the assistant to a perpetually grumpy sod in size small shorts.

Temperance felt a bit of plum standing three feet behind Abel as he unscrewed something from the gate post. After ten minutes, she asked wearily, 'What can I do?'

Abel sighed. 'There are some bricks outside the shed. Could you fetch some? Please.'

Temperance saluted to his back and turned on the spot, just in time to see little Martha walking the other way with her family. 'That's them!' she called to her mum, 'That's the fairies pretending they're normal!'

Temperance shared a smile with Martha's mum. From the mouths of babes: little did Martha know that Temperance spent a lot of her time just pretending to be normal.

The majority of the fruit-picking families started to leave as Temperance was carrying over bricks, two at a time. The heat was starting to get to everyone, with meltdowns aplenty and more than once she heard the magic bribe 'ice cream' being promised to small people.

Soon it was just one seventy-something couple slowly mooching along the rows of strawberry plants, their arms linked and their heads leant towards each other. They looked so in sync. Temperance found herself sneakily watching them in her periphery vision. Had they come to East Prawle for a big wedding anniversary, maybe? Or had they found each other late in life and were now enjoying an Indian Summer romance? Whatever their history, Temperance could almost feel that deep, connected love radiating out from them even without reading them with her powers.

Lasting love. That's what she wanted. That's how she'd

accidentally drawn some dark magic down onto the village: because she had a gnawing hunger in her heart for True Love that wouldn't leave her be.

She felt the hairs on the back of her neck stand to attention: Abel was watching her with intent concentration. 'Have you seriously been carrying those just two at a time?' He didn't bother concealing the tut that punctuated his sentence.

'Yes! What was I supposed to do, tuck them under my armpits as well? Balance them on my head? I have to be careful with my hands, all right? They're the tools of my trade.' Despite the satisfaction in letting the whirl of anger burning in her chest out through her mouth, Temperance wished she could eat the words back up.

He scratched behind his ear. 'Retrained as a brain surgeon, did you?'

'Maybe I did. A lot of things have happened while you've been AWOL,' she shot back.

Abel broke eye contact and studied the ground.

Temperance groped around in her blank mind for an explanation. It was hardly going to get Praveen's gate mended if she just sniped at Abel all day. The sooner they could be civil, the sooner they'd be done and out of here.

'I repair a lot of the vintage clothes by hand. Invisible mending. It's really fine work, hard to do if your fingers have been mangled by a tonne of bricks.'

'They have these amazing bits of kit now called gloves,' he deadpanned, picking up a worn pair from the ground by his feet and tossing them over. 'Funnily enough, you're not the only person who uses their hands at work.'

'Oh, so you're the brain surgeon?'

He turned back to sanding the rusted hinge plate. 'Not

exactly. I maintain rental properties in Bath. Mum does the cleaning service. We work together.' He stopped talking and left an open space in their conversation, as if daring Temperance to pick holes in his line of work.

'Well.' She shuffled her trainers in the dry earth. 'Only the coolest people work with their mums, that much I know.' She gave half a smile as a peace token. 'What do you need me to do now?'

'OK. Stack those bricks so they're parallel to the gate. We're going to prop it up on one end, so we can slot it back in its hinges.'

'Do you fix many farm gates in Bath?'

He took a side step towards to her and lowered his voice. 'I'll be completely honest: I'm just giving it a shot. Looked up a YouTube video. Praveen was so desperate to get it sorted, I couldn't say no.' Abel's mouth lost the hard line she'd now grown used to seeing and instead pulled back into a lopsided grimace.

Temperance bit her bottom lip. Now he was close to her, she could see where perspiration was making his T-shirt cling to his body, the line of reddish dust across the back of his neck where he must have rubbed sweat away with his hand. She shook her head. Now was not the moment. In fact, the moment was *never*.

'Music. We need music. Always makes work go faster, right?'

'My playlist, though. It's too hot for your angsty girl rock – we need something calmer. Only Debbie Harry when it's below twenty-three degrees in my book.'

Temperance was too startled to say anything for a second. The heat must *really* be getting to Abel if he was suddenly willing to recall something from their shared past. He'd always teased her about her love of the great female rock icons – Debbie, Stevie, Tina. But Temperance had always been unflinching in her dedication: she had two ears and a soul, didn't she?

She fought to repress her goofy smile. 'So what do you suggest?'

Abel wiped his hands on his shorts and fished out his phone. 'All this dust I can't get it to read my fingerprint. Can you . . .?' He held it out to her. 'Yes, thanks.'

Perspiration prickled at her hairline. As she picked up his phone, Temperance felt the calloused patches on his palm graze against the soft pad of her thumb. 'I don't . . . know your code.'

Abel looked at her, his grey-green eyes direct and piercing. His face a blank picture of neutrality. 'Same one I always had. You choose whatever. Because we really have to get this job finished.'

'Course.' Her fingers tapped out the code that somehow a part of her brain had kept locked away in a safe all these years. Maybe in a filing cabinet called 'Useless Abel Gulliver facts that will only cause you pain'. That's how much they'd trusted each other, when they were younger: all secrets out in the open, nothing hidden or forbidden. But now Abel dodged the simplest question, the smallest interaction.

Temperance rushed her way through selecting a playlist of noughties hip-hop and put the phone down on a log behind him. It didn't feel right to have access to his stuff, not now.

She cleared her throat and reminded herself what it was she was supposed to be doing: helping a neighbour then getting out of there. 'Bricks it is, then.' Temperance wiped her clammy hands on her back pockets and got back to work.

'Are you really sure you can take it? I'm going to slide it in slowly, but it's heavy.'

Temperance swore under her breath. 'Yes, I'm sure! Just do it already.'

Abel was standing behind her, hot bursts of his ragged breathing landing on her neck. He had the top bar of the gate on his shoulder; the bottom bars rested on bricks but it was still a big piece of wrought iron to manipulate.

'Get ready to take a bit more of the weight then, I'm going to move in three, two, one . . .'

Suddenly, Temperance felt the weight hit her own shoulder, like a mad scientist had cranked up the gravity in the field, and her knees felt like they might buckle. But in another moment Abel was in front of her, lifting the gate and again he took the brunt of it. With a clank that sent vibrations along her arms, the hinges slotted into place and Abel sprinted to kick away the supporting bricks.

The gate gave a smooth swing towards the field and Temperance pulled it back, moving the latch to hold it closed. 'Amazing. Gate Repair 101 with Abel Gulliver.' She put her hands on her hips and smiled. There'd been nothing magical about the work she'd done this afternoon, but the satisfaction went just as deep.

'Dedicated labouring skills supplied by Temperance Molland.' The shadow of a smile played at Abel's mouth before he quickly pushed his lips together into a flat line. 'I'd better get the tools back.'

'What a team!' Praveen called from the hut, leaning out of the window. 'We've missed you round here, Abel. Haven't we, Temperance?' She gave a wink so unsubtle it could be seen from space. 'Can't thank you enough, darlings. Make sure you take as many strawberries as you can carry home as a thank you, yes?'

Temperance was exhausted, but she couldn't shake the dream of a fresh scone blanketed by juicy strawberries and weighed down by a pillow of clotted cream. Truly the only satisfying reward for a sweaty day of squatting in sacks and being an unpaid, unwashed farmhand. She grabbed two abandoned punnets from one of the furrows and passed one to Abel. 'Every man for himself.'

Maybe it was the gruelling heat or how brain-fried Temperance was by the dreams and the doom and the worry, but she fell into a silent search with Abel. He took one side of the planted rows and she took the other. The only sounds were the birds, Praveen's distant radio and Abel's occasional huffs.

'Buggers have stripped the place,' he said, mostly to himself.

Temperance kept her eyes on the spikey green leaves and the scorched soil. She tried to block out the sight of Abel's forearms as they moved the plants gently aside. She tried not to think about how solid they had felt under her touch at FairyFest. She tried not to notice how she could so easily, so innocently, move her hands next to his and brush against them. She tried to remind herself that this was the grown man who rolled his eyes at their festival, who'd deserted his hometown and even now stomped away from crowded dance floors. Not the adolescent she'd once known who would have shared his findings evenly between her and Susie without hesitation. Because they'd felt like a unit back then: undistinguishable from each other, almost. Temperance told herself that was the only reason she was feeling these pangs of attraction to him: it was just an echo of the past, nothing real in the here and now. She was being haunted by her own crush from the past and those feelings would get her nowhere.

'Susie once tried to convince me I was allergic to strawberries, do you remember?' Temperance blurted out, before she realised she wasn't just talking inside her head any longer.

'Hm? No. No, I don't. Sorry.' Abel hunkered down into a crouch, his empty punnet at his side.

'Ah.' She felt a lump at the base of her throat and swallowed it down. Of course he wouldn't remember, not the silly memories of a girl who had the cringiest of all crushes on him.

Temperance took a deep breath and went on, faking confidence in her own anecdote now to style it out. 'It was my twelfth birthday, this big picnic on the green. You were there but anyway . . . I had this huge Victoria sponge with cut strawberries on the top. I don't know if me having all the limelight was getting to Suse, but she tried to convince me – in her gobby seven-year-old way – that I was super allergic to strawberries and if I ate any of my own cake I would freak out and rip all my own clothes off.'

Temperance spotted a tiny strawberry and twisted it off its stalk.

'When I tried to point out that I'd definitely eaten strawberries before and had felt OK, she put on this little stony face and said that it was all part of the medical condition – I would forget the crazy things I'd done instantly. And that mum had sworn her to secrecy about it. For my own good. She literally had her grubby little hands on the plate, pulling it towards her. So I did what any good big sister would do.'

'Oh yeah?' Abel said in a faraway voice. He was probably thinking of his real life back in Bath, Temperance thought, but she was fed up of pretending Abel hadn't been a huge part of her life once upon a time. He'd been there, he'd seen it all. And if he really didn't remember then she would replay it for him, scene by scene, until he did.

'Yup. I called her on her bullshit. Popped a strawberry in my mouth, started crossing my eyes and chanting French verbs. Even started rolling down my socks until she freaked out and screamed at me to stop. You calmed her down with some Frazzles.'

'Right.'

Temperance watched his face for any flicker of recognition, but there was nothing. She shook away the prickle behind her eyes and turned her attention back to the ground, moving further along to the end of the row.

The heat was going to her head, that was all it was.

'Right, here's some.' She spotted three fat strawberry plants, chocked with untouched fruit, nestled under a bush.

Abel side-stepped along with her. 'Don't know how these got missed.' He reached out his arm, to the biggest straw-berries shaded under the knee-height bush, squatting down again.

But Temperance blinked and suddenly saw what the plant concealed: large shards of broken glass in the soil, under the leaves and almost invisible in the shade. And Abel's hand moving dangerous close to a jagged shard. A wink of purple light bounced from its tip.

Doom.

'No, wait!' Temperance thrust out her hand and felt her magic connect with the material of his T-shirt at his shoulder, magnetically pulling him back without thinking about it, her hands following seconds later, holding him around the bicep and dragging him a step away from the bush.

Abel froze as her fingers made contact with him. His breath

went slow and deep, like he was barely able to contain his anger. He kept his eyes staring down, lines appearing at the corners as he held his focus.

They stood like that for a beat too long, Temperance feeling the rigid muscle under her hands that refused to relax, Abel doing nothing but breathing and waiting for it all to be over.

'Glass – broken glass . . . right there,' she breathed.

'I would have been fine. We're not kids anymore, Temperance,' he said finally, quietly. He circled his shoulder so that her hands fell away. 'You don't need to look out for me.'

'Wha—I'm not . . . I just didn't want you to get slashed!'

'Listen,' he spoke plainly, 'I'm just here to get some fruit for Gran, help Praveen and then head back.' He screwed his mouth into one corner and then shrugged. 'So now we're done, I can walk you home, I suppose.'

Temperance felt her jaw go tight. 'No worries. Like you said, I'm not a kid anymore – so I can make my own way back. Thanks.' She said the last word like it was a rotten strawberry in the dust.

She watched him walk away, his shiny red shorts still ridiculous, but there was no laughter bubbling up in her throat now.

Why was Abel Gulliver the stormy-purple bruise she just couldn't help pressing? Temperance wished she could throw a rock at his back and yell, 'Hey arsehole! I'm trying to save your life from some nasty magical shit here! Your cooperation would be nice!' But that was the last thing she could ever admit. She wished, too, that she could click her fingers and somehow restore all the mess now spiralling out of her control in East Prawle. But what would make everything so much less messy was if her heart could just believe that this wasn't the

Abel that Temperance had once loved. This was a new man, disconnected from that kind, funny teenage guy. So if her heart could just stop soaring from the smallest touch, stop seeking out the tiniest hint that he cared in any way about their past, maybe she wouldn't feel so battered every time they spoke. Maybe she'd be able to focus on the job at hand and chase away this doom and send Abel back where he belonged.

But when did a heart ever listen to what was sensible?

Her eyes were still faithfully trained on him as he strode further and further away. On his way out the farm, Abel paused to pick up an already-full basket of strawberries and then disappeared into the lane.

15

Chapter 15

'More hiking, so soon?! Wow, you guys really look the part this time.' Stevie gave a cheeky little thumbs up from behind the cash desk.

Temperance closed the shop door gently behind her and felt something gritty under her feet. Weird. When she looked down there was a thin line of bright white powder running across the shop floor.

'Yup we really . . . caught the bug the other day. Stevie, did something get spilled over here? It looks like sugar, maybe? Or salt.'

Stevie had her fingers steepled under her chin, her eyes trained on Temperance's boots. 'Oh really? Um, I can sweep it up. If it's causing you a problem?' She bit her lip.

'No worries, I'll do it in a sec. So anyway, we're off somewhere a bit further afield. For a . . . challenge. Thanks again for watching the shop solo. It should be a nice, quiet day. Nobody will mind if you want to read a book back here.' Temperance smiled.

Temperance could feel the laces of her mum's boots pressing

into the top of her feet. This 'F' sounded confident enough in their advice, but should Temperance really trust someone so explicitly when she'd never met them? On the other hand, what choice did she have but go on this mad ramble? Susie was fully onboard to try the sedative route on Mark, specifically his leather jacket. If there was anything to take a gamble on, it was keeping East Prawle in one piece, after all. So here she was, in her old camouflage tracksuit from her short-lived leisurewear phase, her mum's boots starting to cut off circulation below her ankles and somehow she was ready to go foraging.

She felt like a witchy Bear Grylls.

Stevie hopped off the stool and came around to the shop floor. 'Cool, thanks. A few eBay listings are coming to an end, so I need to watch those. By the way, bit of a random question, but do you guys go to church?' Stevie looked her dead in the eye.

Temperance almost choked. 'Church?! Um, no, that's . . . not for us. Why?!' She quickly pulled her composure together. 'I mean, if you want to start going, we could find out the service times for you. We have a tiny church here, but to be honest I only ever went inside to go to nursery there. A long time ago.'

A memory popped into Temperance's head, as clear in her mind's eye as if she was gripping a pair of her childhood dungarees. One of those memories that was impossibly huge considering she was so tiny when she made it. The first day she'd gone to the playgroup, having just turned four, Temperance had clung on to a very pregnant Lee's leg. 'Don't want to! Please! I'll stay home with you!' Fat tears plopped out of Temperance's eyes and onto Lee's jeans.

'Oh sweetie. I'm just so tired. Mummy needs to have lots of naps before your baby sister comes. But I'll be back at 2pm to pick you up, OK? Besides, there are lots of kids here, see?' Lee pointed to the six or so children careering around the church, pushing toy diggers along the pews and playing with dollies beneath the small stained-glass windows.

'It's really fun,' the vicar's wife knelt down to say. 'And we have snack time soon. A biscuit and some squash. You could help me put out the cups.'

Lee saw her opportunity at the word 'biscuit' and prised off each one of Temperance's pudgy fingers, before waving and beating a swift retreat to the door.

Temperance's little eyes flicked around the scene – the loud children, the stuffy smell, the vicar's wife grinning at her, a little bit of lipstick caught on her teeth.

'Noooooooo!' she wailed, and ran off to hide behind thick velvet curtains.

That's where Temperance found the box of Play-Doh. And where, twenty minutes later, a five-year-old boy found Temperance, a chunk of dough with very noticeable bite marks held in her hands.

'It's not *real* food,' he said kindly.

Just then, the curtain was pushed back and Temperance's hideout was flooded with light. 'What's going on here, then?' the vicar's wife asked, looking at Temperance, whose face was going blotchy with pink patches of burning shame.

Behind the woman's back, the boy stuck his finger in one of the other Play-Doh pots and rubbed it on his gums. 'We were eating it,' he said loudly, showing flecks of bright blue in his teeth.

'Goodness!' the woman snapped. 'You hooligans! It's not for eating! And it's extremely dear. I shall have to tell your parents about this!' She grunted out a breath.

Tears filled Temperance's eyes, but she wouldn't look at the vicar's wife. She fixed her gaze on the little boy with the blue smile.

That was the first time she met Abel.

'I'm not a churchy person either,' Suzie pulled her back to the here and now, 'I was . . . um, just wondering if religion was a big deal to you. And I'm . . . um, interested if it's an essential English thing that I'm missing out on.' She squinted at Temperance slightly, watching her face closely for any sort of reaction.

'Not so much for us.'

'Right. Right. Hey. I also wanted to ask,' she swallowed, 'about your merchandising system?'

'OK.' Temperance shook the rose-tinted nostalgia from her head. That kind of soppiness wouldn't help anyone right now.

'Like – what is it? Because you've got sizes all mixed; colours, seasons, fabrics – all mixed. So . . . what's up with that? It's like no vintage store I have ever come across. And I've been in a lot.'

Temperance gave a hollow laugh as she skirted her eyes around the shop, desperately hoping a neat explanation would jump out and tidy things up for her. 'Well. Yes. That *is* interesting that you should ask that . . .'

'I'm not criticising,' Stevie rushed on to say. 'But in terms of shopper experience, it's quite a hard job to browse around without much *flow*. For example, I'm going from,' she walked her fingers along the wooden hangers on the rail nearest her, 'a suit vest to some red velvet hotpants to . . . what's this . . . a Liberty maxi skirt. A unique mix, you know?'

'We're, um, a pretty unique shop!' Temperance kept her voice bouncy, aware she wasn't really answering any of Stevie's questions.

Stevie suddenly stepped forward and lowered her voice. 'I could rearrange it for you. The whole shop floor. By era or by size – you choose. I can have it done like that,' she snapped her fingers. 'And frankly it would help me sleep better at night. Like, a whole lot better.'

'That's a big job for your first few weeks, I couldn't possibly ask you to do that.'

'Please?!' Stevie squeaked.

'Honestly, you know, it's the way my mum likes it and I don't want to mess with that. Not without her around.'

Stevie's chin dipped down and she went back to her post by the till. How could Temperance tell her that what looked like a bomb of fashion had been let off in Try Again was actually a very finely honed magical system? The clothes that had come in and received the Molland brand of deep cleaning were racked on the left side of the shop: the entirely clean, almost-new-again clothes. But on the right side were the garments that had come in with shiny, happy memories. Lee and her girls loved to send out these hats, skirts and suits into the world with new owners who could unknowingly enjoy their glow of second-hand joy for years to come. They grouped these clothes by their feelings: romantic tops with loved-up slacks; excited handbags next to optimistic day dresses; confidence boosting boob-tubes with empowered espadrilles. And the Mollands knew just how to matchmake their shoppers with their shiny, happy things: an exhausted-looking parent who'd had a sleepless night of sweaty camping could be steered towards a belt that would help pull them together with a touch of swagger, or the local teen nervously anticipating their first-ever job interview who needed not only a smart suit jacket but a subliminal boost of Bad Ass confidence. There was a system here, just one that only the Mollands could see.

Temperance sighed. 'Susie will be back any minute with the car, so I'd better head out and wait for her. Give me a call if there any problems, OK?'

'Sure.' Stevie gave a half-hearted wave. She watched Temperance walk over the green and then fetched the broom from the office. With a few sweeps, the salt line she'd carefully sprinkled earlier was all cleaned away. It certainly didn't seem to cause a problem to Temperance.

Interesting. But it doesn't explain everything.

Stevie went and placed both hands on an enormous orange faux-fur coat. She kept her hold and closed her eyes, in the best imitation she could manage. Temperance didn't realise it, but Stevie had seen her a handful of times now, touching some of the garments with an almost reverential, spiritual air about her, and in total silence. Like she was listening for something. But even though Stevie let her fingers sink into the deep pile for a good ten minutes, she couldn't hear a thing.

With a sigh, she went back to her work.

'Wine gums?' Temperance asked.

'Naturally. Glove box.'

Temperance rustled open the packet and offered it to her sister, who was keeping her eyes on the road in the driver's seat. Susie took a handful and knocked them back. 'Mhm. I love the first mouthful when wine gums are still delicious. Three more chews and they'll be disgustingly sickly.'

'Not that that would stop us ruining this whole bag.'

'True. Oh.' Susie slowed down, joining the end of what looked like a long tail-back on a narrow county lane lined with thick hedgerows. 'Balls.'

'I wonder what's going on?' Temperance asked no one in particular. 'It's not changeover day.'

Susie raised her eyebrows. 'I'm sure it will pass soon.'

Two hours later, an empty wine gum bag beneath Temperance's feet and every shred of conversation they could explore been and gone, the sisters crawled past a big, red Range Rover, its two left wheels somehow two-foot high into the hedgerow and the vehicle now stuck at an unhappy angle. A middle-aged man with thick gold bracelets had his head in his hands just in front of it. A tractor driver in the next-door field slowed down and yelled out the window, 'You can't park there, mate!'

'I KNOW!' the man shouted back, his voice croaky with emotion.

'Now then, I'm only pulling your leg. I've called my son: he's coming with some chains and we'll pull you out. Don't go anywhere!' He chuckled and the Range Rover man's face went as red as his paintwork.

'Now just another ninety minutes of driving and we'll be there,' Susie grumbled. 'You sure we couldn't have just bought some dried herbs online?'

'Do you want to wait five-to-seven working days while Mark sneaks about with his plans for East Prawle? Besides, the kind of quantities we need might have . . . alerted authorities.'

'What do you mean?'

Temperance pulled out her phone and read from the screen. '*Atropa belladonna*. Attractive, psychoactive, dangerous.'

'That would make quite a good Tinder profile,' Susie cut in, but Temperance only rolled her eyes and kept going.

'Heart-shaped leaves and purple flowers. The toxins within can cause hallucinations, paralysis and even death. Atropa comes from *Atropos*, one of the Three Fates in Greek Mythology who could bring death at will.'

Susie swallowed. 'Sheesh. Hence all the rubber gloves and face masks?'

Temperance nodded. 'I'm taking no chances. If we park up at the location I gave you, then walk as deep as we can into the woodland, I reckon we'll be way off the beaten track and we won't bump into anyone.'

'Sounds like a plan to me.'

The plan shouldn't have involved two wrong turns, a loo break stop and a refuel too, but it did, and after all that, dusk was falling as Susie parked the car in a stony layby close to the postcode Temperance had found.

'Did you bring torches, by any chance?'

'Nope. Phones will have to do.'

'Right. We'd better go quick then, while there's still a tiny bit of light.'

'We'll be *fine*. It won't take us that long.'

Within ten minutes of trudging into the woods, clambering over a bent-down wire fence, the thick canopy overhead drank up the little pinkish light still available and the sisters were waving their phone torches around, swerving tree trunks that loomed up out of nowhere and trying not to fall into the clutches of bramble bushes.

Susie flinched, looking over her shoulder. 'Was that a . . . *howl*?!'

'Suse. Get a grip, love. Probably just a pigeon. Or an owl.'

'A growling owl?!'

'There was no growl. Just keep walking. I think this way is good.'

'You think?'

'I just . . . feel it. Like we're going somewhere really, truly wild. The kind of place magic gravitates to. Ahead for maybe ten more minutes.'

A creature sounded again, not too far away, with a rustle of leaves. Even Temperance had to admit it sounded a bit wolf-like. She kept her eyes on the tiny beam of light in front of her and her mind on tracking down those heart-shaped leaves.

After a dozen more stumbling steps, the trees cleared into a rough circle. Temperance felt something flutter in the base of her throat. 'We're here. I know it. This is the spot. Start looking for the flowers. Really deep purple and a bell shape. Gloves first, though!' She flung a pair of marigolds at her little sister.

'You didn't fancy those nice little suede driving gloves from the shop? I've got a soft spot for those.'

'Wasn't thinking fashion. I was thinking deadly poisons.'

Temperance crouched down and gently walked her fingers through the undergrowth, her eyes searching intently.

Again something jostled the bushes behind them, a blur moved through the undergrowth, and Susie twitched at the noise. 'OK, what the fuck. Something has followed us, Tee!'

'It hasn't!'

A howl sounded behind them. 'I swear! What if it's a magical space guarded by a magical *thing*? I saw something black and hairy move over there. How far are we from Bodmin?'

Temperance tutted and kept up her mission. 'Far enough that the Beast would need a good bus ticket to get all the way here. Are you helping or what?'

Susie shivered. 'I'm freaking out, though! Anything could happen out here and what would we do? Fight off a giant, raging beast with a pair of secateurs?'

Now Temperance could feel the dark trees closing in on her, twigs snapping not far away, a snuffling, getting closer and closer-

'Wait!' Susie grabbed her sister's arm.

'Quiet! You're giving us away!!' Temperance hissed.

'Not that. Heart-shaped leaves, just over there, see?'

The sisters moved as one, hearts racing in unison, flashes of their phone lights showing the sway of heavy purple blooms hanging over smooth, luscious leaves. Seductive, worryingly so.

'*I knew I felt it*,' Temperance whispered to herself, her squeaking rubber gloves reaching out, her fingers almost at the leaves.

'Rufffff!'

'SHIT!' Susie screamed, falling backwards into thorny branches. Temperance threw her arms up in front of her face, stealing her breath for what was about to attack.

'Pooky!' a sing-song voice sailed over them. 'Where are you? Oh, hello. Are you all right?'

A wet panting under her chin made Temperance open her eyes again. A mini Dachshund was licking her knee while happily, heavily breathing.

Under one of the trees a woman in a bright green parka stood, a head torch on a blue strap around her forehead and a dog lead held at her hips 'Pooky, don't bother that woman. Heal!'

The dog skipped off, giving a high-pitched howl in delight as he headbutted his owner's shins.

'Hate to be a killjoy but the main bit of the park is closed, you know. I can show you out through the dog walker's footpath. With all this huge woodland on the premises they let us have free range.'

'The park?' Susie wheezed, untangling herself from a persistent vine.

The woman pointed her thumb over her shoulder. 'Woodlands Theme Park.' She squinted in their direction. 'Had a day on the Pirate's Ship, have we? Bit . . . dizzy?'

'Tell me you did not just Google "woodland" and then followed the first postcode you found?' Susie muttered, loud enough just for Temperance to hear.

Temperance suddenly wished for the ferocious force of Pooky again, to keep her safe in the face of a narked sister.

'Stop,' the dogwalker said sharply, and Susie's jaw hung down silently, assuming she was about to get told off for petty squabbles. 'You need to stand up and move, right away – that's all deadly nightshade there in the undergrowth. You shouldn't go anywhere *near* it.'

'The funny thing is, it's precisely why we're here. We're going to harvest it to use in some experimental magic: to turn a super ambitious man into a meek little kitten who only wants to nap. Magic is in our blood. We're witches! So all good in the hood.'

That's what Temperance would have loved to have said, if only because it involved less brain power than trying to come up with a convincing lie.

Luckily, Susie leapt in, 'Yes, you're right! It is deadly nightshade. The colloquial name, of course. We are herbologists. At the University of Exeter. And we're here to collect some samples for . . . lab work. Hence the safety equipment.' She waved her rubber-clad hands. 'Sorry to have alarmed you.'

The woman hesitated before turning on the spot and moving away, crinkling in her parka. 'Well, good luck. Come on, Pooky.' She disappeared back into the trees.

After five minutes or so, Susie risked a hiss at her big sister. 'No one around, you said! A magic you could just *feel*?! Turns out it must have been the smell of candyfloss in the air, tingling your Spidey senses or whatever. Christ, Tee. We were so nearly busted! Luckily I can think on the spot. Luckily *my* intuition hasn't gone completely arse over tit.'

Temperance's eyes went wild and her cheeks flared with anger. 'You were happy enough to let me do all the planning in the first place! Didn't see you offering all your genius intuition *then*.'

'I've been pretty focused on *saving our home*, if you remember. And I didn't see you offering to drive any of the four-hour-long mission to get here, hey?!'

'And herbology isn't a THING!' Temperance all but roared. 'It's from *Harry* sodding *Potter*! It's not an actual university subject.'

Susie was speechless, her mouth opening and closing like one of the crazy golf obstacles in the theme park. 'It isn't?'

A laugh at the back of her throat caught Temperance by surprise. Soon, she had her hands braced against her thighs, doubled up with laughter at the fact they were arguing about who was the biggest idiot. It was clearly a photo-finish situation.

Susie could barely breathe, she was laughing so hard, tears running down her cheeks. 'The Beast of Bodmin . . . is a . . . a . . . sausage dog! Hahahaha!'

Temperance pushed her marigolds against her collarbone. 'Oh god, I needed that. Phew. I suppose we'd better crack on, in case that vicious guard dog comes back.'

'And Pooky.'

'Ha! Better put on the masks, too, while we're at it. You

ready, Professor Sprout?'

Susie shook her head. 'I'm never going to live this down, am I?'

'Not in this century. Cut close to the ground, remember. We need plenty of that free poison if we're going to throw Mark off his dirty little game.'

16

Chapter 16

There was no reason for Susie and Temperance to drink their coffee 'in' at the Piglet Café, seeing as it had a shared wall with Try Again, apart from the fact that it made it easier to plot their magical shenanigans without Stevie overhearing.

I'd love that. Was beginning to think that night really was a dream . . . How about The Fortesque at 7pm? X

'Hooked!' Susie cackled happily, taking a slurp of her chai latte and revelling in Mark's reply.

Temperance scratched her scalp. 'So are you going to just barrel up to him, rip his jacket off his arms and run for it?'

Susie frowned. 'No. Because I need to get it *back* to him again, without him twigging anything is weird.'

'Sure. You don't want him to suspect you're going to be dipping his leathers in organic poison. Sure.'

She flicked her long, red hair behind her shoulders. 'I'm doing it Mata Hari style. On the surface I'll be a smooth and sexy double agent, but underneath: the cold heart of a killer.'

'How much caffeine have you had this morning?'

'Enough to keep me sharp. I've got to keep my head in the game if I'm going to get through a drink with him and *not* detach his head from his body. Bloody mega-rich thinking they can come here and squeeze the life force from our village, just so they can make a quick buck to add to their mountains of gold guarded by dragons, or whatever . . .'

Temperance put her hand over the top of Susie's mug. 'I'm cutting you off.'

Susie wrestled it free again.

'But are you really OK doing this?' Temperance asked. 'We could think of another way. It feels pretty . . . icky that you're going to have to pretend to like him, on a date. What if he tries to kiss you again?'

A blush swept over Susie, but she pulled her mouth into a grimace. 'I'm not even going to get close enough for him to try. He's completely shallow, when you think about it. Using his lips and body like that . . .' she trailed off, her eyes clouding with a memory.

'Hello? Suse?'

'Hmm? Yes. Exactly. One on one would be too intense. But I was thinking.' She shuffled her chair closer to her big sister.

'Yes?'

'Double date?' Susie's voice squeaked.

'Ha ha. Wait, let me just ask Invisible Boyfriend. Hey,' she turned to the empty chair at their table, 'do you fancy The Fort tonight with Suse and Salcombe's version of Lex Luthor? No? You're washing your invisible hair. Fair enough.'

'I wasn't thinking of a *real* date for you, just someone to up the numbers so I'm not trapped in a corner with Mark,' she said his name like she was retching up bad sushi.

'Let's bring Stevie.'

'I did think of that, but she's bound to notice that we're heading home with a nice bit of vintage leather, and being all sweet she'd get it back to him on the double. Before we have time to tinker.'

Temperance swirled her half full mug of builder's tea. 'It's a bit late for me to ask any of my old college friends – no one's that local to Salcombe, and it's a bugger getting the bus home. It would look pretty suss if I tagged along like a third wheel – he might abandon ship before we get a chance to get the jacket.'

Susie went quiet, drumming her fingers against the table to a jittery beat only she could hear. 'There! There he is!' She pointed through the café window. Walking up the path from the beach, his wetsuit rolled down to his hip bones and a surfboard under one arm, his hair dripping, was Abel. 'I bet Abel fancies a drink in Salcombe. For old times' sake.'

'What?! He can't stand me, remember? He even got mad because I stopped him grabbing a handful of broken glass. He'd rather bleed to death than let me near him. I'm telling you, Abel has no interest in old times' sake, not when it involves me. It's not going to fly and I don't want to—'

Susie yanked open the café door and yelled across the green. 'Miagi! Good surf?'

He froze on the spot as he clocked Susie and Temperance through the window. His eyes ricocheted around the landscape in front of him.

'Nowhere to hide this time, buddy,' Temperance muttered through almost-closed lips.

Susie beckoned and, after a beat, Abel started to walk slowly towards them.

'Come on.' Susie scooped her sister up, hooking her arm in hers and pulling her outside.

It would be awkward enough in any situation to be presented with a bare, unadulterated, *ripped* male torso, but the cherry on top for Temperance was that Abel's discomfort obviously ran deeper than her own.

He leant his board on a nearby garden wall and rested one hand on the opposite shoulder, as if to cover himself as much as possible. Perhaps he was worried she'd make another lunge for his biceps again. Abel couldn't meet her eye even for a moment. And that was hard, because Temperance was adamant that she should hold eye contact and not be tempted to intensely inspect just how much chest hair Abel had grown since he was eighteen (a lot), or how it held onto the seawater and kind of glistened, or how it trailed down his six-pack, circling his belly button and then down . . .

Eye contact, for God's sake. Eye contact!

'Alright, Abel?' Temperance forced her voice to be level.

'Yup,' he grunted, shifting his weight from foot to foot.

'Cold out this morning?' Susie asked.

'Yup. But I just can't resist the surf here. I've missed it.'

'And did you have a lovely long *walk* again before you hit the water?' Temperance's snort of derision slipped out before she realised she was even capable of such an annoyed little piggy noise.

Abel flashed a look at her, quickly, before studying the stones of the bus shelter closely. 'Not today, no. Have you been playing hide and seek again? In a *sack*?'

'Umm.' Susie looked between them in confusion.

'I have, actually. But none of the kids wanted to ask the big, mean, grumpy Bad Fairy to play.'

'Oh, I'm gutted,' he deadpanned, his hand gripping his heart.

'Right.' Susie frowned. 'You know what else you've been missing, Abe?' Susie flipped into her biggest smile. 'A pint in The Fort, maybe throw a few darts too, for old times' sake. With us. Tonight.' She waggled her eyebrows.

'With you *both*?' he asked, his voice controlled.

Temperance found herself clenching her fingers together tightly. She wouldn't let this get to her. She'd been an idiot, on the night of the festival, to let the magic of her costume hypnotise her into thinking there was something – scratch that – *anything* between her and Abel Gulliver still. She'd let nostalgia in the strawberry field make her think that a shred of their old friendship still existed, somewhere. Clearly nothing had changed from the feeling Abel had left woven in his teenage hoody: he was disgusted by Temperance, he could barely tolerate her presence. But she'd meet him there – she'd tolerate him for long enough to sort this cloud of doom she'd conjured up and then she'd let him scoot back to his real life. Done. Over. The only thing she should expect from Abel was that he'd run away again. At least this time it wouldn't be such a gut-wrenching shock.

She forced herself to not roll her eyes and look away, and that was when she saw the tattoo on his shoulder: three simple wave lines stacked in a row. He really had missed the sea, then.

'Suse is right. You should come,' Temperance said flatly. 'There'll be other people there too, don't panic.' She chewed her bottom lip.

Abel shook out a little more water from his hair, almost raining seawater on her in the process. 'OK. I'm in. Anything to get out of the village for a night. I'll meet you there.'

Abel was taking his sweet time getting their drinks, evidently in a long rambling chat with the man behind the bar. Temperance was trying not to be the weird third wheel, but it turned out that things were plenty weird enough between Mark and Susie without her interference. Susie might have been aiming for Mata Hari, but what she was delivering was pure Emily Maitlis: firing off direct questions, one after the other, without letting her date catch half a breath, though still with an air of confident 'don't fuck with me' sex appeal.

'I bumped into Will the other day. He said your parents have a place here. That true?'

Mark rubbed at the back of his neck. 'Yes, but . . .'

'Yet you've been staying at the campsite in East Prawle. That's odd. Care to explain?'

His eyes flicked to the beams running along the low ceiling. On any other evening they might have added to the intimate, welcoming vibe. But tonight it was as if these great big oak beams were pressing down on the three of them, forcing them into the sticky old carpet and making the atmosphere altogether claustrophobic.

'I like hanging out with those guys, and they offered me a spare sleeping bag. It also meant I got to spend more time with the charming staff at The Witch's Nose.' Mark's eyes twinkled but Susie's barely blinked in response.

'Hmm. Oh, here's Abe with the drinks.' Susie snatched up her half of cider and took a grateful gulp.

'Cheers, then.' Mark held out his pint a moment too late, but Abel came in to meet it with his own. 'Cheers. Nice to meet you properly, Abel.'

'You too.'

'Susie says you're another local?'

'Once upon a time,' Abel replied, licking the foam from his top lip. 'Not anymore. I live in Bath now.'

'Lovely,' Mark replied politely, all the time looking at Susie. 'But what a place to grow up – East Prawle. Must have been idyllic when you were a kid. The sunshine, the sea. It's such a jewel of a place.'

Abel nodded. 'Being on the beach every day is hard to beat.'

Mark nodded along with him, as if they were sharing the same memory. 'Shell-hunting, sandcastles, beach cricket with your whole family. Though my dad could never resist smashing it way out into the water, so he'd have a quiet twenty minutes while we went to find the ball.'

Abel stilled and stared into his pint. 'If you say so. My dad wasn't around for that kind of thing. Barely one nappy, in fact.'

'Oh god. I'm sorry, mate. I've put my foot right in it.' Mark's eye went wide and an awkward silence draped over them all.

Temperance broke in. 'You weren't to know you're sitting with The Absent Dads Club. Suse and I didn't have ours in the picture either. We still don't.' She shrugged and gave a jokey grimace. 'But you can't miss what you never knew.'

Temperance's dad was another market trader that Lee met when she was still selling vintage, come rain or shine, from her stall in Bristol. It wasn't exactly a deep and meaningful thing, and by the time Lee realised she wasn't alone in her own body, he'd moved onto a different market rotation and was long gone. Susie's dad had been a bit of a crazy fling on a short holiday to Iceland, with Temperance a toddler cared for by some good friends in the village for the week.

'I want you to know I'm not ashamed,' Lee often said when the subject of dads came up. 'If you can take anything from it, let it be that even adults don't always learn from their own pasts, but they can still be very happy with their lot. Very.' And at this point she would kiss them both wetly on the head, whatever their age, as they tried to squirm away.

The idea of family was always a blurred one in East Prawle: Margie sometimes felt like a gran, albeit one that would tease you rotten. Gary at the bakery was the soppy uncle who cried when you passed your driving test. Besides, having a dad didn't always look so great if some of the holidaying fathers were anything to go by: they'd be snappy over repeated ice cream requests, or they'd miss a springy cartwheel on the green because they were checking cricket scores on their phones. And Temperance was yet to see a dad – even one of the good ones – do anything that Lee hadn't done for them. She was fun, she was firm, she was reliable. Hell – she was magic.

Mark rubbed his fingers across his forehead. 'Fuck. I really am sorry, guys. That must have been tough. For everyone.'

'The mums probably had it worst.' Abel shrugged. 'Being two parents in one. Paying all the bills, stressing about the future. And in my case, having to raise the son who looks exactly like the man who did a runner. Who needs a reminder like that at the breakfast table?'

'But you and Diane are as close as anyone could be,' Temperance said quickly, her heart suddenly hurting for him.

'Yeah,' Susie chimed, 'you're your own person. Not just a carbon copy of your dad. And your mum loves you. She always used to boast about you winning the county hurdles, remember?'

Abel smiled. 'See? A natural runner. Maybe it is all in my

166

genes.'

Susie laughed and elbowed him in the ribs.

'She's right, though. You're nothing like your dad, Abel. You never could be.'

'Thank you, Temperance,' he replied quietly.

Susie looked between the two of them and cleared her throat. 'Speaking of families,' she turned to Mark. 'There's a Beston portfolio company based in Salcombe, Mark. Is that a coincidence?' She squinted slightly.

His eyes widened. 'No, no coincidence. My parents set it up.'

'Right.'

'Are you OK?' Mark asked, his usually mild manner slipping. 'Has something . . . happened here?' His index finger swiped the space between them like a window wiper trying to clear a deadly fog.

'I fancy a game of darts!' Temperance leapt in with forced enthusiasm. 'I'll go and borrow them from the bar, shall I?'

Not a flicker of recognition from Abel. Their last summer together – just before he split – their gang of mates would trek into Salcombe whenever they could to try their hand at being cool, playing darts and getting served underage. Would it really cost him that much to say just one, 'Do you remember when . . .?' Apparently it would.

When Temperance returned, Susie was over at the jukebox and Mark look relieved to be out of the interview chair and chatting to Abel. A rapid set of synth chords played out, with Rihanna growling 'Na na na na na' over the top.

Temperance plonked the darts down on a little table and put her hands to her temples. 'Oh man, Suse! 'S&M': I haven't heard this in so long!'

Susie made her way over to Temperance, a winding motion

167

in her shoulders and hips as she went. 'You used to come back from a Salcombe night out and play it on a loop in your bedroom. I was twelve and had *no* idea what the lyrics meant. Got a bit of a shock when mum explained why I couldn't blast it out of the car speakers on the school run.'

'Yeah, it's not all that family friendly, right? I didn't get most of it back then. But the beat is just so . . . satisfying.' The music snaked its way into her head and heart, drawing up long-lost memories of adrenalin and rum-fuelled nights that felt like they would never end. 'You know, the first ever time I got into The Fort, Abel bought me a gin and tonic and assured me it was a proper grown up drink: it would make me look legit. I had two and started weeping about climate change. You put this on and started grinding with Tim Havers to cheer me up, do you remember, Abe?' she turned to face him, the memory of the scene brightening her whole face with an unstoppable grin.

Abel's eyes were on the space ten centimetres above Temperance's head. She wasn't even sure he'd heard her. In the silence of waiting for him to speak, Rihanna listed all the things she liked to do with whips and chains, being an unashamed bad girl. Temperance felt a surge of red-hot embarrassment travel from her toes right up to her hair follicles. How did she keep forgetting that clearly Abel would rather gouge his own eyes out than relive the old days? Somehow, she kept falling into unconscious ways to sexually harass him too, grabbing at his sweaty body in the strawberry field, leering at him in his wet suit and now making him relive a memory of dry-humping in a public place.

After a significant pause, Abel said, 'Not really, sorry.' And just like that, he took the bulb from her lighthouse yet again.

He wasn't going down memory lane – he was tarmacking over it.

Mark laid his arm along the back of Susie's chair and she felt his thumb lightly brush the back of her neck twice. Despite herself, a charge of something thrilling shot down her spine.

It's all part of his game! She reminded herself, hunching forwards in her seat and away from him. Never in her life had Susie had trouble moving on from a guy. Why did the one that she just couldn't shake thoughts of have to be a corporate sell-out?

'I'd love it if you could give me some paddleboarding lessons,' he said warmly. 'I'm a bit of a klutz, but I bet you could sort me out. Maybe if I get halfway decent we could follow the estuary as far as we can, make a day of it?'

Get me alone so you can dig up more insider info? I don't think so.

It took all of Susie's mental powers not to growl at him.

'Hmm. Maybe. Anyway, let's throw some sharp objects. I'm really in the mood.'

'Are we doing teams?' Mark asked. 'I think the sisters will be deadly together, Abel – let's split them up. I'll take Susie, if that's OK with her?'

She flashed the briefest of smiles in his direction. 'But we play darts with drinking forfeits, you know,' she said coolly. 'So I'll go and get some shots in, to be ready.'

Mark's eyebrows pushed up. 'Right. Guess we aren't bothering with dinner then? Fair play. I'll do anything but sambuca. It destroys me.'

Two hours later, the little pub table was Velcro-like with spilled sambuca. Susie had been expertly bodging all her throws,

169

meaning that she and Mark took the forfeits – except that she'd feign disgust and let Mark valiantly take a shot on her behalf. As a result, he was three super-king-sized sheets to the wind, while she had merely a nice buzz from a few ciders.

Temperance was starting to worry just how sensible an idea it was to let Mark keep playing darts – a drunk person throwing small arrows was just the kind of thing the *doom* hanging over them would love to make use of. Sure, she'd had a lingering desire to throttle Abel now and again when he'd only grunt in reply to a question, but a dart in the neck was a whole other thing. When no one was looking, she slipped them under the table and onto a windowsill, behind a lamp.

Susie wasn't lobbing questions at Mark anymore, but she was still sneaking up on him with the odd curveball.

'You like the pub, don't you? The Witch's Nose, I mean.'

Mark leant his head back on the padded cushion behind Susie. 'Yeah. Certain things about it I like *very much*.' His wink was so drunken that it made his whole skull move.

'And what do Beston portfolios like about it, in particular?'

Mark's eyebrows clumped together, his brow deeply wrinkled. 'What? What are you saying, Susie?'

Temperance knew they needed to keep Mark sweet until a chance came to lift his jacket subtly – they couldn't risk him storming off now. 'I think we could all do with coffees. I'll get them.'

At the bar, the middle-aged barman talked to Temperance over the hiss of the coffee machine.

'You're not on the gin tonight, then?'

'Sorry?'

He gave a dry laugh. 'You don't remember me. I had a lot more hair at twenty-five.' He patted his bald spot. 'And you don't sport a 'tache these days.'

The memory hit Temperance like a freight train and her hand slapped over her mouth.

'God, I'm sorry. We were such plonkers.'

'Who isn't at sixteen, seventeen? And it certainly gave us a good laugh. Though, whoever you nicked those clothes from probably wasn't laughing when you returned them.'

'Eurgh. No, they weren't.'

It had been the most perfect summer Saturday. Temperance, Abel and some friends from their gang of bored teens – Clara, Helen and Tim – decided to sneak off to the granny flat that Tim's parents rented out in high season. And that they hadn't realised granny had left stocked with booze when she passed.

They giggled and swigged their way through mouthfuls of apple brandy, bad red wine and something with a homemade label that stripped Abel's nose hairs when he took a sniff. Feeling pretty pissed and cocky, they set their sights on something bigger.

'Let's go *out*,' Helen said.

'Really out out. Like out in Salcombe,' Clara chimed in.

Tim agreed: 'Yeah!'

He could never decide which girl he fancied more so he kept his efforts nice and even.

'But we might not get served: I'm not eighteen just yet. I only managed two rounds in The Fort before they busted me that other time,' Abel said. 'And someone might recognise us over there and shop us. I don't want my mum to kill me before I reach actual adulthood.'

Temperance laughed into the back of her hand, ending with a wet snort of hilarity that caught on around the group.

'What? What are you thinking, Tee?'

'Disguises,' she managed to say through her laughter.

So while Lee had shut up for lunch and taken eleven-year-old Susie back home with her, Temperance and her mates had sneaked in to Try Again to perfect their 'over-twenty-one strangers from out of town' looks. It quickly got out of hand.

When they reached Salcombe, emboldened by sneaky booze and a 1950s tweed suit, Temperance Molland burst into The Fortesque pub, strode up to the bar, slammed her briefcase on a stool and demanded 'Five pints of Guinness, please!', stroking her glued-on moustache. Behind her, Clara and Helen wore fake fur stoles and long ropes of plastic pearls, while Tim proudly bore an eighties ski jacket in fluro colours. Abel's suit was four inches too short in the leg and uncomfortably tight around the chest. 'We'll get a table,' he said gravelly into Temperance's ear and it sent a weird and new shiver down the side of her neck.

The twenty-something barman waited until the others had sat down, before he leant over the bar to speak to Temperance in a hushed whisper. 'Don't suppose there's any ID in there?' He nodded to the well-used briefcase, which probably hadn't been out in the world for a good twenty years.

'No need, my good man!' she said in her best Brian Blessed impression. 'My acquaintances and I are all over twenty-one and in much need of fresh liberation!'

'Libation?'

'Exactly so!'

The barman ran his hand through his thick blonde hair. 'Being an adult with *finer* tastes, I hate to tell you that our Guiness is off tonight. But what I can offer you is five lemonades. Good sir.'

'Well, I . . . er . . . yes, we'll have those, please and thank you.' Temperance doffed an invisible cap, her vision swaying all over the place. It was hot in this suit and nylon moustache.

She carried the drinks tray over and the others giggled, but with diminished gusto.

'Maybe we should just leave,' Abel offered.

'When we've come all this way?' Clara protested. 'I'd rather drink lemonade in a pub as a grown-up than drink it on the green like a kid.'

'Quite!' Temperance twirled the end of her moustache, and it fell off in her hands.

Abel stuttered a laugh. 'Lemonade it is, my good fellows!'

They spent a very happy hour in The Fort that afternoon, playing Rihanna on the jukebox on repeat, having two rounds of 'vodka and soda' and throwing darts. But they sadly couldn't club together enough money for any kind of food. The heat under their layers of disguise burbled at their very liquid, very mixed stomach contents.

Temperance went green.

Abel went white.

'Are you going to . . .?'

'Are you . .?'

Temperance broke first, yanking open the briefcase and emptying her entire stomach contents onto the green silk lining.

'I'm *mortified*,' Temperance said to the barman, as he put the coffees down in front of her.

'Really, don't be.'

'*A moustache*, though?! I'll promise to forget it forever if you will. And then it dies with us, hopefully.'

'But there's your man there, too.' The barman nodded in

Abel's direction.

'He won't remember. He barely remembers my name.'

He leant to one side, against a pillar. 'That's not how he told it to me earlier. Rumbled him too, didn't I? Seeing the two of you together is what brought it back – a right striking couple. Anyway, your man said he spent hours scrubbing the inside of that briefcase the next day, so your mum would calm down a bit.'

'Oh. Yeah. Still, he's not *my man* and it was a long time ago. We were just idiot teenagers.'

'Ah, but those are the things that shape you, don't you think? Even if they were idiotic. Or maybe especially if they were.' He rubbed his hands together. 'Now then, you need to get one of these to that mate of yours. He's not doing well, is he?'

'God, yes. I'm Temperance, by the way.'

'Jimmy.'

'Pleased to meet you again, Jimmy. My good sir.' She tipped an invisible hat and carefully carried the full tray of hot drinks away.

After two steps, Abel was by her side. 'I can take that.' He put his hands under the tray but Temperance didn't pull away.

'Thanks but I'm fine.'

'Really.'

'No, *really*.' She shook her head firmly, her curls dancing in front of her face.

He pulled gently but instantly on the tray. 'Please. What do you imagine Mum or Gran would say if they knew I let you carry a full try like this? My hurdling hero status is on the line.'

Temperance couldn't quite see him clearly through the brunette curtain over her vision, so she couldn't be sure how tongue-in-cheek he was being. From the range of Abels she'd seen over the last few days, he could be either wryly self-deprecating or stone-cold arrogant. She decided for the sake of their weird little drinks party to hope it was the first one.

'OK. Thanks, then.'

As he took the weight of the tray from her and she pulled back slowly, she felt his fingertips catch against the inside of her wrist. Temperance hated herself for the jiggle above her diaphragm that betrayed her every time she came into contact with Abel Gulliver.

If only you were a pullover, or a pair of pyjamas, Abel. Then I could read you and find out what the hell is going on in your head.

Out on the street, Mark took in a big lungful of crisp, salty air. 'Ooof. We really should have had that dinner, Susie. I had this project I was going to tell you allllll about, very exciting, might have . . . we're all pissed, yeah? It's not just me?'

'Hmm,' Abel managed, making a non-committal grunt.

'No, no, I'm feeling it too. And so *cold*.' Susie did a pantomime shiver, running her fingers up and down her crossed arms.

Mark blinked a lot. Then the penny dropped. 'God, have my jacket! Of course!' He slipped it off and onto Susie's waiting shoulders.

'What a *gent*,' she said with chocolate-dipped venom. 'Night then! Tee, Abel: shall we?'

'Well, uh,' Abel looked from Mark's weaving figure and back to Susie, 'I think I'll just take a walk with Mark, see him home, stretch the legs. No need to wait for me.'

'But we've got the last water taxi booked,' Temperance broke in. 'After that, you'll have to get a regular taxi all the way around the headland.'

'No worries. I'm fine.'

'Of course you are.'

'What's that supposed to mean?' It could have been the sea breeze playing tricks on her ears, but his voice almost sounded hurt.

'Nothing.'

'Good.'

She should have left it there. Temperance knew she should. But talking to Abel Gulliver was like scratching a scab. It wouldn't help things heal over, it wouldn't make anything better, and ultimately it would only mean a pitted, unpleasant scar left behind, but she just had to know if the fresh, shiny version of Abel from her memories was hiding under this crusty, unpleasant exterior.

'Yes, God forbid you let anyone help you save an hour of your time and fifty quid, just to get you back to our sad little village.'

He blew out through his nose, his lips forced together tightly. 'I have never said . . . Ah, look,' he grunted and Temperance could almost see the countdown of numbers rolling through his head as he forced himself to stay civil. That's how much her world had shifted on its axis since the day he left: just a few feet away from where they stood, she had had some of her best teenage memories hanging out with Abel, and yet, right now, on this neighbouring spot, she was being given every sign that she was the last person he wanted to be in proximity of. 'Don't assume you know what I need, Temperance,' he said cooly.

The sharp jab of his words actually made her eyes water a little bit. She rapidly blinked it away. 'Why would I? I hardly know you.'

'Ooooooh.' Mark breathed sambuca fumes across them all. 'Trouble in paradise, is it?'

Abel turned away to catch Mark as he lurched worryingly close to the harbour wall. 'Definitely need to get you home, buddy.'

Mark's eyes, glassy and hooded, did their best to focus on the scene at hand. 'I think we've got one more drink in us, eh? Suse – let's not end the night here.' His arm swung out across the nighttime vista of bobbing boats in the sea, the tiny lights of East Portlemouth visible over the estuary.

Susie wasn't even bothering to make eye contact with him now. Her patience had well and truly worn out. 'I don't think the RNLI boat serves drinks,' she muttered.

'But on such a beautiful night,' Mark sing-songed, 'we should drink, we should dance, we should talk about our passions in life. Tell me about your village, Suse; tell me about the people, the pub, the gorgeous rolling fields down to the sea . . .'

Everything in Susie's body went rigid and for a moment Temperance was worried she was going to have to hold her sister back from doing some actual bodily harm.

'We've got to get that taxi, remember, Suse?' she nudged.

'Yes. GoodNIGHT,' Susie snapped, clutching Temperance's hand and marching off to the moorings, the jacket held tightly around her.

Chapter 17

'Do you think this is how serial killers start out?' Temperance asked, poking Mark's jacket down again as it tried rising to the surface, like it was trying to climb out of its poisoned bath and run for help. A tin bucket in the back garden might not have been as legitimate as their old-school witches' cauldron, but both sisters were a bit nervous about leaving anything noxious behind on the ancient cast iron pot.

'You're not *meditating*, Tee,' Susie growled quietly. 'F said meditating on what we want Mark to *be* was important. You can't just wait to read what's already there, like we usually do. So stick to the mantra: *meek, mild, as ambitious as a child.* That's what I'm doing. That's how we take this sod down several hundred pegs.' She straightened her posture, sitting on a beaten-up beanbag out in the small garden behind their house.

Susie went back to her mediation, looping the mantra over and over in her head. *Meek, mild, as ambitious as a child. Meek, mild, as ambitious as a child.* She imagined the leaves of the belladonna plant reaching out under the water, twisting tightly around the sleeves of Mark's jacket, like a kraken about to drown a wooden ship. F seemed mighty sure that this plant had extreme powers, so Susie was going to trust that it would leech the confidence out of Mark, if she encouraged it in just the right way. She screwed her eyes even more tightly shut, feeling a muscle twitch along her jaw as she played out imaginary scenes in her mind, like a twisted Geppetto setting his puppets up to fail.

Mark would be nervously stuttering and stammering through a business pitch, the PowerPoint fails to load, his fly is undone. Eventually, he is laughed out of the room in disgrace. He's carrying a box of office supplies out of a building in a cardboard box, dejected and despairing. No one will return his calls. He sends off email after email but they fall into a void of nothing. He's finished, and he knows it.

Susie stuck her tongue into her cheek. She didn't want him to starve, just stay the hell away from ambitious property development.

Mark is retraining as an estate agent. He takes a job in London, driving a Mini and wearing a cheap suit. He can pay his bills. But loses all his friends. And self-worth. And dies single.

OK, that last bit is too much. But the suits are definitely shiny and itchy.

But a hero can't just take out the bad guy, Susie knew, they had to shore their castle up from any other attacks. Taking deep breaths from the centre of her being, Susie dropped her head onto her chest, sitting deeper into her subconscious and the images she was casting out into the universe.

She imagined good luck raining down on East Prawle, like a glittering summer shower. It touched the buildings, the locals, the beaches. The people there are happy and unchanged. Their lives will go on as they always have, undisturbed by developers. A precious pearl still in its oyster shell.

Usually when Susie read an emotion in something, the pictures she saw would be exactly as real life, if slightly cloudy or grainy like a badly-preserved family video. But as she was concocting all these visions from scratch, they took on big, bold cartoonish colours. Everything in her mind's eye was clear and vibrant as she willed it into being. There was a tingle in her fingertips, just like she had when reading other people's clothes, but it was hotter and more spikey than usual. More like a static shock than a warm bath, but Susie chose to see that as a good sign that the belladonna was really working.

'The Fairy Princess!' a sweet little voice gasped from behind them, breaking Susie from her trance. Temperance turned to see one of her fairy minions from the festival looking though an upstairs window of the holiday cottage next door.

'Hello again, Martha!'

'Where is your fairy dress today?'

Temperance looked down at her striped jersey skirt and strappy vest. 'I only wear it for very *special* fairy occasions, with my special apprentices. Otherwise, I keep it secret, hidden behind a rainbow.' She tapped the side of her nose and the little girl gave a thumbs up.

'Is that a fairy potion in your bucket?'

'*That sounds really inappropriate,*' Susie whispered.

Temperance cut over her, quickly. 'Not today, just . . . dying some clothes a new colour.' She used the garden cane she was stirring the bucket with to lift the jacket out briefly, the purple water sloshing over the side a little, causing Susie to jump.

Martha peered down. 'Is it for your good fairy friend?'

'Huh?'

'Bad Fairy who we made good. He picked strawberries with you, too. I've seen him surfing at the beach. *I* think,' she checked over her shoulders, 'that he's a mermaid as well. But that's between us.' She stuck her finger up her nose twice.

Temperance gave a light-hearted shrug. 'Who knows what he is, love! He's certainly a mystery to me. Is that your mum calling? You'd better go!' She waved and turned back to the bucket, submerging the leather jacket once more, forcing it into the murky water.

'It's weird with Abel,' Susie said. 'Sometimes I see these flashes of the old Miagi and then – whoosh – the shutters come down. He can be fun at the pub with Margie, but then a vibe killer out in Salcombe with us. He's someone totally different these days. Abel used to be so fun, so up for anything. It's weird that we still don't know why he left like that. I can't get anything out of him. Back in the day, he was pretty much,' she folded her arms, tucking her hands into her armpits, 'a brother to me.'

'Maybe he was just better at fooling us all when we were younger. Maybe this is the real him and he just can't be arsed to put a gloss on it anymore.'

Susie flicked her eyes to Temperance's. 'You can't mean that! You guys were thick as thieves – and he was your first crush! And clearly you loved him enough, once upon a time, that when you cast out for your true love, that's who the universe brought your way. Him. *Abel.* That can't have all been smoke and mirrors on his side. He must have cared about you too, Tee.'

Temperance blew a long breath out through her nose. She felt something in her stomach tighten. She didn't want to believe it either, not really, but time and again since Abel had come back to East Prawle, he'd proved that he felt nothing for Temperance. Nothing for her now and not even a shred of warmth for what they'd once had together all those years ago. Maybe it was time to share with Susie the only proof she had. Temperance turned on her heel and stalked into the house.

Five minutes later, she returned with a sky-blue hoodie, a washed-out transfer of a white seahorse on the back. Temperance handed it to her little sister, her forehead wrinkled. 'Read this for me. What do you feel?'

Instantly, as she took the hoodie, Susie's mouth turned right down at the corners. Her shoulders hunched over as if she'd been winded in the stomach.

The memory dragged her in, even before she was ready for it. Sickness swilling at the pit of her being: bitter, angry. A shameful feeling of disgust. A heart-thumping panic to run away, to get far away from this awful mess. Two teenagers sat in the pub garden, knees touching on a bench, then lips meeting nervously. But from the point at which they kiss, thick black ripples are radiating out around them, turning the picture grey and muddy. Abel is packing a bag now, Diane watching him anxiously, her words muddled and warped, indistinguishable.

Susie opened her eyes. 'Shit!' She looked dead at Temperance. 'You're there, Tee! You're kissing . . . you're kissing Abe! But it's all ringed in this dark disgust. What . . . what is this?'

Sharp jabs stung her fingertips where she would usually feel a warming buzz after reading. Susie threw the jumper down onto the scrubby grass, pushing it a further foot away with her powers so that it turned a somersault in the air. She needed as much distance as possible from this toxic memory.

'The night Abel left, I'd gone to meet him at the bus shelter like we'd planned. He wasn't there but he'd left his hoodie behind, with a note. The note said he was sorry, he had to go, but when I picked that up, I knew the truth of it. He was so grossed out and embarrassed by the fact we'd kissed that he couldn't bear for anyone to know, or to face me again. So he left.'

'Oh, Tee, Tee,' Susie jumped up and wrapped her arms around her sister, cinching her into a tight hug. 'I don't . . . I can't believe it Why didn't you tell me any of this before?'

Temperance pulled back. 'You were so little and you were already heartbroken that he'd gone. Besides, it was pretty hard to have a frank conversation when I spent three weeks in my room ugly-crying.' She nudged the hoodie with her sandal. 'It was the first thing I ever read with magic, can you believe it? It taught me how powerful those leftover emotions can be. Not so good for my ego, though.' She gave a hollow sort of laugh that fell flatly between them.

Susie gasped. 'You've kept it all this time? We could have cleaned it. Or *burnt* it at the very least. Temps, why would you hang onto something like this?'

She bit her lip for a moment. 'My head couldn't work it out: my best friend vanishing into the air. I had these dreams that he'd turn up at our door with a bag of Doritos and a huge apology, begging me to be his girlfriend. Even *years* later. It was,' she cleared her throat, moving on from the tiny crack in her voice, '*pathetic* of me. So, each time I had that dream, I had to remind my heart of the truth: he didn't love me, he didn't want me. It was all a silly, one-sided, teenage thing. Clearly my heart didn't fully get the message, hence the magic dragging him back to East Prawle when he still can't stand to

183

be near me. But I'm going to fix that. Reverse the cast. Use the magic to send him away again. At dawn.'

'Dawn: like, tomorrow?'

Temperance nodded. 'First thing tomorrow.'

Wedding dresses were not designed for napping, that much Temperance knew to be true. To be able to get into the dress while it was inside out and still fasten it up somehow, she'd needed Susie's help. So to save Susie also waking up at an ungodly early time to catch daybreak on the beach, the sisters had got her into the dress before bedtime and Temperance had tried to sleep on the sofa. But not only was it tightly cinched with boning and lacing, and giving out rustles like a cat tearing through a stack of paper bags, this time Temperance was not dulled to the powers of the dress as she had been on FairyFest night, with a gallon of booze in her system. Initially, falling asleep was fine – the thick hue of royal blue pure love made her feel truly content and at ease, so she could drift off in a minute. But then a red kick of hip-rolling lust would surge through her dreams.

And oh those dreams. They were so real. And so *hot*. Temperance learned two things about her subconscious that night: it was horny and it was cruel. Her brain dug up the filthiest of dreams, but all about a man who wouldn't share a water taxi with her, let alone a bed.

At first, Temperance wasn't even aware that she was dreaming. The living room door swung open and Abel walked through, his wetsuit pushed down below his navel again, wet footprints glittering in the lamplight. Temperance could see his chest rapidly rising and falling, like he'd just run all the way back from the beach. She was about to open her mouth and tell him to get lost but the words got stuck in her throat as she took in the curve of his biceps, the stepping stones of his abs.

Without saying a word, he strode toward Temperance and knelt over her on the sofa, his thighs outside hers. There was a steely certainty in his eyes. Abel's right hand reached out and held her chin, then ran down her neck and her shoulder, all the way along her arm. His touch was tender, but when he reached her wrist the movement stopped and his fingers gripped suddenly, raising her hand above her head. Before she could say a word, he'd scooped up her other hand and now had both wrists pinned to the cushion behind her. 'Stay,' he growled as he sunk forwards.

His sea-cold lips found the soft skin at her neck, her collarbone, then the top of her breasts. Temperance wriggled to bring her hands down to his bare torso, to feel that new-to-her chest hair, those steps of muscle. But each time she tried, he only repositioned his hold and gave an impatient sigh. And then his lips would start again, exploring every part of her body available, the rough warmth of his tongue drawing ley lines over her skin, drawing deep on a powerful longing she had kept buried for so long.

Temperance was caught between lust and frustration, her head swimming with the mix. She tried to push her hips up against him, demanding to play her own part in what was building between them, but she was powerless against his tall frame, his solid muscle.

Just as she whispered, '*Abel. Abel, please,*' she woke up , breath heaving and sweat along her hairline.

Temperance blinked into the darkness, willing the images to fade away, to slip just out of consciousness like most dreams did when the spell was broken. But she could see it all in perfect recall, could feel the weight of him still over her, somehow.

It didn't take long for the wedding dress to lull her into another deep sleep, but then the dress did its thing. In the next dream, Abel appeared silently in front of her once more, but Temperance wasn't going to let him be in charge this time: she stood and went to *him* without an invitation, weaving her hands into the hair at the nape of his neck, pulling him down to her, pausing when their lips were just millimetres apart.

'Now *you* stay,' she murmured against his mouth, feeling a flip behind her navel as he smiled a wolfish grin in response. She kissed him softly at first but then ran out of patience, her mouth wanting more, wanting everything, her tongue exploring boldly, her teeth holding his bottom lip until he groaned to be released. They moved hard and fast against each other like this was a frantic dance they knew from muscle memory, and yet it was all so electrifying and brand-new: Abel's hand pulling her hair back to angle her neck to his lips, the other strong hand on her bum, dragging her in flush against him. Not wanting to lose the upper hand, Temperance pushed him back, back up against the door, but clearly Abel wasn't going down without a fight. He turned on his heel and span her around with him so that her hands were braced against the rough wood and his were free to grab at her hips, run up her sides, over her tits, squeezing hard. He was right behind her, his body like an outline of her own. Breath on her neck, each deep, throaty sigh making her push back further against him.

'*Now, Abel.*'

She was awake and staring into the black again. The clock said 3.17am. She knew she needed more sleep, but she was almost afraid of where the dreams would take her next, and yet she wanted to go there again.

They're at the bus shelter. Teenagers once more. A perfect summer's day. Abel's hand is open on his thigh, as Temperance sits next to him on the bench, drawing circles over his palm. Their eyes are locked together, barely breathing. She works up the nerve to explore as her fingertips tingle: the thick muscle at the top of his leg, built by hours spent on a surfboard. Temperance can feel how strong he is, even over his shorts. Then the softer skin on his inner thigh, finding a gasp from the back of his throat as she moves. The noise makes her feel bolder, braver. Her fingers trace the hard shape pointing up towards his stomach now, under the fabric. Abel shuts his eyes and his head tips back against the shelter wall, a low growl coming from deep in his chest. Her hand trembles as she slips it beneath the elastic waistband and finds him impossibly hot and rigid: this is what she's done to him. It's like a river running down her spine, this ego boost, this invitation. The feeling pools between her legs: she's so wet from just what she can do to him. She wants to know more.

Abel moves forward, kissing her like he's been in the dessert and she is the water. When he breaks away, her hand is still stroking him, still absorbing the delicious, satisfying hardness there.

'Someone might see,' he whispers, but it's not really a complaint or a warning. Temperance feels her heart bang against her ribs. He pulls his blue hoodie over their laps, a makeshift barrier, so she can keep her fingers wrapped around him, she can keep turning him insensible with each shudder of pleasure.

'Come closer,' he says into her hair, and her hips wriggle next to his. Abel's hand snakes under the hoodie, finding the button of her jeans, clumsily wrestling with it while his mind is on what she is doing inside his shorts. 'I need to feel you too.'

187

As his hand slips inside her knickers, parting her and finding out for himself just how turned on she is, Abel has to cover Temperance's mouth with his to stop her crying out.

'Sshhh,' he almost laughs against her lips. 'The people on the green will hear.'

Whether he knows it or not, he's found just the right spot, just the right pressure, to send flashing lights up behind her eyelids. She's terrified that someone might see, but she's terrified that Abel might stop: the pulse of lust filling her whole body turns her light-headed, almost.

Temperance can feel Abel straining to keep his shoulders and hips still, to concentrate. 'Just . . . don't move your hand, OK? I want to see if I can . . .'

His finger traces tiny, delicate circles. He kisses the side of her neck until she feels dizzy, until the feeling builds and every muscle she has clenches, until this new energy courses along her nerve endings and makes her feel she will float, until she almost can't breathe, until she . . .

'Abel!' She collapses against him, entirely spent and entirely delighted.

Her mouth tries to find his again. Except he's not there. She's on her sofa – twenty-nine, not seventeen – her breath ragged, her body on fire.

That dream felt particularly cruel: painting it like a memory, like something she'd really experienced, when it was total fiction. Temperance couldn't take it anymore. OK, so the dreams were *fun,* but they were a surreal vision of a future she could never have. They were a tantalising taste of everything she wanted but just couldn't find. She wanted love, but she wasn't going to find it with someone who detested her, that was for sure.

With every follicle of her skin on edge and her mouth aching, she forced herself to stand up.

'This dress will kill me,' she said into the dark room, searching out the torch on the table by the fire and switching it on. 'The minute Abel Gulliver is back in Bath, we are doing some heavy pagan shit on this.' She touched the red belt at her waist and her knees went weak for a second, unintentionally reliving the feeling of Abel pressing her against the door, his fingers over her hardened nipples, his lips sinking into the back of her neck. 'You'll be first to go, you spicy little thing.'

Temperance finally caught her breath on the walk to the beach, trying to close off the hundreds of R-rated images the magic had conjured up of her and Abel on the sofa, in a bed, in a car, hot and heavy on the bus shelter bench. . . Instead, Temperance turned in to the hoots of the owls in the trees, the insistent crash of waves on stones, the wind chasing through ivy. Anything she could find that was not hot. That would not make a granny blush. She needed it PG so that she could get her head in order and concentrate on the job in hand.

'Don't move your hand, OK? I want to see if I can . . .'

Temperance shook her head like she could knock the dreams out onto the ground. This was serious. This was not the time to live in a Judy Blume fantasy. It was time to take action.

It was still pitch black, so Temperance had plenty of time to get down to the beach, start a fire and practise reciting her spell in reverse. The dress was heavy and cumbersome as ever, but with no one around, she could use her powers to heft a lot of it. She was finding that the more she used her kind of magnetism to draw the silk up off the floor, the more she could lift several thick layers in one go, like she was strengthening a muscle. But Temperance was wearing her Marigolds just in case, to save herself getting nonsensical with love and lust.

With the fire gently licking away at some driftwood (she couldn't look at it for too long or the dressing gown belt started giving her flashbacks again, specifically to Abel's tongue on her throat), all Temperance could do was sit and wait for the day to arrive.

And for the millionth time over the last twelve years, she found herself wondering just what it was that she'd done wrong. How badly did you have to kiss someone to convert them from your best friend to your worst enemy? Clearly the dream version of Temperance had some killer moves, but what had she done that day in the pub garden that had turned his stomach so completely? It must have been something really so horrendous that Abel hadn't been able to explain it face to face, instead he'd chucked all his worldly possessions in a car with his mum and left Devon.

Temperance had a few other kisses before that day, and none of those boys had renewed their passports and left town. Mind you, they were botched, sloppy moments of panic. What she'd shared with Abel was something much more memorable.

It had felt so natural in the moment. After a day at sixth form, they were rolling cutlery in napkins, sat together on one of the picnic benches in the pub garden. Something they'd done a million times before, though admittedly usually with Susie doing cartwheels around them. Temperance was turning seventeen in a few days and Abel was teasing that she wouldn't in a million years guess what he'd got her.

'Well, last year you bought me a double ice cream cone. So this year am I getting sprinkles as well?'

Abel rolled his eyes, his grin never faltering. 'Nope. Way off.'

'A hot glue gun?'

He laughed. 'No! Who else in the world would go from thinking ice cream to a glue gun but you, Temperance Molland?'

'Exactly.' She straightened her shoulders, pulling up her frame. 'That's how amazing I am.'

There was a lull as Temperance expected him to shoot back, *yeah, amazingly lame.* But Abel didn't say anything, just kept smiling down at his little mound of shining cutlery as he wrapped and rolled.

A nervous twist in Temperance's stomach made her fill the silence. 'If you won't tell me, I'll just have to go through your search history.' She snatched his phone from the table before he could get there pressing it to her chest.

Abel's eyes went wide. 'Hey!' His hands lunged for the phone, but Temperance dodged away quickly, holding it over her head.

But this tactic was no match for the extra inches Abel had rapidly grown over the last few summer months, and he stretched out his arm, wrapping his fingers around her wrist.

Something about the way he held her, gently but with power, and how she was now just inches from his face, her body stretched along his, seemed to charge the air around them. Their hands lowered slowly, in unison. He dipped his head down, found her lips with his and just pressed them there for a moment.

Temperance was both surprised but also strangely at ease – as if a part of her knew this day was coming, as if her subconscious was giving her a slow hand-clap and saying 'At last!'.

She opened her mouth, her tongue meeting Abel's, and even though her eyes were closed her vision was filled with a glowing sky blue.

Still holding onto the phone as if for dear life, with Abel's fingers only tightening on her wrist, Temperance felt his other hand rest on the space between her neck and her shoulder, as if keeping her rooted on the spot, in the moment. Not that Temperance felt she could operate her own legs right now, even if she'd wanted to run away. All she could think about was how alive her skin felt where he was touching her, how there was nothing strange at all about the fact they were kissing, the synchronised way they tipped their heads to either side, the warmth of his breath on her top lip. It was the first time, but it felt as natural as if they'd been doing it for a decade.

Temperance had no idea how much time had passed before a raspy voice said, 'Ahem, that's enough of that.' She had looked up to see Margie, a washing-up bowl balanced on her hip and her hair tied in a gingham scarf. Temperance moved half a step away from Abel in that moment, her fingers reluctantly breaking contact with the golden skin on his forearms. The smile on her face was concreted on, no matter how much she tried to play it cool. Abel was blushing up to his ears, but likewise he had the grin of someone not at all sorry. Temperance walked home with a skip in her step, not knowing that that kiss was not just their first but also their last.

Two days later, he was gone.

Trainers kicked off by a rock, Temperance rooted her feet in the chilly, damp sand. Double-checking over her shoulder that she was truly alone, she twirled her fingers, setting the hem of the wedding dress into a gentle sway, the friction keeping Temperance's legs warm in the cool night air.

It wasn't time to dwell on the past – where had that ever got her? Frustrated, alone and now with the village in a whole lot of magical trouble.

The memories she was preserving in the time capsule of her heart needed to be set free, left to weather away to dust, to return back to the pure energy of emotion that linked the universe. Ironic, really, that she was so talented at washing away the leftover memories of others with her magic, when here she was, still clinging to the echoes of things that happened twelve years ago. Not letting go.

That would all tonight.

She held her hands together at her heart and took deep, steadying breaths, right down into her core. The crash of the waves seemed to get louder, the cool air nipped more forcefully against her skin.

It's true love I'm after, Temperance spoke inside her head, hoping to make the message clear and simple to her soul and to the magical forces all around her, *not raking over a teenage tryst. Abel wasn't the one I needed here, OK? Let's sort this out and set him free. Get out from under this doom cloud. Then everything can be the way it should be.*

Set him free. Set me free.

Streaks of inky blue nudged between the black sky and the grey sea. The sun was waking up. Temperance turned her palms out and up to the sky. In a low voice, she stated, *'Abel Gulliver is not The One. Though I have spent long, lonely nights wishing for love, even calling on nature's wonder, I will set him free. For my will is as strong as yours, and my magic as great. Love can have all power over someone else, honestly. I swear.'*

Temperance kept repeating her words, closing her eyes as the dawn emerged. She pictured Abel climbing back in his van, starting the engine and driving out of East Prawle without a backwards glance. She imagined herself happily working away in the shop, oblivious as he left her life silently for the second time, and how freeing that would be.

I will set him free. I will set him free.

She searched her body for any strange sensations, any magical twinges or tickles. Her feet were warming up, but maybe that was because the first rays of dawn were hitting the sand. Then again, maybe taking magic away felt different to reading it or casting it. Maybe it felt nothingy because you were leaving a void behind? The clothes that she washed at the store often felt empty, neutral, once they'd had their old emotions teased out from them. Maybe this is how she should feel after releasing some toxic magic. Like a blank canvas. Ready to start again and paint a new picture.

Abel Gulliver is not The One. He's not and he never wanted to be.

It was done. It was over.

18

Chapter 18

Temperance ran for her life.

The wedding dress was ripped down to shreds: just one layer of the skirt still hanging on, the hem singed, ragged and pulled to bits. The sleeves and the red belt had come off somewhere behind her in the woods, but all she could think about was running.

Running from the clap of thunder, the white burst of lightening, the roll of smoke around her head. The fire was spreading; it was spreading to the village. She had to get there. Before . . . before . . .

Suddenly, someone was standing on the path in front of her, screened by thick, grey smoke. But were they blocking the path or had they come to rescue her?

She opened her mouth, her hand at her throat.

But she couldn't make a sound.

Temperance sat up in bed.

'Shit!' she yelled, bringing Susie bursting through her door. 'What? What's happened?'

Temperance dragged her hands down her face. 'It didn't work! This morning, at the beach: it didn't work. I had the nightmare again, only this time it was worse.'

Susie flopped onto the bed next to her. 'Oh fuck. So we're still in doom times?'

'Seems like it.' Susie got her phone out her back pocket and started typing frantically. 'I'm having a major magical crisis and you're texting?!'

The little sister bit her lip. 'Not texting. Googling.'

'What?'

'Witch premonitions: storms and fire.'

Temperance gulped back a sticky lump in her throat. 'What does it say?'

'Well, the first history site that comes up is about this woman, Mother Shipton. Born in the 1400s.' Her eyes scanned the screen. 'She lived in a cave, with a skull-shaped rock pool. Made herbal potions for those in need. And . . . accurately predicted the Great Fire of London and the Spanish Armada.' Susie shivered.

'I was hoping you'd find something a bit more reassuring than that.'

'Me too.' Susie squeezed her big sister's hand. 'We'll email F again, see if they have any other tricks up their sleeve. Some bigger magic. How are you feeling?'

'I mean, pretty wired, what with the magic and the – um – broken sleep before dawn and then this. I suppose I—'

Susie sucked in air between clenched teeth. 'Is there a chance you could pull all of that together in the next half an hour and come to the pub with me?'

'What? Now?'

Her little sister nodded. 'It's actually 11.30 – you slept in.

And seeing as his jacket was dry, I texted Mark to come for lunch. He'll be there at twelve. Time to plant some devious little magical seeds, Tee.'

Temperance gave a sigh of defeat. 'OK, I'll get up. Let's hope this bit of F's advice actually does the trick.'

'And one more thing?' Susie held up a finger.

'Yes?'

'You really need a shower. You smell like you've just done the marathon in an acrylic knit.'

Temperance swung her legs out of bed and snatched a towel from her radiator. 'You could have at least brought me some tea.'

Temperance picked slowly at the crab salad sandwich Susie had ordered for her by way of an apology as she started her shift at the pub and went into the back to start prepping for the evening rush She watched the door, waiting for Mark to stroll in. So much depended on the belladonna having the effect F had promised them. Who knows if there would even be a pub to have a crab sandwich in in two years' time if it didn't?

She'd been trying to ignore the presence of Abel in the room as he aggressively rubbed down the bar top, using about ten times as much CIF as you'd need to clean the hull of a boat. Every time his forearm muscle tenses and flexed, Temperance would have another flashback to the saucy dreams she'd had. Each reminder was a cocktail of overwhelming sensations: a squeeze of annoyance across her forehead that Abel Gulliver could still have such a visceral effect on her; a lurch of guilt in her stomach that she was somehow harassing him by making Dream Abel carry out every single one of her sexual fantasies without the real Abel's knowledge; and a deep tightening between her legs when her libido betrayed her better sense, aching to experience those dreams all over again.

As Abel leant right over the bar to reach the far edge, scrubbing away with a particularly vocal huff, Temperance saw a flash of him bending her over the desk in her living room and she snapped. 'What is UP with you?'

His head whipped up. 'Sorry?'

'You're treating that bar like it owes you money. Are you OK?'

'Yes.'

'You're sure.'

'Yes!'

'OK. Whatever. Suffer alone. It's really none of my business.'

Abel gave her a long stare before throwing the jay cloth in the sink and stalking around to her table. 'Sorry. I'm . . . I had the weird dream again. That one I told you about? Last night. Except this time there was a fire coming towards the village, really close to the pub. And I knew Gran was still inside, so I was banging on the door, but for once in her life she'd locked it. The dream . . . it's shaken me up, OK? Scared the shit out of me, if I'm honest. I don't like the idea that something could happen to her and I'd be too far away to help.'

Temperance slightly regretted her snappy tone and softened her next words. 'Margie has a big network of people here who love her. We'd never let anything bad happen to her. We are always around.' Temperance had meant to sound reassuring, but maybe her intonation had lingered too long on that final 'we': the implication being that she and Susie were doing a better job as surrogate grandchildren than Abel was doing as a real one.

'Right. I appreciate that,' he picked at his thumb, 'but all the same I'm going to extend my stay a bit, really make sure she's OK once the birthday party stuff has died down.' He said it as excitedly as if it was four back-to-back dental appointments.

Temperance felt her heart unclench just a little – more time to puzzle out the spell she'd cast over them all was a good thing, at least. Who knows if she had the powers to be as on the money with her predications as Mother Shipton, but she wasn't going to let it get far enough to find out.

'She'll love that,' Temperance said encouragingly. 'Not that she's a wilting little wallflower when you're gone or anything, but I can see the extra spring in her step at having you back.'

Half a smile lit up his face. 'It was fun watching her kick out a lairy holidaymaker who rested their pint on the pool table. She told him to go back to Centre Parcs where he belonged. I think she threw in a few extra swear words just for me.'

'I legitimately learnt all my swear words from Margie as a kid. Well, Margie or *you*.'

'Oh right, because you were a goody-two-shoes? It wasn't my idea to steal flakes from the ice cream man, remember? And yet somehow, *I* got the massive lecture from Gran about "leading you astray". Typical.' Abel grinned, blinked, then quickly went back to wiping down glasses.

Temperance felt her breath catch for just a second. Abel Gulliver had actually admitted to having a past here in East Prawle. It shouldn't have felt so momentous, but it did. Now she'd heard it confirmed with her own ears, and had glimpsed some sliver of warmth in Abel, Temperance was too curious for her own good. She wanted to see what else he might open up about. 'Must be nice, though, a Gulliver get-together for Margie's big birthday?'

His mouth folded back down into a line. 'Yes – although it's always weird, seeing Gullivers in a big group.'

'What do you mean?'

'It reminds you who's not there. Who never turns up.' Abel rubbed unnecessarily hard again at the bar, as if he could polish out his anger. 'And I don't enjoy that part.'

Temperance bit her bottom lip. She hadn't meant to stir up memories about Abel's dad like that. Even if he could be a cold, rude arse at times, he didn't deserve for that kind of a wound to be opened. She could kick herself. Trying to dig deeper to expose his happy roots to the village, she'd actually uncovered a deep, dark well of sadness. And perhaps another reason why he'd been happy to turn his back on the place he grew up in. For each good memory, there was obviously a sad one lurking just behind.

'I'm really sorry, Abe, I didn't mean . . .'

He looked up and met her eyes. 'It's OK. You get it, more than most.' His eyebrows scrunched together as he moved to start wiping down the big coffee machine.

'If you ever wanted to talk—' she ventured, but her words were cut off by a giant blast of steam shooting out of one of the shiny steel pipes, dangerously close to Abel's face.

'What the?!' Abel stepped back, his forearm shielding his eyes.

A stab of pins and needles shot up Temperance's hands, as if she was reading the strongest magic. She sprinted over to where he stood. 'Are you OK?'

Abel nodded, wiping moisture away from his skin.

Temperance threw a tea towel over the guilty pipe and slid her hand around the machine to unplug it. But she found that it was already unplugged.

Her blood went cold.

The door was rolling closer.

'Fuck me, that was hot.' Abel had his fingers pressed into his closed eyes.

Temperance turned to him. 'Can you see OK?' She took his hands away, moved them down to his sides. 'Open up. Can you see me alright?'

The skin over his nose and forehead was flushed still but when Abel opened his grey-green eyes to her his gaze was unblinking and direct. He spoke slowly. 'I can see you, Temperance.'

Her hands were still holding his. 'Good. That's . . . good.' She slipped her fingers away and stood back. 'Margie should get that machine checked out.'

'I'll tell her. Maybe something fell in there and set it off. I swear that steam looked purple as it was coming at me.'

'Um, right.' Temperance tried to gulp back the lump in her throat.

'Actually, can you watch the bar for me? I'll tell Gran about her demon machine.'

Temperance nodded numbly. 'No worries.'

She went back to her sandwich and was silently worrying about what other inanimate objects might start magically attacking Abel, when Mark popped his head around the heavy front door. 'Hello? Are you open?'

'They're open.' Temperance waved him in.

'Temperance, hi. Is Susie around? She's promised me the perfect fish and chips to help put an end to my three-day hangover. Fair, when she was the one behind the sambucas. I could have sworn I told her that was not my poison.'

Temperance trilled out a fake, tinkling laugh at the word 'poison'. 'She is a one. Must not have heard you properly over the jukebox. I'll go and get her for you.'

She sped off to the kitchen, nipping quietly through the swing door. She didn't see Susie straight away, but she did see the broad back of Abel as he rolled an orange back and forwards along the stainless steel counter with one hand and pressed his phone to his ear with the other. The way his hand moved, slowly and smoothly, had Temperance back in the dream where she was up against the wooden door, his hands all over her, squeezing tight . . .She shook her head like a wet dog to dispel the image.

'. . . much rather be hanging out with you, too. I don't like it but it's something I've got to do. I know, babe. Maybe another week? Yeah, OK.'

He turned on the spot and locked eyes with Temperance, his jaw falling open ever so slightly.

'Sorry,' she blurted, her stomach trying to make its way out through her mouth, 'looking for Suse.'

Her heart was pulsing in her ears as she walked blindly towards the pub garden instead, finding Susie polishing silverware at one of the tables, under an umbrella.

'Mark's here. In the pub.'

Susie's eyes lit up with a manic energy. 'Go time!' She snatched up the jacket in a bag next to her and went inside.

Temperance picked up a fork and napkin, rubbing at a water mark. She decided that it was much safer out here with the cutlery.

Twenty minutes later, from over the fence she heard Mark and Susie open the pub's front door.

'I thought it was a good place to moor at the time. Maybe it's not. And I'd hate to get caught in anything choppy today. I could just call a taxi to take me home, leave the rig here.'

'Hmmm,' Susie said without commitment. 'You could.'

'I don't know quite what to do . . .' his voice trailed off. 'Oh, um. I brought this for you. But maybe you already have it.'

'*Rough Guide to San Sebastian.* Oh. Thanks.' Susie's voice was flat.

'I knew one of the guys at the boat club had been, so I borrowed it off him this morning. He said you can keep it. If you like. I think you'd have a great adventure there. And I would—'

'The other night,' Susie suddenly cut in, 'you said you had an exciting project you wanted to tell me about. But we didn't get a chance to talk about it. But I've got a little time now?'

There was a pause on Mark's end. 'Did I say that? I suppose . . . it's still up in the air, though. Lots of hurdles to go over. Might not get very far at all with it. Red tape, you know. A solo project of mine, and my family . . . aren't always easy to convince. Now I think of it, I really should rush back. Don't want to piss off my dad. Goodbye, Suse.'

Temperance heard footsteps on gravel as he crunched hurriedly away. After a good beat, Susie yelled out, 'Hear all that?'

'Yup.'

'I'd say we're in business. Or more like – he's not. Ha! Belladonna, you little beauty.'

Chapter 19

From: TinyTempsM@yahoo.co.uk

To: FEverything@hotmail.com

Subject: Help again! PLEASE

Hi F,

I know I'm bothering you twice now in the same week, but doing everything in reverse DIDN'T WORK (using your caps style so you can feel how much I'm freaking out here). I did clothes inside out, daybreak, same beach, and I really, *really* meant what I was saying. The only things missing were my old purple beanie – Susie had left it at the pub – and 12 litres of Malibu. Which I now cannot drink again as long as I live.

I totally told the magical world to take this guy back – but I had the dream again that night and so did he. What else can I do?! I feel like I accidentally knocked over some cosmic dominoes and they've kept tumbling and tumbling and now they're about to push over Stonehenge or something. HELP. If these dreams come true . . . it would destroy our village, our way of life.

T x

P.S. The casting on the leather seems to have worked a treat, so thanks for that one. Susie says double thanks.

Temperance shut her laptop and fiddled with a frayed shirt collar she should have mended weeks ago. Her desk was turning into more of a mountain range of mess than normal, and that was saying something. Whenever she got a spare half hour to do some mending or patching for the shop, the usually calming, meditative stitching couldn't compete with her inner monologue, screaming at her that she'd jinxed the village, cursed Abel and then stuffed up the one hope of reversing it all. And inside *that* monologue was a tiny, squeaky voice in a right sulk saying 'Abel's got a girlfriend!'

'Obviously he does,' she muttered to herself, picking some pins out of a little strawberry-shaped cushion and then jabbing them back in again. 'He's a grown man. An *attractive* man. Who wears a wetsuit as well as David Gandy.'

'Did you say something?' Stevie popped her head around the office door.

'Just . . . running through my to-do list out loud. Sorry. Everything OK out there?'

Stevie nodded, her pixie cut gelled into cute spikes today and working with her baggy denim overalls, undone on one shoulder. Some thick nineties R'n'B vibes going on, and Stevie really carried it off.

'I'm going to take my break soon, if that works. And I thought, when I come back, I might get into there.' She waggled her fingers towards the tiny drawers at the far wall, where the Mollands kept all their dried flowers and herbs.

'What? Why?!'

'There are a few pieces at the front – that big orange faux fur and a couple cord skirts on the right rail there – that I noticed the other day were giving off a bit of,' she wrinkled her nose, 'very *slight* mustiness.' She held up her hands. 'Which is not an attack. You really have the sweetest-smelling vintage shop of all time. But those are giving off a tiny whiff, so I thought I'd do my bit and give them one of your patented lavender baths.' She smiled sweetly.

'No!'

Temperance had had a crush on that mega bright seventies orange fur nearly her whole life. Not only did it look the coolest, but when you put it on you felt its almost chemical, magical burst of joy and the sense of what a treat it was to be alive. It made you want to spin on your tip-toes, belt out 'Groove is the Heart' and throw some serious shapes, whether you were on a dance floor or just at the butcher's. Just as they'd always called Stevie's catsuit Frederica, this coat had always been a Cassandra to her. There was no way she was going to let Stevie accidentally wash any of Cassandra's power away. Temperance had never told Susie or even her mum this, but she harboured a secret plan to buy that coat from the shop should she ever fall actually REALLY properly in love, and wear it to leave her wedding reception in. She just knew it would look so awesome with a short cocktail-style wedding dress and crisp white Converse. The only problem would be keeping Cassandra unsold in the shop that long.

And finding the actual love of her life, of course.

Temperance stammered, 'It's . . . uh . . . you know, these seventies synthetic fibres. So delicate. They've got dry cleaning instructions like they're written in Klingon. I always worry if we get them wet they'll just disintegrate into nothing.' She saw a crease appearing on Stevie's forehead, as if the fib was trying and failing to get into her brain. 'But how about,' her eyes scanned her cluttered desk, landing on an old Liberty handkerchief that she'd been thinking about reusing for patches, seeing as it had a cigarette burn in one corner, 'we use this.' Temperance grabbed it and made for the little drawer that she knew contained dried lavender heads. She plonked a handful of those into the handkerchief, dragged the hair bobble out of her bun and used it to tie it up into a mini parcel. 'Plonk this in a coat pocket. Fanny's your aunt. A *subtle* sweet smell.'

Stevie tipped her head to one side, looking first at the ratty little lavender bag and then at her friend. Her forehead was still creased. 'If you say so. I'll see you in an hour, Tee.'

Temperance felt bittersweet about her new friend casually usually her nickname after only a week or so of working together. She loved that she'd got to know Stevie so fast, that they had their equally strong love of vintage fashion to bond them, that Stevie was clearly a 'Yes, and' person, up for a last-minute fancy dress party and rummaging about in a store as well organised as an over-shaken snow globe. But she also felt guilty that she had to keep Stevie at arm's length at times – denying her very sensible suggestions to remerchandise the shop or deal with slightly stale smells. But what choice did she have? Their family magic was sacred, it needed sheltering from prying eyes and sinister assumptions. There was only so close Stevie could get to the Molland sisters.

Perhaps Temperance could make it up to her soon by organising a few classic English trips for the off-season, show Stevie some of the sights that made up their patchwork culture: Birmingham's delicious curry mile, a raucous Brighton drag show, the breathtaking feat of Hadrian's Wall. There might be things she absolutely couldn't share with Stevie, but Temperance could definitely help her new friend get closer to her mum's heritage.

Temperance decided to make up some flower cocktails for the next batch of clothes that needed treatment from the estate sale boxes, so she'd be ready to go once the shop was closed for the night and her witchy tasks began. A generous scoop of lavender, another of rosemary and then a delicate smattering of the dried yellow rue leaves. They were small, but they were mighty at drawing out lingering heartache. Twelve years ago, Lee had run right through her rue supply when she had to wash the misery out of Temperance's tear-stained duvet. That had been one for the record books, she'd said at the time, trying to find any small glimmer of humour for her crushed daughter. Without much luck.

Temperance added each kind of flower to a paper bag with a heavy sigh. There had been so many happy garments within the same box that housed the powerful wedding dress and silk robe. So many breadcrumbs on the trail of a joyful life well lived. But at the very bottom of that box, thrown in without any hint of being folded, were two black dresses and one charcoal grey suit. Not that old, not much noticeable wear and tear and beautifully made by some luxury brands. But from the first touch, Temperance could fully understand why they had been given away. She and Susie had already taken care of a black silk shirt, which must have originally been part of one of these funeral outfits, when they washed on the beach the other day. The clothes were all heavy with grief, the weight of things unsaid, of empty, stony hearts. The grown-up children of the fabulous wedding dress lady, Temperance assumed, devastated to face a world without her.

When she had floated the garments from the box and stilled herself to tune into their memories, Temperance had seen a picture of huge floral displays, but ones that brought no joy. The soft close of a shiny black car door. Heavy velvet curtains closing with a coffin just visible behind. And then even more heartache at empty drawers and wardrobes, a once-loved garden now abandoned to weeds. She could well imagine how eager the family would have been to peel off the dark clothes they only now associated with her loss and never see them again.

I guess it's the yin and yang of life, Temperance thought to herself as she carefully folded over the top of the bag and laid it on the windowsill. *You can't create that much love without it leaving a huge footprint. Sometimes happy, sometimes sad. It's a risk to love that big.*

The little bronze bell over the shop door tinkled again – Stevie must have forgotten something.

Temperance decided to lift the mood in her heart. 'Left your sexy catsuit behind, Unikitty?' she called, but Stevie stayed quiet. Maybe Temperance had pushed her away one too many times earlier.

She jogged through to the shopfloor, not finding a unikitty but a decidedly bad fairy instead.

'Oh. Abel.'

He dropped the sleeve of the orange fur coat as if it had singed his fingers. 'Hey.'

The silence was a wedge between them.

'Anything I can help you with?' Temperance asked at last.

His jaw tightened. 'Yes. I'm after purple.'

'Purple?' She looked him up and down – black jeans, black T-shirt, hair still damp from another surf, maybe. A surprising styling choice, but a sale was a sale.

He cleared his throat, then ran his tongue over his teeth. 'Gran has decided that her birthday barbeque will have a theme: purple. You know, like the poem about getting old and not giving a shit, wearing purple and eating sausages.'

'Ohh. I remember that from school.'

'Me too. It was the kind of thing Miss McKenna could recite off the top of her head, walking about the classroom with chalk smudges on her sleeves, remember?' It was as if he'd forgotten himself again, sharing an old memory, and after a beat he cleared his throat and went on. 'Anyway, as she's decided with only a few days to go, I don't have time to get to Kingsbridge around my pub shifts. So . . .'

'So . . .?'

'Here I am. For something purple.' He shrugged. 'Preferably something subtle.'

If this is the doom, it's got a really creative sense of how to mess up my day. 'I'm sure I can find you something. Subtle.'

He nodded. 'Thanks. And Gran said to tell you she's a modern eight, but an old-school ten, whatever that means. Mum's a bit bigger, I'd say.'

'Oh – so you're shopping for your mum too? You're going to be busy.'

A blip of panic made his eyes go wide. 'I was hoping you

could . . . if you might be able to . . .'

Temperance decided she might as well enjoy the chance to make Abel feel as uncomfortable as he'd made her feel since he'd set foot in East Prawl again. Albeit gently.

'Hmm?' She raised her eyebrows with a quizzical lilt, as if she had no inkling at all of what he was after.

'. . . *help me?*'

She nodded. 'We have some purple. Let me pull up some options and you can choose. Ahh!' Her eyes lit up, piercing the neutral 'not bothered' expression she was aiming for. 'We actually have *just* the thing for Margie, only arrived a few months back. It is classy, yet glam, and takes no prisoners.' Temperance went to the rails on the lefthand side of the store, flicking through hangers at an excited pace.

'It sounds like Gran,' Abel replied tentatively.

'Here!' Temperance pulled it out with a flourish. A cocktail dress in a rich, plummy purple, lace overlaid on a satin sheaf, three-quarter sleeves and a fitted pencil skirt. 'Going by the label, it's early sixties and would have been made bespoke for the woman who wore it.'

Her heart sank a little as she remembered the memories this particular dress had carried when it came to Try Again: glimmers of cheerful resilience skirting around a deep disappointment. Temperance had felt it and seen a very fancy dinner, a table at somewhere like The Ritz, with candles and music and a buzz of anticipation. The woman in the dress expected a proposal – but it never came. It had felt like a personal mission to strip away that memory and Temperance carried out the task with extra care and patience. Now all that remained was an absolute killer dress that was ready for a new adventure.

'It might be a bit loose in the hips for Margie, but she's *got* to try it on at least!' Temperance held the dress up against herself, leaning back on one heel to take in the juicy sex appeal of the thing.

Abel studied it carefully. 'Agreed.'

Sheesh. Temperance felt like she'd presented him with the crown jewels and he was thanking her like it was a plastic party tiara. Maybe she should have done that tacky sales patter of offering two crappy things before the good one, so he was too bored/tired/deflated to say no.

'As it is a one-off, and almost fifty years old, it's pretty pricey, I should say.'

A huff escaped his nose as he looked out the window. 'That's fine. Gran's sorted. How about my mum?'

Not exactly an overwhelming moment of gratitude, but Temperance chose to feel good about having one significant sale in the bag today, at any rate. 'Your mum, OK. If I remember it, she's a bit less showy in her style than your gran . . .' She tapped her chin and walked around the shop, Abel stepping back to let her past. 'It'll be nice to see her again, anyway. I always expected her to drop in and see Margie now and again—'

Abel cut across. 'Mum liked the new start in Bath. It suits her. The property management business keeps us both really busy, and we have Gran up to stay sometimes. East Prawle was never really the same for Mum once my dad left, not that I can remember much difference. She's not from here – he was. So there were no real ties.' He shrugged one shoulder, his eyes still trained on the green outside the window.

'Of course.' Temperance watched him under her lashes, her head ostensibly dipped to explore the rails. He said it all so calmly without a flicker of emotion on his face – detaching himself from his hometown. She just didn't understand how that could be.

After a few minutes, she found a lilac mohair jumper from the eighties, but that didn't seem to be a great match for a summer barbeque. The grape-coloured nineties T-shirt that said 'ladette' in block letters also got instantly benched. 'So we don't want a cord; linen is preferable but it doesn't wear well after a decade so we don't carry all that much . . . maybe a denim,' she mumbled to herself, falling into a sort of styling trance. 'I think I remember . . . aha.'

Lee found it really hard to say no to any of the jeans and denim jackets that wound their way to Try Again – even if the Mollands had run out of space to display them. Denim could have such a long, hard life and each crease or badge or tear only added to its unique beauty. It could hold complex layers of emotion and could take a hardcore cleansing when it needed, and still come out unscathed. So underneath the hanging rails were battered suitcases and wicket baskets and even an old bureau drawer full of jeans – skinny, flared, intentionally ripped and accidentally so.

'Give me a hand?' Temperance asked, already having wriggled out a heavy old suitcase and now busy rifling through the rolled-up jeans inside.

'Uh, sure.' Abel picked the wicker basket furthest from Temperance – of course – and pulled it out onto the shopfloor in one fluid motion. 'What am I looking for?'

'I know we had a very dark purple pair of jeans – a noughties bootcut, I think. Nothing too radical and your mum could dress it up or down.'

'OK.' He crouched down on his heels. 'Dress it up or down –

I never know what that means. It's . . . baffling. Do they take girls aside at Brownies or something to explain it?'

Temperance laughed, passing over some inky black loons. 'What are you on about?'

'I get how something can look fancier – with jewellery or whatever. But what is dressing *down*? Going out in an old stained T-shirt that needs a wash? And why even would you want to look more 'down'?

It was almost the most Temperance had heard Abel spontaneously say in one breath since he came back to the village. It was most like the 'old' Abel she had seen in a long time. Like how he'd always try to chat nonsense to the school bus driver, Lily, on the drive back to the village in secondary school. Just to make the same old journey that bit more interesting for her. He wasn't as bothered in Lily's racing pigeons as he made out, but she never twigged in all those years.

But after what he'd just said about having no real ties to East Prawle anymore, Temperance felt dizzy with the contrast in these two opposing sides to Abel Gulliver.

'So I take it your girlfriend never dresses down then? Always a blow dry and a string of pearls on the go? I bet she doesn't buy her jeans from an old suitcase,' she teased.

Abel stood suddenly and dusted off his hands. 'Probably not.'

Temperance felt her throat go sticky. She knew she shouldn't go down this route – she knew it would only make her feel worse – but Abel's girlfriend was the spot she was going to have to scratch. There was so much about his life that was an utter mystery, and now that she had the chance to get some answers, she wasn't going to pass it up. Even if the curiosity put her heart six feet under.

'What's she like? How long, um, have you guys been together?' She aimed for nonchalance as she kept searching for the purple jeans, her hands now clammy.

'Not long,' Abel replied in an even tone. 'Just a few weeks. Maybe two, officially,' he finished.

Temperance nodded. 'Cool.'

Abel rubbed his palms against one another. 'I'm not really into relationships. Not long-term ones. Cass knows that.'

Steady on, Casanova. Temperance allowed herself a kernel of bitterness. Just a little one.

Abel leant down and pointed over her shoulder. 'Those look purple, right?'

'Yes. That's them. And of course your mum could come and switch them for something else if they're not for her.' She stood up, hit suddenly by his scent. Toast, honey and the tang of seawater. Temperance swallowed. 'No hard feelings between old friends.' Her eyes locked with his.

Abel ran a hand over his head and left it resting at the back of his neck. 'So . . . about me.'

'Yes?' Temperance found she was holding her breath. Was he finally going to clear the air about making the greatest of all French exits all those years ago? Was he going to say it had all been a stupid, impulsive mistake and he realised now – now he was so very grown up at thirty – how much he hurt her and how sorry he was?

'So . . . I need something too.'

'You do?' She felt her lungs contract.

Abel creased his brow. 'Yeah. A purple thing? Gran won't let me off the hook. I did try and get out of it.'

You're very good at getting out. 'Of course. Right. We don't have so much menswear, but it's worth a good look all the same.' She turned on her heel and moved to the back of the shop. 'Or you can bend the gender norms. We love a bit of that at Try Again.' She yanked a sequin mini dress from the rail, it was rainbow striped but at least had a healthy line of purple.

'Not sure I could pull that off.' He stuffed his hands in his back pockets.

Temperance scrunched up her lips into an exaggerated knot. 'No. I don't think you could, actually. There are a couple of waistcoats on the rail behind you, if you want to have a flick through. One might have some purple piping or lining inside. Might get you through on a technicality, but not exactly in the *spirit* of our village. There's some men's accessories out the back. I'll go and grab them.'

When Temperance came in again with a large cardboard box that she could barely reach her arms around, Abel on reflex stepped forward to help her with it.

'No, no. I've got it,' she all but snapped, plonking it on the counter. Her hands started to dig through, luckily not chancing upon anything as filthy as that red dressing gown. Now was *not* the time for a bolt of sexual chemistry. 'Black belt, brown belt, black belt. Menswear is so blah,' she said crossly, as if Abel was responsible for all the men's accessories that had ever been designed or made. 'A red pocket square: closer to some sort of flair, but no cigar.'

'You sure there's no purple sweatshirt . . . or a hoodie?'

Temperance felt heat rise to her cheeks with that last word yet he had no reaction. *Yet more proof that he's forgotten everything about us.*

'Why don't you have a look.' She pushed the box towards him and with an eye roll he started searching.

'If the theme was purple plus *Antiques Roadshow* expert, this would do.' He pulled out a purple bow tie, silk with a fleur-de-lis pattern picked out in a darker, plummy shader. It was the kind of bow tie that came ready-tied and with a clip in the back to fasten it.

'Let me see,' Temperance took it carefully out of his hands. She ran her fingertips over the band at the centre, tracing the slight folds in the silk. Her skin warmed as a low hum of contentedness ran up her arm and into her rib cage.

Happiness and pride.

Temperance closed her eyes.

Charged wine glasses, a well-folded sheet of paper, a waistcoat that matched the tie.

Someone gave a father of the bride speech wearing this bow tie, and it had been the best day.

Temperance couldn't deny that she was hoping that the tie might have slipped through the Molland net and was holding on to a depressing sort of drizzle of emotion that she could pass on to Abel with her very best wishes. But she owed it to Margie to do better than that. Her pseudo-granny would be so happy to have Abel there at her celebration, joining in with the theme, and even more so if he was in a good mood. Besides, the thrill of pairing someone with the perfect vintage item they'd normally not look twice at always called to Temperance. She loved not only rejuvenating clothes with her inherited magic, but also seeing the potential in something that hadn't been loved for years and blind-dating it to just the right recipient. If only her real experiences with blind dates were so productive.

'You know . . .' she trailed off, her hand still pressed over the bow tie in her palm, her heart swelling with its memories, 'this could work.'

'You're *joking*. You're joking?'

217

She shook her head. 'In shirts, you're a sixteen-inch neck, right?'

Abel looked genuinely impressed. 'Yes. How could you tell?'

'Comes with the territory. But anyway – get in there and take your top off.' She shoved him towards the changing cubicle with one hand, pulling the curtain around once he'd stumbled inside.

'Tee, what—?'

'It's going to be a whole look, trust me. I just need my scissors.' She dashed into the office to grab her sewing kit and some purple thread. 'And you need a white shirt.' She dumped her mini haberdashery on the desk and went straight to a beautifully tailored white dress shirt, with pin tucks at the front. In the next moment, she pushed it into the cubicle, her eyes averted.

Back at the desk, she snipped the threads that were holding the bow in place, setting the silk free. She then cut off the clasps at the back and speedily sewed the two ends together.

'Do you have the shirt on?'

'Hang on, just doing the cuffs . . .'

'Come on!'

'Alright!' he growled. 'I'm ready.'

Temperance swept back the curtain with an excited smile. 'I've always wanted to be in one of those dressing room montages in movies, where they transform the geek to a cute soundtrack.'

His face remained stony. 'I am not a geek. And those movies are actually *fun*. What am I doing in this? I know Gran will have me on pot-washing duty, but looking like a waiter feels like a step too far.'

Temperance tutted. 'I'll have you know this is a very fancy

shirt – Saville Row.'

'But it's white?'

'Obviously. But then you loop this around your neck.' Temperance handed over the altered purple tie, its happy buzz dancing in her palm again. 'Like you're Daniel Craig, all rugged and handsome after some Bond shenanigans in a casino.' Heat flared along her collarbone as she realised she'd just compared Abel to one of the sexiest men alive.

Abel lowered an eyebrow, threading the tie under his collar, apparently letting her comment slide.

Temperance blustered on to cover up her embarrassment. 'No, no. The shirt needs to be open at the top for the whole thing to work.'

'Ugh, it just took me five minutes to get those buttons done up, fiddly little berks.'

'Some Bond you'd be. Fine, let me.' Without thinking, Temperance stepped into the cubicle, toe to toe with Abel. Her hands set to work pushing the buttons out through tiny, stiff holes. She could feel the warmth of Abel's breath hitting the bridge of her nose. His back seemed to stiffen, making him stand even taller.

With the buttons undone, she pushed the collar open and arranged the ends of the tie just so, smoothing them down over his pecs for maybe a second too long. Temperance was so far into her 'work' mode, that it took a minute for her to clock just how totally she had put herself in Abel's personal space, and this was no dream – she was actually doing it. She should really pull her hands away. She should really put distance between them. But Abel wasn't moving. He was just watching her fingers as they pressed the tie into his shirt, picking up his body heat. All at once she had his smell in her head again

– toast, honey, but something else a little sharper cutting through now. Furniture polish.

A memory of Saturday chores set by Margie came flooding back – spraying and wiping down the leather seats in the pub. Only Abel and Temperance, sixteen and fifteen then, thought it would be hilarious to load the banquets with so much polish that people slipped right off them again. Temperance still got a fuzz of that stomach-creasing laughter whenever her bare legs touched the leather seats, to this day. There's no subtle way to drench a pub chair in sea water and basil to clean away the memories, and no way she'd even risk annoying Margie to that degree.

'Margie's still using Mr Sheen then?' she murmured under Abel's chin.

'Yes.' He half-cleared his throat. 'But she rations me to three sprays a day, now. Seeing as I've got form.' A smile drew in just the corner of his mouth, giving him a dimple.

Abel released a slow breath – not a sigh, not a huff, which is what she mostly seemed to hear from him these days. But a slow, shallow exhale, almost too quiet to hear. The sound you might unconsciously make when you get into a hot bath or sink into the sofa after a long, busy day.

Temperance realised she was still there, in his space. The perfect distance to let her hands skim down his chest or up over his broad shoulders. His smile was still there too, and the dimple.

So many of last night's dreams came her way all at once, at just the hint of his lips curling in such a knowing way.

Abel's voice just a growl in her ear, his mouth against her neck, going down, and down . . .

But then came the twist of guilt in her stomach again – she

220

was painting him into fantasies he wanted no part of. It wasn't right. And besides, it was pointless. He lived in Bath now, where he had a girlfriend. A whole other life. Where moments before she had felt the warmth of nostalgia and safety, a chill now ran over her skin.

Temperance stepped away and forced herself to lace her fingers tightly behind her back. 'See what you think.' She gestured to the floor-length mirror.

'Ah. Oh. Abel licked his lips, then craned his head back as if seeing a stranger from a distance and trying to work out if it could be his identical twin. 'Right. I see what you mean. Not sure I've ever looked so . . . stylish. Thanks. This will do perfectly.'

'I think your Gran will be impressed.'

He nodded and rubbed his hands together. 'I should send a picture to Cass. She'd hardly recognise me.'

'Right. Of course!' Temperance fidgeted with her bracelets, her eyes darting around the shop – looking at anything but Abel. 'I'll leave you to get changed then, and I'll ring those things up.'

'Cool. Thanks again, Temperance.' He pulled the curtain back around, hiding himself away behind a wall of moss-green velvet.

It was exactly the boundary Temperance needed – Abel was off the market and she needed to remember that.

20

Chapter 20

The sun laid the most gentle kisses of warmth on Temperance's cheeks as she stretched out on the green, her toes pushing down into the worn-soft beach towel underneath her.

It was the same beach towel she'd used her whole life: Mickey Mouse on a surfboard, grinning madly, his primary colours now faded from a thousand hours of bright sunshine. It had been the towel she and Lee had taken down with them to the sea when she was a pudgy toddler, and the same towel she'd shoved into a record bag when she was let loose on her own to wander down there with mates. It had been so embedded with happy memories of Abel – sharing a single Calippo as the sun set, playing beach cricket with Clara, Helen, Tim and the others, sketching out plans that the whole gang would apply to Exeter Uni so they could stay together. Forever. It was so tightly packed with these glowing memories that Temperance had used it in her first ever solo magic washing, a few months after Abel left. To try to pretend to herself that they never had been so close, so content.

'You know we have a beach for sunbathing, like, just down

there?' Susie's shadow suddenly turned the heating off.

'I know. But Abel doesn't surf on the green, so I'm safest here.'

'Aha. Still awks between you?'

'Like you wouldn't believe. Got the skinny on his girlfriend, though.'

'Ohh,' Susie breathed. 'That must suck.'

Temperance rolled her shoulders. 'You can't really expect someone who wants to puke after kissing you to stay celibate all their lives. Apparently, he "doesn't do" relationships, so nice to know he's grown up into a proper male stereotype, eh? I bet he has a string of girls all over Bath, pining for a grumpy, near-silent date with him. Maybe I should move to a big city permanently to find love. Maybe that's what the doom is trying to show me – Abel got out and finds women, maybe that's how I need to do it?'

Susie turned out her bottom lip and Temperance squeezed her little sister's leg briefly.

'Only kidding. Besides, that's not the kind of love I'm after. Something beyond two weeks. A forever kind of situation.'

'Eurgh. No thanks. I'm glad I'm not old yet.'

Temperance moved to a swift pinch instead.

'Ouch!'

'Any word from Mark? Another fifteen texts per hour and invites to The Crab Shack?'

Susie smiled smugly. 'Not so much as a DM. And he's not been back to the pub. We sent him deep inside his shell, Temperance Molland. We are a right pair of crafty witches.' She put her hand out, down by her knees, for a congratulatory high five.

'Amazing. So we're safe – the village is safe?'

Susie narrowed her eyes, looking out at the impossibly blue sky over the sea. 'Not necessarily. I might have taken the wind out of Mark's sails, but Beston aren't the only developers out there. We need to keep our eyes open. The Parish Council are doing their best but . . . they need help.' She put her fists to her hips.

'We're not going to have to cast on all *their* clothes, are we?!'

'No, you tit!' Susie laughed. 'I'm going to join them! Join the council. Add my skills in the non-magical way. Distribute leaflets and rant about things on Facebook. Get my Boomer on.'

'Oh my God!' Temperance choked on her laughter.

'What?!'

'There you were, saying you're not looking for long-term commitments and in the next breath you're on the Parish Council? Don't get me wrong: I'm all for it. I love that you're throwing yourself into something. It's just . . . new. Good for you, Suse.'

'It is good for me, isn't it? I'm going to get us both a scoop of honeycomb to celebrate, seeing as mum can't needle us for having ice cream before lunch.'

Temperance smiled. 'I'm pretty sure she hasn't done that since we both left school, but OK. I'll have a waffle cone, please.'

She settled on the towel again, pulling her sunglasses down from the top of her head and grounding herself in the sounds of East Prawle: the low rumble of a distant tractor engine, the seagulls ever-watchful for a dropped chip to swoop on, laughter and happy shrieking from the gardens of the pastel-coloured holiday cottages.

The twitch of doom still hovered around the edges of her

mind, as it had ever since that bonfire on the beach with Stevie and Susie, but she decided that could wait for the morning. She needed chilling time. She needed deep breaths. To switch off. To relax.

The brambles cut into her face as she pushed through the woods, the splice of lightning suddenly turning the whole world white. She could hear them shouting – pleading – for help, just ahead. She had to keep going. Thunder. Rain pouring down her cheeks. And in her nose the acrid smell of burnt leaves, burnt flower buds. The wildflowers. The wildflowers were nearly all gone. She had to get to them. To put it all right.

***

From: FEverything@hotmail.com

To: TinyTempsM@yahoo.co.uk

Re: Help again! PLEASE

Temperance – describe to me *exactly* what this beanie looked like. I'm very serious.

F x

Temperance sipped her first coffee of the day, frowning at the laptop screen. Why was F so concerned about her beanie? She typed out a reply with one hand, the other still wrapped around her mug.

From: TinyTempsM@yahoo.co.uk

To: FEverything@hotmail.com

Re: Help again! PLEASE

It's one my mum knitted for me when I was a kid. It has these big, chunky bobbles all around it, in a cable pattern. Miraculously, it still fits and I keep it around for emergency Devon downpours in the winter or, as it turns out, late night beach spell-casting . . .

Temperance had started frying some eggs a few minutes later when her laptop pinged with a reply.

From: FEverything@hotmail.com

To: TinyTempsM@yahoo.co.uk

Re: Help again! PLEASE

Your mum didn't knit that hat. I did. I made it for her when she fell pregnant with you. I wanted to make her something special. I unwound something unique I'd been keeping. It was a jumper from the first woman to climb Everest: it had the most fearless energy I had ever felt with my powers. Bold, ready for anything, incredibly strong. I enchanted the yarn with a few other things, a bit like a fairy godmother, I suppose, so you would always have a connection to the magic you'd come from. With a bit of a fiddle, I managed to cloak that magic so your mum would never know it was there, or

you in time. I knew she wouldn't want my help, in whatever form it came in.

It was supposed to be a baby hat, but I'm not so good at following knitting patterns (too much like maths homework, if you ask me) so it came out all baggy. I never knew if your mum liked it, let alone used it for you. Seeing as we haven't spoken in all this time.

That must be why the spell amplified in the way it did, and why you couldn't reverse it the other night: because you weren't wearing the beanie. You'll have to try it AGAIN, Temperance. With the hat, with the Malibu, and take your sister too – she was there that night. You can't leave any magical stone unturned.

The frying pan spat an angry drop of hot oil onto Temperance's wrist. 'Fuck,' she whispered, barely feeling the pain.

***

'Fuck!'

'Chug it down, Tee! Jesus, it's just a bit of rum. What is a small hangover compared to removing a jinx over our heads?!'

Temperance could feel the sand whipped up by the dawn's blustery wind getting between the silk bodice and her ribs, scratching and tickling her with every slight move she made. She held the glass bottle up to the weak light. 'I know, I know! I just wish it didn't have those bits floating in the bottom. Ugh. Fine.' She put her lips to the rim and swallowed two gulps, retching slightly as she came up for air.

'Big baby,' Susie muttered, passing her a water bottle.

'Could I get a bit of support here, or what?! I know this whole thing is my mess, but I'm also bricking it that I'm not going to be able to clean it up. Now: checklist.'

Susie bit her lip. 'Wedding dress, check. Robe tie, check. *Beanie* – with hidden magical powers apparently – check. All inside out, check. Malibu, campfire, beach, sunrise. What else did we do that night?'

'Stevie was there.'

'Yeah, but she can't have contributed to it, can she? Being normal and everything.'

'Good point. So . . . we held hands and danced around the fire,' Temperance said reluctantly.

'We were such tools.'

'We *are* such tools. Come on.' Temperance clambered up off the beach towel, feeling several layers of lace and boning plus the fate of her community pulling at her shoulders. She scrunched up her fingers and let her magic take some of the weight. 'We just need to do this, and mean it. Abel needs to be free to go home and go back to Cass.' She shivered. 'It's a cold one today.' She put out her hands, after relaxing her grip and dusting them off on the ivory skirt.

Susie took them and held firmly. 'I'll mean it, all right. I'm taking no chances when it comes to our home, or the pub. And you're going to really mean it too, right?' She gave her big sister a hard stare.

'What does that mean?'

'No lingering hope that if Abel hangs around for longer, that he might remember the good old days more, warm up a bit, forget all about Bath and Karen . . .'

'It's Cass. And God no, Suse! He needs to be gone, for both

228

our sakes. I *want* him gone.'

Susie nodded. 'OK. Good. Just checking. So, what did we say last time?'

'It's too much of a blur. I think we should keep it short and sweet. Punchy, to the point.'

Susie looked up to the sky striped with powdery blue and baby pink, the sun starting to feel its way into the morning air. 'Abel Gulliver we release you.'

'Perfect.' Temperance started moving clockwise around the fire, forcing Susie to amble into the dance too.

'I feel like such a dick.'

'That's not in the chant. Let's not accidentally cast for an army of giant penises to wash up on the beach, OK? Focus.'

Susie spluttered out a laugh and Temperance couldn't help but match it for a minute before she cleared her throat and started the chant for real.

'Abel Gulliver we release you. Abel Gulliver WE release you. Abel Gulliver WE release YOU.'

They moved round and round, both sisters closing their eyes. Temperance felt something click into place and a swirling warmth start to build in her palms, between Susie's, locking them in. It was like they had put two perfectly matched jigsaw pieces together at long last. They could join their magic and do anything, as a sisterhood. The feeling tingled sharply and spread up her arms, into her shoulders. There was a discreet prickling under her hat, as if now that its powers had been named it was happy to get involved and play its part. Temperance felt a heat circle her hairline and surge along her cheekbone and jaw. She focused on painting the outcome she needed, sent all that tingling heat into her mind's eye.

She started to imagine Abel walking towards her – why did he have to be half naked in his wetsuit, even in her own mind?! – and now she should let him stroll right past and hop into his van and drive far, far away. She should.

Temperance would let the universe know she was sorry for taking what wasn't hers, like a toddler sneaking a teddy from the toy shop. She would put the toy back. It wasn't hers to play with.

With eyes squeezed shut, the sisters twirled around and around, a pulsing energy between their hands, and Temperance felt her head go woozy. Was this magic or was she just getting motion sickness?

She kept trying to piece together the vision in her head, as real as day, willing it into life. She wasn't conscious of using her powers on the layers of the wedding dress but they were floating up and out, like the undulations of a jellyfish at sea.

Abel Gulliver we release you. Abel Gulliver you are not mine. Go home, go home. Abel Gulliver we—

'I knew there was something about you two!'

A voice breathed out the words, like it was inside Temperance's head. But when she snapped open her eyes there was no one else by the fire.

Susie stumbled to a stop. 'Did we sort it? Are we done?'

There was a flash of neon pink at the top of the rocks, far too bright to be part of the dawn colour scheme.

Stevie stood in her running gear, her hands pressed against her forehead like she'd just seen a car crash. Suddenly she pointed at Temperance and started clambering down the jagged rock steps to the beach, sending loose stones clattering in her wake.

Susie's head whipped around at the noise. 'What?! Oh good lord, how are we going to explain this?'

Stevie was racing over now, taking big but faltering steps in the sand, her index finger all the while pointing at the Molland women.

Temperance's mouth opened uselessly as the wedding dress flopped down flaccidly. She pulled anxiously at her clothing, as if whipping it all off and streaking along the beach at daybreak would provide the perfectly logical smokescreen they needed.

'I knew it!' Stevie wheezed as she reached them by the campfire.

'Knew . . . what?' Susie tried.

'I *heard* you chanting. *Abel Gulliver we release you.* That's a cast! That's magic!'

'Erm, maybe the wind was playing tricks on you, babe. It does that. It's a Devon thing.' Susie shrugged with faux nonchalance.

'Uh uh.' Stevie's finger was still held out in a sharp point and now it started to wag side to side, her face blank. 'I know what I saw. In Massachusetts we're taught about witches along with our ABCs. And I knew *The Craft*, *Practical Magic* and *Hocus Pocus*! My top three films of all time. I *knew* there was something about you guys.'

Temperance felt her stomach churning and kneading itself into a tight ball. Here it was. The rejection and hostility she had dreaded all her life. Not only had her magic brought doom to East Prawle, but now it was going to drive away her new friend. And then what if Stevie wanted to tell the whole village? A local newspaper? Put it online?! Temperance and Susie could be driven out of the home they love for being 'weirdos' and 'freaks'. No one would want to associate with them – the store would have to close. What would they do for money? How could Temperance ever look her mum in the eye again if she let their precious secret out and ruined their livelihoods?

It felt like Temperance's ribs were being clamped together as she managed to force out some words. 'Listen, we can explain . . .'

'Please!' Stevie's hands opened up into a wide sunburst and a smile filled her face. 'Please, *please*. I wanted to ask but then I was worried, what if I got it wrong? I could really offend you two. I was trying to ask Tee about going to church, just in case I had the wrong end of the stick. And she managed to cross the salt line . . . But all those herbs and flowers, that I'm not allowed to touch, and the way you close your eyes sometimes when you're handling the stock, as if you're listening to it? When you knew Frederica's whole life story like she *told* it to you. I knew I'd *seen* you make clothes, like, *fly* just a tiny bit, you were doing it with the dress just a minute ago! Plus, there was that leather jacket hanging up that you made me swear not to go near.' Her eyes popped. 'You haven't enchanted people into objects? This isn't an Ursula the Sea Witch kind of situation, is it?!' She froze, her breath coming in gulps.

Susie laughed briefly. 'No, but it's worth looking into now you mention it.' She looked at Temperance, raising her eyebrows. Her big sister took a huge gulp and nodded back. 'We . . . um, do dabble. In magic. We are, you know, witches.'

'OHmmmyyyyygoddddd!' Stevie shrieked happily. 'I have never met real-life witches before!'

Temperance felt the shake in her hands start to settle. 'We've never told anyone before. It's kind of a new thing for us, too. It's not something we feel like we can shout about, to be honest. It could be . . . dangerous.'

Stevie clasped her hands to her chest. 'Of course, of course. I would never tell a soul, Scout's honour. I wasn't out to spy on you. I just couldn't sleep so I thought I'd go for a run. Man, it's all so . . .'

Temperance held her breath.

'. . . *cool*, though. Can you, like, do a glamour spell and change your hair colour? Do you have a talking cat? Can you make people fall in love with you?' Stevie was talking like a machine gun.

Susie wrapped her arm around their friend's shoulders. 'It's going to be OK, love. Deep breaths.' She put her other arm out to Temperance and squeezed her fingers. 'It's all going to be OK. There's a lot to explain. Let's do it back at home over some Crunchie bars, shall we? I hear that's the best thing for shock.'

'Sure. OK. But Temperance, why are your clothes inside out?!'

'Crunchies,' Temperance said. 'Two Crunchies each and one hell of a pot of tea. Come on.'

Stevie was so mind-blown to have all her suspicions confirmed, and the Molland sisters were so relieved not to be facing a trial by fire any time soon, that the three women walked away from the beach forgetting that the reverse-casting was not entirely complete.

Temperance and Susie decided not to wake Stevie later that morning when it was time to head over to The Witch's Nose. She looked so cute curled up on the sofa, her pixie cut all ruffled and her hands clutching their family blanket. It was a vintage quilt Lee had found after Susie was born and now the strong maternal love it came woven with was layered up with the Molland's own family ties and bonds. It had always had the power to soothe Temperance after a rough day at school.

Explaining their family powers and answering Stevie's four

thousand questions had taken a good few hours and the whole contents of their snack cupboard. Truthfully, both sisters would be happily still asleep now themselves after all that, but they'd promised Margie they would help with some of the batch cooking ahead of her birthday party this weekend, and breaking a promise to her was just not an option. They didn't want to let her down and they were equally a bit nervous of what she'd say if they ever tried. Even if that meant following an online tutorial about how to pre-cook a giant hog-roast and all the trimmings. So they'd left a note for Stevie to tell her to hang out and fix herself breakfast whenever she did wake up, and they'd be back later in the day. To answer the next two thousand questions.

Temperance had been given the job of peeling and chopping an obscenely large sack of apples, so they could be cooked down into a chunky sauce. It would have been a pretty chilled task – sitting out in the still-closed pub garden, Radio 2 in the background, a bag of peanuts to snack on, and her mind could have happily drifted off – except that after ten minutes Abel had stalked out with an armful of red cabbages and a chopping board.

'They said I was taking up too much space in the kitchen,' he grunted, plonking himself down three picnic tables away from Temperance, letting the cabbages bounce down onto the rough wooden surface.

Only big enough in there for one stuffed pig, huh? She thought to herself and bit down a smile.

'At least you didn't have to carry a watermelon.'

'Sorry?'

'Never mind.'

They fell into a tense silence as they sliced and diced, Temperance almost getting obscured by the mountain of apple peelings in front of her.

'Here,' he said, passing her a big brown paper sack. 'For the compost.'

'Right, cheers.'

A few times, Temperance had the very particular feeling of being watched, but whenever she flicked her eyes to Abel he was staring at the space just to her right, his eyes glazed and faraway. His hand would be holding the area where she knew his tattoo must be, under his T-shirt. Two fingers pressing into the waves. But it had looked far from a new inking to Temperance. Surely it couldn't still be sore?

At one point he got up with a huff and went to the tiny shed in the corner of the pub garden, wrestling with the rusty latch until it opened. He came back five minutes later with some dusty recliner cushions and plopped one on the bench next to Temperance. 'I'm bloody uncomfortable, don't know about you.'

'Oh, thanks.' She slid the purple cushion under her bum and as soon as the back of her knees made contact with the scratchy nylon fabric she burst into intense giggles.

'What?' Abel's head flicked around.

The world's longest game of The Floor is Lava, Susie in her box-fresh school uniform and Abel and Temperance in their threadbare set. They'd used cushions, pub trays and beer mats as their 'safe' stepping stones to get from one bench to another, the September sun poking its way through the tree branches. It had all been Abel's idea, to cheer tiny Susie up after a disastrous first week (where she'd wet herself twice) and they had laughed their way through a good few hours before Margie told them to call off the racket and served them all fish fingers, chips and beans.

Temperance steadied herself and shook her head. 'Sorry. Just, um, got a funny text from someone.' She made a show of checking her phone screen and then went back to her pile of apples, her lips still sneaking in a smile.

'Devon Loves, is it?' he said, without a glimmer of emotion.

'What?'

'Your app. Your dating app. That's who's making you laugh?'

Temperance's head ducked back, like he was about to throw one of his cabbages at her. 'No. Not today.' She was hardly going to admit most of her Devon Loves dates had ended in her eating three Daim bars in front of *Bridgerton*. Totally alone. It wasn't as if Abel needed more ammunition to make her feel like a total reject.

Abel cleared his throat. 'So are you with . . . Uh, do you ever think about . . .'

A gentle tap at the gate behind startled Temperance, sending apple peelings all over the grass.

Abel frowned and stalked to the fence before she could react. 'Who's out there?' he growled.

'Um, it's Mark, mate. Wondered if Susie was around? Or not. If it's a bother. I shouldn't—'

Abel slid back the bolts on the gate and yanked the door open. 'Come in. It's still half an hour till opening, so I can't serve you though.'

Mark ducked in, his hands shoved in his grey joggers. 'Right. Sorry, sorry. I should have realised you'd be busy.' He took in the chopped apples and cabbage. 'Are you . . . making some sort of Pimms?'

'Yes, it's a native Devonian recipe,' Abel replied dryly. 'Apple and cabbage is our custom. Served by a Morris Dancer.'

'But with cream on *first*,' Temperance chipped in, provoking a sudden blast of laughter from Abel, which seemed a surprise to him as much as it was to her.

Mark's eyes flitted between them. 'Right. Right. Silly of me. And now you're laughing. At me.'

'Just breaking the boredom.' Abel clapped Mark on the back, and Temperance felt just as winded. Of course: it was boring for him, being forced to spend time with *her*. 'You're after Susie. I'll let her know you're here.'

Abel walked inside to the kitchen and Temperance could only smile weakly at Mark while they waited. She knew she didn't have to be outright rude to him, but he still represented a very real threat to their way of life. Even if this current version of Mark didn't look like he would pose much of a threat to a paper bag.

Susie barged out, wiping her hands on a tea towel. 'Hello,' she said plainly.

'Hey, hi. Suse. Um, sorry I didn't call first. Or text. I thought about it. Drafted it and deleted it, couldn't get the tone right. Thought coming here in person . . .' he winced in her direction, 'but maybe not. I . . . I, er . . .'

Susie rolled her eyes. 'Was there something you wanted to say? I'm quite busy back there butchering a hog.'

He seemed to shrink into himself even more. 'Blimey, right. Well, it is important. Maybe we could take a walk?' He looked to Temperance and back at Susie. 'Alone?'

After folding her arms, Susie said, 'I don't think so. Whatever you tell me I'll only tell my sister anyway, so you could save us all time and say it now.'

Temperance swallowed. A little bit of pity for Mark was creeping into her heart: seeing him all twitchy and nervous, far from his usually suave self.

He ran his hands down his cheeks and shuffled on the spot. 'OK. Haha. Right. Any chance of a stiff drink first?'

Just as Susie started to reply, disgust in her tone, Temperance leapt in. 'One can't hurt! And it's got to be noon somewhere. Margie won't mind us having a little tipple from her private sherry bottle.'

With a sigh, Susie went inside again and then brought out the drinks.

Mark took a sip. 'Mmm. Tastes like Christmas with my Granny.'

'How wholesome,' Susie deadpanned. 'Now, you wanted to tell me something?'

He carefully put down the little fluted glass. 'I did, I did. Have been wanting to for a while but then . . . kept bottling it.' His neck flushed red.

He's so vulnerable, Temperance thought, *maybe we went too heavy handed with the Deadly Nightshade . . .*

'Go on.'

'I've been working on this project and I wanted to get your take on it, seeing as you are an East Prawle resident, at the heart of the community. Have you ever heard that the village is in a trust?'

Susie nodded, her poker face immaculate.

'Well, my family's business − one of them, I should say − is in property development. The acquisition team have had East Prawle on their radar for years.'

Temperance could sense her sister's body stiffen, saw her tongue run around her teeth like a lioness about to take down her pray. If Mark admitted out loud what they knew he'd been up to, it wouldn't be happy hour for him, that was for sure.

'I thought I'd found a way to ringfence the village, protect it. Based on the cultural significance of this place and its very long history.' He looked up at the unevenly sloping roof of the building, its higgledy-piggledy stone walls, built by hand hundreds of years before, and smiled, the warmth of the old Mark breaking through just for a second. 'Apply for a historical preservation order for The Witch's Nose, and the old smuggler's path down to the beach. That way, extra housing can't be built on the area for the foreseeable. I'd found enough anecdotal evidence and documents through the local archives to build a good case but . . .' He shrugged and picked at his thumb.

'You're saving the village?' Susie all but breathed. 'You *don't* want to develop it?'

A flicker of strength passed over Mark's brow. 'Never! I love this place. I fell for it the first time I visited, back when I was a kid and we'd come to Salcombe for the summer. It wasn't all about who had the biggest boat or the flashiest aga, or any of that nonsense. The minute it came up on the Beston agenda, I started working behind the scenes on how I could help preserve it. But,' he swallowed hard, 'now that I'm at the point of filing the paperwork,' he wrung his hands together, 'I'm not sure. And so that's why I wanted to talk to you. You love this village, but you also know how important family is. If I do this, if I block the path for my family's business . . . well, firstly I'm fired for certain, but other than that I risk my family turning their backs on me forever. It's not like I'd be bankrupting them, but it's not exactly model son behaviour.' He scrunched up his nose. 'And the ripples it would make in their social circles, their friends who are investors. If I do it, there's really no going back.'

Over the course of ten minutes Susie's face had gone from a pillar of marble to an eiderdown cushion. Her eyes were brimming with tears as her lips struggled not to wobble. She rushed at Mark for a hug. 'I'm so sorry,' she said into his neck.

'That's OK, um, it's really all my own fault. I knew it was on the table and a month ago I was prepared to take that risk – it felt totally worth it. It felt right. But recently, I don't know. I just can't seem to make a decision. It's like I don't trust myself. Which is,' he gave a flat little laugh, 'not really me.'

The sisters locked eyes.

Oh boy.

'Would it help,' Temperance ventured, 'if the paperwork got filed in our names, instead of yours? I'm not trying to steal your homework, but maybe then your job is safe, your family won't rumble you?'

Mark tipped his head to one side. 'It's an idea. But it doesn't feel honest. I'd always planned on leaving the firm anyway. A few years out of uni I knew it wasn't what I really wanted to do. There had to be more to life; something better, fairer. I was thinking maybe I could offer an affordable consultancy service to other places that wanted to secure heritage orders, based on what I know about how the developers work and all the red tape. But now, I'm not so sure.' He shrugged.

'You *have* to do it,' Susie said. 'And we'll help you. If your family do decide to turn their backs then . . . they're not much of a family, are they?'

He smiled weakly, the movement not reaching his eyes. 'I suppose.'

The two of them were staring at each other so intently that Temperance felt guilty about breaking the moment. 'Did you ah . . . bring anything with you today, Mark?'

He looked back towards the front door. 'I left my jacket and bag outside, they got a bit wet on the boat ride over.'

'Ahuh ' With all the coolness she could muster, Temperance slipped out her phone and started texting at the speed of light.

STEVIE, R U awake?! Bring tongs & plastic bag from kitchen. Mark's jacket is outside pub. Put in bag, meet at store. DON'T TOUCH, REMEMBER xxx

'So I'll let you guys catch up, and I'll just get this all back to the kitchen.' Temperance just about managed to pick up the two laden chopping boards without creating an accidental salad.

As she went inside, she found Abel at one of the counters, a snorkelling mask over his eyes and a sharp knife in hand. 'Don't say a word,' he muttered, 'it's the onions.'

'Could not be less bothered,' she said quickly, dumping her cargo and legging it towards the door. 'Tell Margie I'll be back later.'

His eyes followed the whip of her dark hair as she hurried around the corner.

21

Chapter 21

Stevie's lips were so firmly pressed together that they had almost disappeared. It was the only way she could trust herself not to blurt out a line from *Hocus Pocus* or even, if really desperate, *Macbeth*. But here she was, living her amateur wiccan dreams, about to assist a real-life witch with real-life magic.

'Luckily I had this ready to use.' Temperance held up a glass bottle with an old-fashioned stopper. Inside were large, flat leaves, what looked like bright green sprinkles and tiny buttery-yellow flower heads, all floating in crystal-clear water. 'I prepared it for the red robe, but I think soul-sapping powers are more important that intensely horny ones.'

'Huh?'

'I'll explain once this is steeping. Remember – tongs at all times. Turns out this baby is pretty potent. It sent Mark from a heritage hero into a timid little country mouse. We need his grit and ambition back because it turns out he was on our side all along.'

Stevie carefully pulled Mark's leather jacket out of the bag by her feet using the tongs from the Molland kitchen. She gingerly hoisted it into the bucket in the middle of Try Again's back garden. Temperance unstoppered the bottle and poured over the mixture F had recommended as a cure-all neutralising potion for really big emotions. She willed everything in her being that it would do the trick. With a beach bucket of sea water as the last ingredient in this chancy cocktail, Temperance stirred it around and around until she felt the whole jacket was submerged. She knelt down, placing her hands around either side of the bucket and closing her eyes.

She hoped that Susie might have guessed what her big sister was up to back in the pub, what with her weirdly specific questions about Mark's belongings. If she did, she'd be trying to keep Mark busy for a while, so Temperance could have a stab at undoing their grade-A royal fuck-up.

'Uhm, should I . . .?' Stevie's voice went squeaky and tapered off when Temperance opened one eye. 'I mean, what do I do now? I'll help however I can.'

'It's kind of a bloodline thing at this point. I'm going to focus on what I want the magic to do while I'm making contact with the jacket. Usually, I'd put my hands directly on it, but whatever we did to it is super toxic, so the bucket will have to do.'

Stevie grimaced. 'You really gave him deadly nightshade, huh?'

'Not *directly*.' Temperance squirmed. 'Just into a garment that he wears most days.'

Stevie played with the hairs above her ear. 'It's not what I thought witchcraft would be like.'

'It's not.'

'Hmm, it kinda feels like . . . I don't know how to say this . .

.'

'It's OK, you can say anything to me.'

'Kinda feels like you drugged him,' Stevie blurted.

Temperance spluttered. 'What? No! We put the enchantment on his *jacket*, not directly on *him*. And we didn't want him to get ill or anything, just take down his capitalist greed a notch or two. Which, in fact, he didn't have. Quite the opposite. If we wanted to poison him, we could have just slipped the belladonna into a sambuca shot, to be honest.'

Stevie grimaced. 'The calm way that you said that is very disturbing to me.'

'But I *wouldn't*. We got it wrong this time, stupendously wrong, but our intentions were good. Susie had a really strong vision and when we put that together with how Mark was acting . . . we just got the wrong end of the stick. But our hearts were in the right place.'

Still Stevie frowned. 'I just think if you're going to play with people's emotions you've got to have . . . maybe, like, two-step authentication? Not just some vibes and hunches, but actual proof of wrongdoing. Feels like a slippery slope, right? Like Sabrina the Teenage Vigilante.'

Temperance sat down on the grass with a thump. 'God. Yes. We were all fired up by our panic and fear, and took some pretty drastic action. You're right, Stevie. We need proper proof before we ever tackle anything like this again. Don't suppose you fancy a side hustle as a coven apprentice too, do you? I think we need some dedicated help on this front, not just in the store.'

'Are you kidding?!' The sparkle came back to Stevie's eyes. 'YES!'

'Brill. First job in this new role is to go and make yourself a cuppa and put your feet up – we have given you a rough twelve hours and you're going to need some decompressing time.'

'How do you decompress in a coven?'

'Same as regular people, really. Netflix, toast. A nice pair of socks.'

'Got it.'

Temperance waved Stevie off and then turned back to her big mistake. She closed her eyes again and placed her hands on the bucket, drawing all the energy she felt into her fingertips and through the plastic.

A cartoon Mark shuffled along the green, dogged by rainclouds chasing him wherever he went. As Temperance let out a long breath she blew those clouds away, into vapour, and the sun was coming out for him again. Next, Mark was carrying a box of his things out the Beston office, but with his head held high and a spring in his step. Racing towards his brave new future. Temperance, next, put him back in the thick of a busy night at The Witch's Nose, holding court and laughing away. She restored the spirit that was his.

That which we dampened in you, we return. Your spark is your own once more. With a big apology.

The energy moving through Temperance felt different, still warm and tingling as it had always been, but now with a stronger core to it, a steely determination. She might make a mess, but she could also fix it. There was power in that.

When Temperance eventually headed back to her shift helping with prep at the pub, she couldn't find Susie anywhere. On her second check on the snug, she almost collided into Abel carrying a huge crystal punchbowl.

'Whoah there!'

'Steady. Gran says this is a proper family heirloom. Which probably means some great great grandfather smuggled it away from somewhere it genuinely belonged.' He looked down at the sparkling facets of the crystal, the rainbow reflections catching in the pub lights, and scowled. Could anything escape the condescension of Abel Gulliver? Even old-timey dinnerware wasn't safe these days.

'Have you seen Suse anywhere?'

'Gran sent her off with Mark to get some last-minute things from Salcombe. Apparently, she urgently needed some posh pickle from one of the delis for tomorrow. But I think she actually just wanted to give them some more time together. They were having a long, deep and meaningful talk out in the pub garden.'

'That was sweet of Margie.'

'We Gullivers aren't *all* bad,' Abel said with the smallest note of warmth to his voice.

Temperance chewed her bottom lip. 'If you say so.'

'Interesting guy, that Mark. He seemed the life and soul that night in The Fort, but today it was like he wouldn't hurt a fly. Literally that he *couldn't*.'

The guilt surging at Temperance for having unfairly mag-icked Mark into such a shell of himself made her snap, 'People can seem one way but then be something completely different under it all.'

Abel's eyes went wide. 'What do you mean?'

'Just . . . just that people change, don't they? Sometimes completely without warning.' She looked straight into Abel's eyes, her meaning clear.

He pressed his lips together while taking a slow breath. 'Sometimes they have to, Temperance. Sometimes they have no choice.' His fingers went white around the punchbowl and he stalked away.

Margie came out into the pub lounge, a duster in hand. 'Your face,' she tutted at Temperance. 'My god, no wonder we're empty this lunchtime with that stormy mug on display. You'd put anyone off their whelks. Oh – while I've got you, girl, tell me how much that gorgeous dress cost Abel. He won't let me pay him back, but I'm planning on sneaking the money into his bag before he goes.'

'Oh, I don't know . . .'

'You *do* know.' Margie narrowed her eyes at Temperance, showing off a flash of her sparkly blue eyeshadow.

'But I . . '

Margie shook her head. 'Your loyalty is with me, remember? Your local landlady and unofficial granny? Not some fool that's buggering off back to Bath in two days.' She checked her slim gold watch.

'Would that be my one and only son you're bad-mouthing?' Diane, Abel's mum, shouldered open the thick wooden door, two small suitcases in her hands.

'Love!' Margie bustled over to her, wrenching the bags away from her daughter-in-law. 'I'll get these upstairs, you sit yourself down.'

'Why does everyone want you to sit down when you've had a long drive?' the woman asked, smiling. 'I need to stretch my legs after all that holiday traffic, thank you. And help you get ready for this big do tomorrow. Which apparently is purple themed.' Her eyes caught on Temperance. 'Oh, Temperance, my darling, you're a grown-up woman!'

Temperance laughed nervously. 'That's what they tell me.' It was hard to be mature and composed around someone who

247

was a witness when you used to pull your swimming costume down to wee in the sea.'

Diane came forward and squeezed Temperance with a rib-cracking hug. 'It's so good to see you,' she said almost sadly, in a hollow voice. 'After such a long time.' She pulled back, her hands on Temperance's elbows, taking her in. 'You're well? You're doing OK? Happy?'

'Um, yes. Course. Working in the shop with Mum. Running it, actually, while she's away for six months,' she replied, straightening her shoulders back a fraction.

'And anyone in your life? Boyfriend? Girlfriend?'

Temprance felt her cheeks boil bright red as Margie rejoined them. 'Diane!' she remonstrated. 'You've no need to worry about that. Temperance is absolutely thriving. Waiting for a catch of the right calibre to come in, OK?' She raised her chin towards her daughter, a tiny movement that seemed to put an end to that line of questioning.

'Of course.' Diane stepped back again. 'Pour me a wine, woman, and stop your harping.' The tense moment passed and Temperance exhaled.

'If you're all set, I'll head off, Margie. I need to dig something purple out of the stockroom for myself.'

The older woman shooed her hands towards the door. 'Yes, off you trot. See you tomorrow in your glad rags – it's going to be a hoot!'

Temperance left Try Again closed to the public for most of the day, letting Stevie have a quiet mooch around on the shop floor as she uploaded some more pieces on eBay, trying her very best to pick up 'vibes' from the stock. Maybe it wasn't the greatest sense of hustle for a new manager, but after everything that had happened over the last few days she felt brain-fried, and not exactly in the mood to politely shoo away the hands of sandy children from their fanciest items, as they loudly complained that their mothers were taking too long in 'the most boring shop on the planet'. But they'd come around. Give it ten years and they'd be back as teens, begging that same mum to buy them some eighties Wranglers or a late nineties Stussy T-shirt in perfectly oversized proportions.

After a huge plate of scrambled eggs on toast at home and two Diet Cokes for a caffeine boost, Temperance dragged her weary bones down to the shop as afternoon mellowed into evening. She let her fingers trail over the rough stone wall of the bus stop as she went by, passing equally weary holidaymakers as they returned from the beach, their hair crisp with dried saltwater, their skin flushed and glowing. Sometimes it was easy to forget what a special place she lived in, especially in the off season when it was deserted and cold. But when you came across someone new to the village drinking in the rows of pastel-painted houses, the flit of a swallow darting between hedgerows, or happily bedding down for an afternoon pint in the pub, it was a useful reminder to be glad to be in Devon, every single day. They weren't going to let anyone tear down East Prawle and replace it with holiday apartments that locals couldn't afford, whatever it took. And Temperance wasn't going to let the doom take hold of the place either.

She blinked as she reached the shop door. She hadn't had the dream again, not since she went back to the beach with Susie, when Stevie had rumbled them. But the reverse casting had been interrupted, so she couldn't be sure it had truly taken hold.

Temperance closed her eyes and pressed her fingertips

together, trying to listen to what was in her head. Could she feel that tinge of doom and gloom to everything still? Maybe. Or was she just imagining it now, because it had been all she could think about for the past week?

She might have said enough to release Abel before Stevie found her: there was a tiny chance it might have worked. And in that case, all she had to do was get through Margie's birthday tomorrow and life could go back to normal. Susie and Mark would keep the village safe with a heritage order. Stevie would be their happy coven apprentice. Abel would go back to Bath. And to Cass. Which was great. And Temperance would focus on running Try Again, maybe swipe right a little bit when she felt ready. Yup, normal.

She opened her eyes and pushed her way into the store, the little bell tinkling overhead.

'Just me!' she called out to Stevie. 'Got to grab *something* purple.' Temperance's eyes scanned the rails where she remembered putting the 'ladette' T-shirt back. She wasn't sure she'd wear it herself but Susie might, and Margie would definitely get a kick out of it. The exhaustion was so deep in her bones that she just needed something, *anything*, quickly, then she'd head back home for a very early night. But it wasn't where she could have sworn she left it. Maybe another guest had nabbed it without her knowing?

'Stevie, have you seen . . .?'

'Ta da!' Stevie pushed a rail on wheels before her, swinging with all the purple garments Try Again had, from light lilac to rich royal plum. 'Margie told me the theme yesterday. She also said I could come along as long as I didn't "hog the hog", but I think she just liked the joke. I don't think she knows I'm hardcore veggie. But a barbeque on a village green feels like another thing to tick off my English bingo sheet. Anyway, I started collecting a few pieces and then it became this kind of compulsive treasure hunt and . . .oh god, have I screwed up? Are these, like, magically problematic or something?'

Temperance realised her face must have gone blank. But not from shock or disgust, just a very tired form of relief. 'No, no, it's great. It's perfect, in fact. Thank you, Stevie. I'm really grateful. Now if I can just find that T-shirt . . . it's got a slogan on it, did you come across it?'

Stevie's mouth formed a tight O of shock. 'Not the 'ladette' one?! Come on, Temperance Molland! You are not only a gorgeous young woman and a talented witch, but you are a studied dealer of fine vintage items and a small business manager. You cannot go out there to a special event in a *'ladette'* T-shirt.' She shuddered. 'You're your own advertising, after all. You've got to sell the shop, sell the dream of vintage. The lifestyle!' Her eyes sparkled and she raised up onto her toes for a moment.

'I do?' With about three percent of her battery left, Temperance would have just been happy to scrape up her unwashed hair into a purple scrunchie and call it a day.

'Damn straight you do.' Stevie nodded. 'There is something here I think you're going to love. I found it in a box from that shipment you and Susie have been working through, so I don't know if it has . . . bad *karma* you might need to work on, but I really hope not.'

'Please be jogging bottoms, please be jogging bottoms,' Temperance mumbled as Stevie turned to the railing.

'Not in my name! it might need some clever underwear to go with it, but it will be totally worth it.'

Temperance groaned. 'Seriously, Stevie I am—'

She was planning on saying she was out. But then she saw the dress. The lightest lilac gingham with a sweetheart neckline going into a halterneck, and what looked like a very fitted pencil skirt. 'Oh my.'

'Oh my is right! Eeeek! Don't you love it?! I just feel in my bones that it's your size. Like *it's meant to be*. And you can't say that's not a thing because you know magic is real. This is pure magic in dress form. Please please pleeeease try it on.'

Temperance didn't need the flutter of the lashes: she was already sold.

'OK. But just ignore the fact I haven't shaved my legs in a fair while.'

Stevie shrugged. 'Who has the time. Or the motivation. You could be growing lime-green body hair a foot long in this outfit and no one would notice because it will cinch your waist and push out your boobs to perfection.'

Temperance held her breath as her hand reached out and fabric started to move towards them. There was the prickle in her fingertips as she closed her eyes and listened closely in her mind's eye. Would it be cloaked in sadness and sorrow? Would it be tied up in anger and revenge? She could totally see someone using a dress this killer to serve a cold plate of vengeance on an ex.

There was nothing. Blissful nothing. It seemed nothing seismic had ever happened to someone wearing this dress and Temperance was eternally grateful.

'Well?' gasped Stevie, and Temperance realised she wasn't the only one waiting on tenterhooks for the reading.

'All good. Totally empty of any big memories. Phew.' She smiled easily for the first time that day.

Stevie squeezed her dainty hands into excited fists. 'Then you'll be the one to leave your important imprint. And while you're feeling good, any chance of another staff discount on the rainbow sequin mini?'

,

Chapter 22

The white paper tablecloths fluttered in the light, August breeze as Margie surveyed the green. 'That'll do, Pig, that'll do,' she said to Temperance and Susie who both – unknowingly – rolled their eyes in perfect synchronicity.

Along with Abel, Gary, Praveen and a few Witch's Nose regulars, they had laid out four trestle tables end to end down the grass this morning and then had spent a good hour 'prettying it up' as Margie had ordered. Abel had collected all the glass ramekins from the kitchen and filled them with tea lights; Gary had gently laid his own granny's embroidered napkins into wicker baskets for the bread rolls later (which he'd now gone home to finish baking). The Molland sisters had been dispatched with some secateurs and a bucket to the wildflower meadow at the top of the cliffs so that they could put together some sweet, organic arrangements in jam jars along the table tops. 'And free,' Margie had wagged her finger. 'If I'm getting closer to my pensionable age, I've got to watch that income, my loves. You can't eat flowers so I'm not paying for them.'

Temperance had wanted any job but that one, having been haunted by the idea of this very wildflower field burning to a crisp all week. Her nails scratched at her palms incessantly as they walked along the path and Susie had told her to go home – reading her mood, her worries – but Temperance was determined to see this through. The nightmare hadn't crept up on her again, so it was high time she unclenched and learned to live in her village normally now. No more twitching at the sight of one white cloud, no checking for the nearest fire extinguisher. And now Margie's table was blooming with poppies, rock roses and marigolds. It would definitely do.

'Like your twelfth birthday,' a voice said behind Temperance. With a flinch she turned around.

'Abel. Didn't see you there.'

'Oh I remember!' Susie piped up. 'You were having this weird Famous Five obsession that summer and you wanted us to have lashings of ginger beer and honey sandwiches as a picnic on the green. Cake and strawberries. Mum found that massive tablecloth and we all wore bows in our hair.'

'I didn't,' Abel said gruffly.

'No.' Susie raised her eyebrows. 'But *you* set up the treasure map so we could pretend to chase down some ruffians who'd stolen the, I don't know, crown jewels or something.'

'The church candlesticks,' he said through a sigh.

'Oh, yes.' Temperance kept her eyes on the horizon, watching the seagulls riding the warm air. She needed to fix her eyes on anywhere but Abel Gulliver right now. If she turned and saw him being cool and dismissive about one of her favourite childhood memories, she might just cry. She'd been so exhausted by the past week that she felt more thin-skinned and vulnerable than ever.

Diane approached them from the pub, carrying two mugs. 'Teas are up inside. Brought yours out, Marge.'

'Thanks, love.'

'What are we talking about?'

Susie grinned. 'The time Miagi set up that elaborate treasure hunt for Tee's birthday party, when she was twelve. He made maps for us all and stained them with old tea bags, remember, Abe? Singed the edges with your lighter, Diane, and got a bollocking. And then the candlesticks we had to track down turned out to be made out of loo rolls covered in tin foil.' She snorted a laugh through her nose.

'Hey, that was some *Blue Peter* level stuff!' A smile cracked into Abel's stubbled cheeks. 'And it's not like I used sticky-backed plastic. It was all recycled materials. I hid them in a cave at the back of the beach. They'd gone soggy by the time you read the map.'

'It was special. I'm glad you remembered it at last,' Temperance added finally, her eyes still averted. Her heart had gone from being shrunken with vulnerability to almost filling her chest with pleasure. *He remembered.*

'Right,' Diane spoke up quickly, 'Abe, you get back inside now, babe. There's a love. Plenty to do. And we shouldn't keep the girls from getting ready, making themselves presentable. Off you go, come on now.' She virtually shooed him off the grass and back to the pub.

A look passed between mother and son and he shook his head ever so slightly, a flush creeping up his neck.

'Ohhhkayy,' Susie drawled. 'Nothing more you need us for, Margie?'

'No, all set. See you at 12.30, you pair of scrumpets.'

Temperance shrugged at Susie and they walked off, arms

linked.

A good strapless bra could do the work of ten men, keeping cleavage supported and bouncy and at just the right level. The bra Temperance had finally found at the back of Susie's underwear drawer seemed pretty substantial: some sturdy underwiring and three hook-and-eye fastenings. Crucially, it couldn't be seen while she wore the lilac halter and Temperance felt a lot more relaxed about the whole outfit now she could be sure nothing deeply private would escape from it. What this bra couldn't handle, seemingly, was changing a beer barrel.

Temperance and Susie had been at the bar, assembling the first drinks orders of the guests at Margie's BBQ.

'Oh balls,' Susie hissed. 'This barrel's nearly finished. I'll have to change it. Could you finish the G&Ts for me? I'll be ten minutes or so.'

'Sure.' Temperance's phone buzzed on the bar and she picked it up.

From: FEverything@hotmail.com

To: TinyTempsM@yahoo.co.uk

Subject: Earth to Temperance . . .

Lovely girl, how is it going? I haven't heard from you again. Did you go back to the beach? I realise you could be ghosting me for several reasons:

1. **Your mum has heard we're needlessly communicating**

and has hit the roof and hexed you silly, even from afar.

2. You sorted your magical snafu and are now busy living a beautifully balanced life without need of my witterings.

3. Or, it's all gone so horrifically wrong that your whole village has combusted and you've no means to brush your teeth, let alone send an email to an old witch.

I must say I am dying to know which one is closest . . .

If for whatever reason you don't want to reply, let me say one last thing: magic is a gift, but that doesn't mean all we do is take from it. We witches can receive and intuit power that passes most people by, but we have to give back to that power – recharge it – to keep the balance around us in check. It's like a cashpoint, maybe: you can go and take out enough money to make you feel filthy rich, but it's your own account you're running dry. And eventually you'll be in its debt.

You inadvertently took something big from the magic world, asking for a true love to be plonked down in front of you. And now it wants something big in return. I'm not trying to put you off the witch's life, my dear, but it's a relationship, like anything else. It takes work, it takes sacrifice.

Let me know if I can help.

Your friend,
   F x

Temperance blinked at the words as they settled into her brain. She owed F a proper reply, a full explanation of everything that had been happening. Once the party was over, she would take the time to write a thoughtful response.

Just as Susie went to swing through the kitchen doors and head down to the cellar, a woman with a high ponytail and a Breton striped top burst through the pub's front door. 'Could someone help me? I'm totally lost and my car's GPS has no signal here.'

'I'll point you back to the big road. It's easier if I draw you a map and point out some landmarks, follow me.' Susie grabbed an order pad and pen, and headed outside with the stranger.

And so here Temperance was, five minutes later, flushing out the beer barrel line with cold water and working the pump to clear it through. A job she'd done enough times in the past to help Margie or Susie out on a quiet evening that she could do it with her eyes closed. But right now she had her eyes very much open and vigilant to the fact that the vigorous pumping action was testing the elastic limit of her bra and squeezing her boobs together in an almost cartoonish way. Thankfully there was no one else around to see it.

'My god.' Abel's voice was a half-breath half-cough and Temperance stood up quickly and awkwardly, bracing herself for the criticism he was surely about to deliver. What had she done wrong this time?

He blinked rapidly, closed the heavy oak door behind him and then knelt down to take over the job. 'Gran wondered what was taking so long with the drinks. I couldn't find anyone at the bar, or in the kitchen.'

'Oh, sorry. Susie had to nip out to help a lost grockle.'

'You can't do this on your own.'

Temperance bristled. 'I *can*. I have plenty of times over the last twelve years, it's just you weren't around to see it.'

Abel exhaled through his nose. 'What I *meant* was that it should always be done in a pair, just in case. These full ones are bloody heavy, you know.'

She fiddled with the halter at the back of her neck. 'Yes. Right.'

'I don't mind helping.' He started up the pump work, producing much less jiggle than Temperance had in the same position.

There was an awkward five minutes of silence between them, as old beer spluttered into the ice cream tub at their feet.

'What did Margie think of your outfit?' Temperance asked tentatively.

He smiled wryly. 'Loved it. Said she's thinking of making it the new bar staff uniform.'

She laughed with relief. 'I'd like to see that. And I wouldn't mind the commission.'

'Not that it will really affect me,' he went on. 'I'm back to Bath with Mum tomorrow. Back to normal life.' He pronounced the word normal clearly and definitely, as if it was some kind of warning.

'I think the line's clear now,' Temperance mumbled, the wind taken out of her sails. Abel untwisted the pipe and moved over to the new barrel. 'Could she not make it then: Cass?'

His eyes flicked up at her. 'I told you: we're not serious. Besides, I didn't think *I* was coming until last week, until you all ganged up on me.'

Fury puffed up Temperance's cheeks. 'I didn't do anything! Jesus. Sorry for asking just an innocent question.'

Abel snatched a beer glass of the shelf behind him and turned on the tap in the new barrel, drawing out a few inches of beer. 'Here,' he thrust the glass in Temperance's direction.

'Oh, peace offering, is it? I graciously accept your apology.' She curtsied, taking the beer and swilling back a mouthful.

'Nope. Just needed to test the barrel and I didn't want to be guinea pig,' A cheeky flash of the teenage Abel lit up his face with a smile for a split second.

She smacked her lips. 'Charming!' But she couldn't stop herself smiling back in response to his very brief show of warmth. 'Tastes OK to me.'

'Good.' He started screwing on the hose.

Temperance didn't really know what to do with herself while he worked. She suddenly felt totally incongruous in her skin-tight fifties pin-up outfit, her red lipstick and winged eyeliner. Like she was a supermarket egg who'd stuck on some plastic gemstones and fancied herself a Faberge. Abel would see through it all – he knew who she really was. The girl who always had sand in her scalp from beach cartwheeling; the teen who'd tried to 'style up' her own goth fishnets and ripped one leg clean off.

She thought about making an excuse to go first and leave him to it, but she didn't want to give Abel the impression that he was actually succeeding in bothering her, that his wall of grump was actually an obstacle in her day.

'Done,' he muttered, standing up and brushing his hands off on the back of his thighs. He kept his gaze on the wine racks behind her. 'We should get back. After you.' He motioned towards the door.

Temperance twisted the old ceramic handle. Nothing. She yanked her elbow back sharply. Not budging. 'Of course,' she said to herself.

Abel sighed behind her shoulder and leaned over, nudging her out of the way. 'Here. Give it a bit of muscle.' She picked up the smell of him again as he moved near: honey on almost-burnt toast, salty seawater.

Temperance stepped backwards, feeling the rough stone wall on her bare skin. Although she tried not to pay attention to how Abel's jaw clenched, how the muscles in his forearms jumped into action as he heaved at the door, there was hardly anything else to watch, seeing as she was squeezed into a tiny galley with him.

'What?' he spat. 'No, we can't be . . .' He pulled and pulled but the ancient wooden door wasn't even creaking.

'It must have expanded after the rain last night,' Temperance offered.

He glared at her, as if she'd drawn up the weather report herself to cause just this problem.

'We *have* to get out,' Abel said gravelly. He kept yanking and yanking for another five minutes before kicking at the door and throwing his hands into his hair. 'Perfect!'

If Temperance had been looking for a final summary of just how much Abel Gulliver disliked her, before he packed his bags for the city again, this would have done the job nicely. The idea of being cooped up in a cellar with her made him want to tear his hair out. But Temperance fought back against the cold, clammy feeling behind her ribs. 'At least we have plenty to drink,' she said lamely.

'It's not funny!' His face was pale.

'I didn't say it was!'

He strode back to the door, pummelling it with both fists. 'Hello! Hey! We're stuck! We need to get out.'

Temperance grimaced. 'Susie might still be on tour guide duty, or already outside with the others.'

Abel growled and squeezed his eyes closed.

'Alright, calm down. I'm not infectious or anything. Ten minutes won't kill you.'

At the mention of ten minutes, his eyes pinged open, as if she'd said 'three millennia' instead. 'It could be longer than that, you don't know.'

A realisation suddenly jabbed Temperance painfully: what if this was the doom? What if it was sealing them into the pub so they'd be cooked slowly while a wildfire took the village and everyone in it? Temperance pressed her hands against her sides to stop them shaking. 'You could be right.'

'Let's do it together, OK?' He nodded her over to where he was standing.

Temperance walked closer, the fitted dress only really allowing her to take small, sauntering steps.

Abel cleared his throat. 'You touch it first. The knob. The *door* knob,' he stuttered.

She put both her hands on the handle and his hands came around them, engulfing her fingers in warmth and a locked-tight grip.

'On three, we turn and pull. One, two, thr—'

'Eeee!' With their combined action, somehow the door popped open like someone had magically buttered its hinges, sending Abel and Temperance crashing into the wall behind. Temperance's head snapped backwards, catching her cheek on one of the stones that made up the ancient basement. 'Ow, shit!'

Trying to untangle themselves from each other's limbs on the floor, Temperance felt Abel's hand snake up her neck, this thumb moving gently over her cheek. 'Are you OK? Is it bleeding?'

She sat herself up. 'I think it's . . .'

'Was it your head? You didn't black out, did you?'

His hand was still there, cupping the back of her head, holding her upright almost. She felt herself sink back slightly into the strength of his arm. It felt good to let go for just that moment, not have to put on an act around him, not to pretend to be the steady one in this whole mess. She reached out one hand out to touch his crisp white shirt, the bow tie hanging loose just like she'd styled him to wear it, the slippery satin contrasting with the hard wall of muscle that hid underneath.

'Tee? You don't feel sleepy, do you? Don't fall asleep. Look at me.'

Abel's face filled her vision: squinting, looking between her eyes intently, his top teeth biting down on the corner of his mouth. How could anyone feel sleepy when their heart was rattling in their ribcage like it had just been jump-started with a car battery? She could see the rise and fall of his chest; wondered how *his* heart was behaving behind his ribs right now. There was a fuzzy light around the edge of her vision but it wasn't any kind of head trauma, it was because her lungs were too scared to move and break this spell, so now she was running out of air.

Temperance looked deep into the green-grey eyes that she knew almost as well as her own. Almost-slate grey flecked with bursts of moss green. So much about Abel Gulliver was *just* as it had been. He cared about his family, he loved to surf, his smile – when it broke free – was just as luminous. That adventurous, open-hearted boy had to be in there somewhere, he had to. Still there behind the glares and the awkward silences and the staring into space. And as much as Temperance wanted to find any trace of her first love, that irrepressible teenager, she also wanted to explore the man he now was. The width of his shoulders, the strength in his back, the texture of stubble on his more angular jaw. Because as much as she told herself she didn't care that he was curt and aloof and bored around her, that it would be great when he finally left the village again, when she got this close to Abel all she could think about was the crackle in the air between them, the invisible rope that he did his best every day to unknot. But they were in a tangle there was no way out of.

'I'm here,' she just-about whispered. She wrapped her fingers around his wrist.

'Tee, I . . .' Able let out a long, deep breath, looking down at her hand. His eyes half-closed, as if he'd felt a small jolt of pain. Then he shook his head just once, as if denying an argument going on inside his mind. Abel tilted his chin to one side and slowly pressed his lips against hers.

Her lips pushed back eagerly, feeling his fingers now moving through her hair. She moved up onto her knees to face him fully, never breaking contact, not caring that a stray piece of gravel was digging sharply into her skin. Here was the new Abel that she wanted to explore, now inviting her in. She wasn't going to hesitate, the door could be shut in her face again in another heartbeat.

Temperance ran her hands along his forearms, over his biceps and to his shoulders, gripping him tight, fixing him in place so this moment would never end. Their mouths worked furiously together, picking up pace: tentative kisses swapped out for hungry ones. Temperance wanted to consume him: his lips, his skin, his muscle. She wanted to know every inch of him.

Abel's hand cupped her chin, his thumb rubbing along her cheekbone, the rough callous on his palm now on her neck. He crushed his chest against hers, wrapping his arm around her waist to pull her tight, all the way in. His hands roamed over her back as he murmured through his kisses.

Temperance wasn't sure she was remembering to breathe, but her fingers were moving, tugging the shirt away from his waistband. Feeling the skin at the base of his spine and hearing his responding groan as she touched him.

Please don't let this be a dream. Please don't let this be a dream.

Suddenly, without saying a word, they were moving in seamless sync, lying down on the cold floor, Abel's body moving to cover hers. It was like her fantasies on the sofa that night but better: it was real.

His hands were holding her hungrily, his kisses fast and feverish. She could feel how much he wanted her, pressing into her hip. Abel moved his kisses to her neck, giving what was something between a growl and moan into her skin. His fingers snuck underneath the halter neck of her dress at her collarbone and Temperance wished it wasn't so well made, wished he could just break it free with one swift movement so more of her would be exposed to him. Temperance's fingers dug through his hair, wanting to know every texture, every taste.

Abel's hand was on her thigh now, sliding inside the tightly-fitting skirt. Higher, higher, his fingertips brushing the fabric of her underwear.

Something deep with Temperance loosened, melted, as if a wave was washing down the sandcastle she'd built over the last twelve years to protect her heart. Her hands moved across his back, pulling him closer to her.

'Abel.'

She whispered his name.

And the spell was broken.

Abel pulled away, sat on his heels, his eyes blinking and his head shaking. 'No.'

Temperance felt the chilly cellar air flood around her, the absence of his body and his heat. 'Wait, I—'

'What have you done?' He looked stricken, his eyes watery.

'What have I done?!' Every inch of Temperance's skin felt alive still, but the instantaneous wrench from connection to isolation had her head spinning, her emotions leaping around from lust to rage. 'I didn't do anything – you kissed me!'

Abel was still shaking his head, tucking his shirt back in furiously. 'We can't do this.'

'I hate to break it to you, but we just did.'

'No.' He stood all the way up and Temperance clambered ungainly, one foot at a time, to mirror him. He spoke down to his shoes. 'That dress – I come in and you're in that dress. At the festival – we danced. And being here, the memories, The Fort, it's like old times. But . . . but it can't be. I can't explain, Tee. But this is wrong.'

A bubble of rage burst behind her ribs. 'Why can't you say it, even now? All this blame . . . on the dress?! On nostalgia or whatever.' Her hands flapped in circles like birds trying to escape a cage. 'Twelve years and you can't say it. You can't just say: "I don't want you, Temperance Molland. You embarrass me, you make my skin crawl. I don't want you."'

He reeled back a step. 'That's not it. That's never been it.'

'Then what is it?' Temperance grabbed at his arm, not with affection but to make him turn and look at her again.

'Because I want you too much, Tee. I can't control how much I want you.' He walked over to the door, closed it again and leant against the wood.

Tears prickled at the edges of Temperance's vision. 'What? How . . . how does that work? You left me. No warning, no real explanation. You just left and never came back. People don't do that to the people they care about.'

Abel's head tipped back and he pressed his hand over his eyes. 'It was a few weeks before your birthday and I'd been working on this present for you, for ages, really. In secret. I couldn't wait to see your face when you opened it. All I wanted was to make you happy. And that's when I realised I wanted you to be *more* than just my best mate. But I didn't know how to tell you. What if I messed it all up? So I didn't say anything. I thought maybe the present would say it for me.' He took in a deep breath. 'The morning of your birthday, Mum comes in as I'm trying to wrap it at the kitchen table and she sees it too: that I'm in love with you. So she gave me the Gulliver Talk.'

Temperance frowned. 'We all get that talk, Abel.'

He shook his head wearily. 'Not this one. This is . . . just for the Gulliver men.' His eyes suddenly flicked to hers. 'You're not going to believe this when I tell you. It sounds mad – I know it's true and it still sounds insane to me. It's a bit,' his hands were held out at his sides, 'woo woo, if you know what I mean? But it's why – when I had that dream that Gran was in danger, I had to come back. Because those things can be *real*, Tee.'

'Go on,' she urged. After so long, it seemed like Temperance was going to have her answers. But they were starting to sound more complicated than she'd ever imagined. Her heart being pulled apart by both terror and relief.

'Right. You already know my dad left my mum not long after I was born? Did you also know my grandad left Margie not long after she had their third kid? And if you go back through our

268

family tree – well, it looks more like a family telephone pole, because the branches with the men just vanish. They all leave. Uncles, cousins, all of them. There are plenty of weddings, but no anniversary parties.'

Temperance fiddled with an unpeeling wine label. 'You think you'll be like them, a bad dad? So you don't want any sort of commitment, is that it?'

He sucked in a breath. 'I don't think I might be like them, I *know* I will. Because it's in my bloodline. Mum literally took me through the big family album. All the way back to the Victorians. There are wives and kid, but that's it. The men have all gone. They'll be blissfully happy raising their families one day, in another county by the next. Gran hoped it wouldn't be true for Dad, but it was.'

'So you think it's like . . . a personality disorder in your genes maybe?'

'No. Not that I would choose that, but at least it would be more straight-forward to explain.' Abel gave a cold, dry laugh.

'I've heard a lot of weird shit in my time, Abe, believe me. Just . . . *tell me.*'

He cracked his knuckles. 'Family legend goes that we were smugglers, the Gullivers, way back. And we were damned good at it. Until one Gulliver went too far. Jack Gulliver. He had an agreement with a local woman – she would help him with safe passage and he would split the rum haul with her. Only he cut her out, thought he'd get one over on the lonely old hag everyone laughed at, the woman who danced under a full moon.'

Temperance felt a wave of *doom* crawl over her skin.

Oh no. No no.

'The legend goes that she,' he squeezed his eyes shut, 'oh

269

man, this sounds nuts. She was a witch.' He said the word like it was spiky on his tongue. 'And her revenge on Jack taking what was rightfully hers was to curse him and all the Gulliver men that followed. They would never again hold on to what they loved.' Abel put his hands to his hips. 'Pretty clever as curses go – didn't stop him loving, but made sure he and everyone around him would feel the misery of love being taken away. Over and over again. Mum felt it when Dad walked out on us. Even though he'd always said the curse was bullshit – boom, it worked on him too. So mum wanted to warn me, when she saw how much I . . . what I was feeling for you, Tee. She couldn't bear for you and I to go through it all. She loves you like a daughter, you know? The best thing we could think of was just leaving. No chance of me breaking your heart, put all the memories of Dad behind us too. A clean break.' He shrugged.

The wine label was now a hundred tiny pieces at Temperance's feet. 'But Cass? Or the next fling you have. You're going to do this to her one day? You're not bothered about that?'

Abel stared directly into her soul. 'I did my best to stay away from any kind of relationship that could get serious, that could potentially trigger it.' He threw his hands up for a beat. 'I'll admit I haven't been a monk – it's a bit of a tall order to stay celibate your whole adult life. And I like Cass.' Temperance felt the words sting at her already-bruised heart. 'But it isn't what I feel for you, Tee. It isn't a drop in that ocean.'

'*What you feel*? So you still . . .' Temperance jumped hungrily on the present tense.

'No – no I'm not going to hurt you, Temperance. I could never do that.'

His mouth opened again but then he snapped it shut,

wrenched open the door and strode away.

23

Chapter 23

'Abel, wait!' Temperance kicked off her sky-blue kitten heels and tried to break into a jog as Abel ran across the green, down towards the beach. Not having the legs of a six-foot-man and her thighs being encased in fitted gingham, she wasn't getting all that far that fast.

The heads of Margie's guests whipped around at the noise.

'Oi!' Margie called from the head of the table, regal and relaxed in her purple lace number. 'Where's my Tanqueray and tonic, then?!'

Temperance ignored her and continued her shuffling speed-walk. She'd get there. If he was going to the sea she'd catch him eventually.

She could hear Susie calling her name, but she just waved her hand, as if to silently communicate 'Things have gone batshit, I'll fill you in later.' But a hand clasping her shoulder literally stopped her in her tracks and she turned on the spot to see Abel's mum.

'Diane, I know the drinks are late but I've got to speak to Abel. It's . . . it's complicated.'

Diane pursed her glossy lips. 'Oh, don't I know it. Come with me, Temperance. Margie can get her own sodding gin. We need to talk.'

Temperance had only very rarely been upstairs at The Witch's Nose. The pub downstairs felt like Margie's living room, open to all, but going upstairs was like peeking in her underwear drawer.

She lowered herself awkwardly onto the chintzy velveteen settee and sunk right down into its softness.

'Not really the time for a cuppa, not if he's told you what I think he's told you?' Diane raised one eyebrow.

'He told me. About Jack Gulliver and the witch.' Her cheeks started to burn.

With a nod, Diane went to the little shelves on one side of the ancient sunken fireplace and pulled a thick leather book from the bottom corner. 'I know it sounds crazy. Phil told me I was crazy, even though it was his family history. But now he runs tourist boats in Thailand, so I hear. Has never reached out to his son.' Her lip twitched. 'But this is the proof: all these families, with one very important piece missing. The kindest, sweetest men you'd ever want to meet, but once the curse hit them—' She snapped her fingers.

Temperance leafed through the creaking album pages: pictures of Diane and a little Abel in the nineties; Margie and her kids in seventies' stripes of orange and brown; some photos from the fifties; black and white dog-eared pictures from further back, and back. And not one of a man beyond his early twenties, at the very best.

'I couldn't let my Abe become that. He had the purest heart of any of them. You two, like brother and sister for so long – I

273

told myself that's the way it would stay. I *wanted* to believe it. But you both got older, and I could see his face changing when he was with you, how he'd made you this lovely present, so . . . I had to break it to him.'

She plopped down next to Temperance.

'He went green in the gills. The *shame* he felt, these big tears falling on his hoodie. He was destroyed at the very idea he could ever hurt you. But I knew he wouldn't be able to turn those feelings off, like a tap. God knows I couldn't for Phil. Not for a very long time. The only way was to go away and stay away. No updates on the village from Margie, no visits: no temptations. So I'm sorry, my love,' she squeezed Temperance's knee, 'that we bolted. It was the best we could do. A hard but clean break.'

The shame he felt. His hoodie. The disgust, the panic she'd felt in hoodie when she'd found it in the bus stop, all those years ago, it wasn't about her. It was about what the Gulliver curse might make him do.

'Oh, God.'

'Don't blame him, will you? He's tried so hard to keep himself distant from you this week. Always texting me in a panic that he was going to slip up. Just being in the same room as you turns him upside down. It's hard, Temperance, awfully hard. But it's the only way. You'll write me off as a nut job now, all this talk of curses and witches, what have you, but even if you do, I've said my piece. And I've done my best by you all.' Her lips formed a flat smile.

'It's really the only way?' Temperance asked in a small voice as Diane stood and moved to leave, to rejoin the party they could hear going on through the window without them.

'I'm afraid so. You don't want you heartbroken by a Gulliver, darling. Believe me. They fill your heart up like no other, till it doubles in size, it feels like. Then when they leave you, all you have is that huge emptiness.'

A cheer went around the table on the green, the clink of glass on glass singing up at Temperance as laughter rippled through the crowd. She had never felt more on the outside of something.

And then the thunder came.

Temperance took the stairs as quickly as her pencil skirt would allow and followed Diane out through the thick, oak door in the porch.

The laughter she'd heard just minutes before turned to groans and boos as thick raindrops, like splattering pearls, hit the party on the head, landed in their drinks and started making Gary's baps soggy. But Temperance was only vaguely aware of the panic at the lunch table. She couldn't take her eyes off the clouds. The rolling clouds. The *purple* rolling clouds.

It's coming. The doom is coming. The premonition fulfilled.

'Well, this wasn't on my weather app!' Margie hollered crossly, gathering all the plates she could muster. 'All hands on deck – get this lot inside, loves! The show will go on.'

Diane squeezed past Temperance to head back inside and reappeared in a moment with a stack of bar trays. 'Hang on, Marge, this will help.'

Temperance felt welded to the spot by the scene in front of her. All those nightmares: now they were on her doorstep. And she had no idea what to do next. This didn't feel like a campfire-and-a-bottle-of-Malibu problem. This felt *huge*.

The words of F's last email came back to Temperance and she felt the air get pulled out of her lungs. Whether it was a lack of faith or some Wiccan telepathy, F had hit the nail right on the head: the trouble had found them, and there was no more time for bodged solutions. They needed something big. Why couldn't she have been born with Gandalf powers to whistle up a couple of giant eagles right now?!

Susie raced in, sliding a full tray of drinks effortlessly on the bar, her calm hands not matching her milk-white face. 'Tee . . . what do we do?!'

'I . . . I don't know, Suse. I just don't know.'

Stevie skittered in behind them as more of the party guests filed into the pub, looking for a dry safe-haven. She spoke in a low hush, 'I'm guessing that these purple clouds are like—?'

'Yup.'

'Holy shit.'

'Wiccan shit, more like.'

Stevie dipped her head in closer. 'So what now?'

Susie wrapped her arms around their friend's shoulder. 'We can't ask you to get involved, babe. It could be dangerous. You keep everyone tucked up here, let them help themselves to ales and crisps. Temps and I will,' she looked up at the ceiling, 'figure *something* out.'

A wounded pinch screwed up Stevie's neat little face. 'Hey, I'm a coven apprentice. You can't shut me out just when I could actually be useful! Besides, I was on that beach the night Tee did her accidental casting. Maybe you need me to complete the spell, to reverse it?'

With a frown, Temperance mumbled, 'She might have a point.'

'I do? See! So do we head back to the beach and dig out the wedding dress again?'

'No, we have to go bigger. I don't think just trying to

276

apologise again for what I did will work, it's like we have to strike out more than that. And there's something else.' Her eyes were wide.

'Something else beyond a purple storm and potentially the end of our village?!'

Temperance grabbed Susie by the wrist, and then Stevie. 'Come to the loos with me. Quick.'

Margie watched the three women hurry off to the back of the pub and leant over to Gary. 'These girls, they can never go to the bathroom alone, can they? Hang on – has anyone seen my Abel?'

Susie unlocked the cubicle door and stumbled out, her eyebrows disappearing into her hairline. 'Those poor Gullivers. I had no idea. Do you think Mum knew, Tee?'

With a shake of her head, her big sister replied. 'I don't think so. I feel like she would have told us if a centuries-old curse was at work right under our noses. And I'm really sure she would have tried to break them out of it if she could. I want to find a way to help too, but obviously that's going to have to go second on the list after "Saving our skins from a magical hurricane and being struck by other-worldly lightening."'

Outside, another boom of thunder filled the sticky afternoon air.

'If this wasn't so trippy – and terrifying – it would actually be kind of ironic, you know?' Stevie asked, only getting blank stares in response. 'You made a spell to bring back Abel, your true love. But he's under a curse that will always push him *away* from love, in the end. Like two magnets with the same kind of end always spinning and twisting each other away?'

'It certainly is a fuck-up of epic proportions,' Susie said,

277

leaning back on the tiny old radiator in the ladies' room. 'Maybe now is the time we call Mum with an SOS, Tee?'

'I don't know what she could do on another continent.' Temperance felt her heart sink further down, like a lead balloon. 'And F kept telling us that it has to come from me, since I'm the one that kick-started it all. God, if I could just take it back I would! I'd give anything, *anything*!'

She caught sight of herself in the bathroom mirror. It hadn't been replaced in generations and the surface had brown dots of age. Somehow, Temperance felt like she'd aged a good ten years just in the last week. Her red lipstick was now entirely gone, thanks to that boiling hot fifteen minutes with Abel on the cellar floor. The skin just under her collarbone still had the heat of a blush from when she'd felt herself come back to life under his touch. But knowing what'd he given up, to save her from heartbreak – family, friends, his home: his whole life, really – she desperately wanted to take that burden from him. It wasn't fair. He'd given so much and got so little back in return. And here she was, the author of her own tragedy, who'd tried to call in the love of her life like he was a takeaway pizza. With little thought and even less effort. Abel had taken the hard path, for her, and it felt like she'd just stayed tucked up in a feather bed all these years, blissfully ignorant. She'd given up nothing.

Temperance saw herself nod in the mirror. Only she knew she hadn't moved.

Wait – what?

She gasped. 'I know. I know what it is I have to do. I've been trying to reverse the *wrong* curse. Stevie, tell me that thing about the irony again, about the magnets. You've just cracked it, and literally on your second day as coven apprentice.'

'Oh my god, for real?'

'Temps, what are you thinking? Your eyes have gone funny.'

Temperance pressed her palms together. 'We're going to need some things. The wedding dress, the belt tie. My beanie. A couple of sturdy buckets. The firelighters from the pub. Abel's hoodie – the one he left behind, with all the disgust in it. And a few raincoats.'

'Raincoats, right. What kind of powers do they need to have? Do they, like, enchant the water not to be wet or soemthing?' Stevie asked.

'No, they're just waterproof. It's cats and dogs out there.'

'What are we washing?' Susie ran her fingers through her hair.

'Nothing. We're way beyond that. I'm not going to run from the wildfire in my nightmare any more – I'm going to start it.'

24

Chapter 24

'Tell me again when you learned how to control a wildfire safely?!' Susie yelled over the howling rain. The wind was bullying all three of them on the clifftop, pushing and pulling them in any direction it pleased, their shoulders going one way, their legs another. The rain had gone from big flouncy drops on the green to hard little bullets being pelted by the storm right into their faces. The beach below them was, by now – naturally – deserted, the holidaymakers sprinting up the rocks for cover at the first sign of clouds. But Temperance, Susie and Stevie had walked into the eye of the storm.

They were standing by the wildflower meadow that just hours before they'd collected posies from. But there would be nothing pretty about what they did next.

'Pour the water right around the edge, then the fire won't travel beyond that. Like a salt circle – it keeps everything inside.' Temperance spoke firmly, but inside she was really only making it up as she went along. All she had right now was the courage of her convictions and she couldn't show any chinks of uncertainty to the others. 'Keep the clothes in the bag until we're ready, Stevie, OK? So they stay dry.'

Stevie nodded and clasped the top of the giant Bag for Life closed. It wasn't exactly how she'd pictured helping out in a wiccan ceremony: standing in a sweaty yellow raincoat in the middle of a storm, some firelighters in her pocket and a huge wedding dress punched flat into a Tesco bag. But she'd take it.

'Done.' Susie put down the empty bucket. 'So, are we doing this? Really?'

'Really.' Temperance's tone was as firm as the rocks they stood on. 'Suse – don't repeat what I say, OK? Just keep up your own mantra, promise?'

'Of course, but could you just tell me—'

'There's no time. Stevie – firelighters?' Temperance knew it wasn't the most authentic way for a witch to start a fire, but she needed this to take in a big way, in the rain, and fast. She took them from her new friend and moved deep into the knee-high flowers, her dress still limiting her movements. 'For fuck's sake,' she hissed, bending over and ripping at the side seams with her bare hands. Stevie couldn't help but let out a horrified gasp.

Temperance placed a pile of firelighters in the dead centre and set them ablaze with an old Zippo, hurrying back at a satisfying speed now that her thighs could move independently. She watched the fire grow rapidly for five minutes or so, as if it loved that the air was charged with threat and drama and was feasting on it, growing hot and fat.

'You two, hold hands.' She beckoned the others together. 'And then we begin.'

'Gulliver men, we release you,' Stevie and Susie said in unison, taking up the chant. 'Gulliver men, we release you. We release you, Gulliver men. Gulliver men, we release you.'

After a steadying breath, Temperance turned her face up the bruise-blue sky and the clouds tumbling along at a stomach-lurching speed. The wind tried to knock her over again but she planted her bare feet firmly on the sodden ground. Flames started to creep now to the outside ring, sneaking up the stalks of ferns and flowers and uncurling wisps of black smoke into the air that were instantly taken out by the storm, like an impatient child who can't wait to blow out their birthday candles and stick their face in the cake. The heat tinged at Temperance's skin but she wouldn't step back. She wouldn't allow herself to be cowed.

Temperance took a lungful of the metallic air swirling around her and held out her right hand, her finger pointed. The bag by Stevie's feet started to shift of its own volition and the bodice of the wedding dress rose from the top. Soon the dress was floating in mid-air, its long train whipping around precariously in the storm.

Stevie's eyes were like saucers. She would have been whooping with delight, if she was able to break the chant.

Temperance flicked her wrist and the dress flew to the air in front of her. She didn't have her fingers on fabric, but somehow the flourish of pure love still seemed to travel through her, giving her the extra bolt of courage she needed right now. Temperance pulled her arm right back, and with a pushing motion sent the dress deep into the flames, the red flash of the satin robe disappearing into the fire with it.

'I called for a love that had no place being mine. I used my magic to cheat a man's free will.' The wind tried to push back Temperance's words, but she only went louder. 'I renounce that love: it doesn't belong to me. I didn't earn it. I give you back this pure love and desire, to repay the debt.'

The fire tore into the wedding dress, pulling it down deep into its amber heart and gobbling it almost whole.

Next, she pushed back her hood and yanked off her beanie, the rain now stinging at her scalp, another gale trying to rugby-tackle her ankles. From her pocket she took a tiny pair of embroidery scissors, snipping into the headband and working free an end of the purple yarn.

Susie's voice was strong in the chant, but her eyes were hollow as she watched Temperance unwind row after row. 'We release you, Gulliver men. Gulliver men, we release you.'

Temperance pulled and pulled, looping the crinkled yarn around her other hand until she reached the top of the crown and snipped into the last, securing knot. She squeezed her fingers around the wool, a pulse of steely strength kicking into her heart. 'And now, to send back the danger hanging over our home, I will give to you this talisman,' she yelled. 'It has a powerful protective spell, made from strength and care. I give it to you, to ask that my chosen family are kept safe forever. Those who find their home here will always be welcomed and treasured, I make this vow.' She lobbed the yarn into the fire that now crackled and spat dangerously close to her feet, but didn't cross over the seawater moat Susie had poured out. The wool fizzled almost like a sparkler on Bonfire Night, with shards of white light bursting from it and flying into Temperance's face, buzzing around her ears, until it vanished in mere seconds.

From the bag, Temperance snatched up Abel's hoodie. Though she had felt it a thousand times and could recite the disgust and fear in its fibres like she could a Stevie Nicks lyric, as that chilling emotion ran up from her fingertips, icing the blood in her veins, she felt a new low to it. All these years she had thought that Abel was sickened by her, by the thought of them being together, but in fact it was his loathing for *himself* that had woven its way into the soft jersey. And though Temperance had come to relive it now and again over that time, Abel had been stuck with it in his heart, day in and day out. How devastating that must have been for him to carry around. How lonely.

She could have used to her powers to lift it up, but Temperance wanted to feel that connection to the past one more time, a last echo of what she and Abel had meant to each other back then. Now that she knew all of its negative feelings were really about protecting her, it felt less like a dirty secret and more a badge of honour.

She wiped at her eyes with the fabric and drew back her shoulders. Her voice started to scratch as she called out her next vow. 'To my sister of old who was wronged by Jack Gulliver: I see your pain. He had no right to cheat you, to laugh at you. Jack Gulliver has paid the price. His debt is clear. It is time to release his descendants from this misery. It was never their burden to carry. I give to you a taste of their pain, so you can know how deeply they have suffered, a thousand times over. It's time to let them rest. Abel Gulliver and all his kin should be free to go and find real, unshackled love.' With a flick of her wrist, the hoodie spun into the air and landed in the heart of the roaring flames.

Stevie was by now trying her best not to flinch as they kept up their mantra at top volume. The heat was aggressive, pinching at their faces while the storm tried to freeze them out from behind.

'My last gift,' Temperance shouted, 'to lift the Gulliver Curse, is this very meadow. My mother, sister and I have picked these flowers and used them to enhance our magic. I burn them today to show you that I renounce my power. I renounce *my* magic, so that the village and the Gulliver family will always be safe. I give this freely, with my whole heart!' She held her palms open and up to the furious sky.

'Tee, no!' Susie yelled.

'Don't stop chanting!' her big sister shouted back in response. From the corner of her eye, Temperance saw that the bag by her feet wasn't totally empty. A Malibu bottle was rolling slowly from side to side, maybe caught on a breeze or maybe doing its best to get her attention. She smiled. 'It's only right.' Unscrewing the top, she shook the last measure into the flames.

The flames roared up like a totem pole for one terrifying second, right up over their heads, and then were gone.

The fire was out.

No smouldering, no smoke. Temperance crouched down and inched her fingers towards the blackened ground. Completely cold.

Susie and Stevie's voices stopped their mantra.

'What the . . . did you mean for that to happen?' Stevie said in a cracked whisper.

'Look – Tee!' Susie yanked her sister up by the elbow and pointed to the sky. The clouds were rolling back fast, back to the horizon, like someone was rewinding a movie on double speed. Their colour faded from purple to blue, to soft pink and then nothing. The wind fell away.

Temperance searched for the last cloud that was still raining down on her, keeping her face wet, when she realised it was her own relieved tears.

'We did it.' She felt her ribs loosen, her forehead unclench.

'I think we did it.'

'I think *you* did it,' Susie corrected. 'But your powers, Temps, you . . . how could you give up your powers like that?' Her bottom lip trembled with the question.

'It had to be big. Not just to undo what I'd done, but for all those Gulliver generations suffering. It had to be big to correct that balance. And it wasn't like I had a mega yacht or a mansion to chuck in. It was the biggest sacrifice I could make.'

Susie joined her in a full-on weep. 'But it doesn't feel fair.'

They hugged, Stevie coming behind and doing her best to wrap her petite arms around them both. 'I'm so proud of you, Tee. And just *think* of the wicked memories these raincoats are going to have now.'

Except you and I won't be able to feel them. Just Suse. Temperance kept this echoey little thought to herself.

'Temperance!' a low voiced boomed out from the path, Abel appearing a second later. 'Oh thank God, we saw the flames from the pub. What are you doing?!' Before she could speak he had almost pulled her off her feet into a bear hug, his arms crushing around her.

When they stepped apart Temperance wiped more tears from her cheek. 'Um, so you know how you told me something a little bit woo woo? I've actually got one of those stories too, it turns out. I need to tell you about it, maybe once we've had a chance to get back and dry off.' She looked down at her mud-and-ash-splattered legs, the ripped skirt now showing off a serious amount of flesh, and patted the hair plastered to her skull.

Abel's eyes flicked away from her thighs. 'Sure, of course. Here, I brought these for the three of you.' He handed over bobbly beach towels and the women grabbed at them gratefully.

As they started a slow stagger back up to the village, none of them really knew how to make small talk after what they'd just witnessed. Susie walked at the back of the group and she couldn't help but smile as a memory of a failed, soggy surfing lesson came back to her. If you took out the raging fires and ancient curses, it was just like old times.

25

Chapter 25

'A witch.'

Temperance put one hand to her chin. 'Yeah.'

Warm, dry and in her favourite pink joggers with the rainbow stripe up the side, she felt more like herself than she had in weeks. The neckline on her Blondie T-shirt was still stretched out, her hair was pulled back into a bun so dishevelled it needed its own therapist, but she was at peace. At last.

Temperance rested her feet on the kitchen chair in front of her, and sipped more of her Irish coffee. Margie had wanted them all to dry off by the pub fire with a round of whiskies, but Temperance knew she needed her own shower in that moment and to get out of clothes that involved a strapless bra, at the very least. All the party guests and villagers were still in shock about the Armageddon-themed afternoon: a thunderstorm, a random fire, three bedraggled women cartwheeling their way across the green to come home. Abel insisted he see Temperance safely back, all ten steps of the way.

He'd waited silently downstairs while she got changed and was now drumming his fingers against his legs, leaning back on the counter top.

'Like . . . eye of newt, leg of frog? A *witch* witch?' His face was unreadable.

'Not so much cackling, or the foraged proteins, but a witch.'

'Like the kind of witch that hexed Jack Gulliver?' His face was pale.

Temperance shook her head so hard she felt slightly dizzy. 'No, no. We'd never curse anyone like that. We're into herbs and flowers, good memories. We've just been quietly doing our thing under the radar.' Temperance had lived her adult life in fear of people knowing – especially people close to her. But now that she'd brought Stevie into their witchy world and she'd offloaded the entire weird story to Abel, she felt oddly free. No more shame. No more cold sweats of panic. He deserved to know the whole truth after sharing his. It would be up to him what he did with it.

'Except for the part where you jinxed the whole village. Developers nearly swooped in. And you reversed a centuries' old curse. That wasn't so quiet.'

'No.' She gulped back the sweet coffee. 'I'm sorry what I did brought you back here, against your will. I'm sorry you got dragged into all of this. But the curse is gone now – no more monk's life for you.'

Abel held his bottom lip with his teeth. 'I don't *feel* different, though. Am I supposed to?'

Temperance shrugged. 'Don't know, sorry. Never lifted a centuries' old curse before. There's a first time for everything. But I felt something shift out there, in the flames. I sort of . . . bartered for it. A trade-off. And the storm certainly pissed off fast enough, so I'm taking that as a definite sign. These last weeks I've looked at you and felt *doom*, but now,' she took

289

a pause to really study him, his drawn brows, his darkening stubble, 'I feel nothing.'

'Um, thanks, I guess,' he muttered, his eyes widening. 'It's a lot to process. This has been hanging over me my whole adult life and now – if it really is gone . . .' He pulled the purple bow tie out from under his shirt collar and laid it next to the kettle.

Temperance's eyes fell to the tie. The Temperance of yesterday could have held it in the palm of her hand and read all the big emotions at war in Abel's head right now, giving her a shortcut to understanding him that would otherwise take forty-eight hours of deep and meaningful talk. Did he feel a whole new wave of revulsion knowing she was a witch? Was all this stuff about powers and curses and sacrifices just too much, sending his head spinning? The old Temperance could have held the tie and seen fear or despair or overwhelm or disgust. But using magic to jump to the front of the emotional queue hadn't exactly done her many favours this summer. She felt blank without her powers, and perhaps once the reality sunk in she'd grieve it deeply, but for now that blankness felt light and refreshing.

No one's fate was resting on her. The past was no longer chasing her down.

Who knew if lifting the curse would change anything between her and Abel? That wasn't why she'd given her magic to dissolve it. She'd done it because it was the right thing to do. Now she knew he wasn't living his life in a vice of shame and denial, she could rest easy. That felt like a gift in itself.

Besides, Abel had spent most of his adult life under a magical curse. He was hardly going to jump into the arms of someone born and bred a witch. And he had a life away from East Prawle. Magic spells didn't tie all those things up in a neat bow.

He cleared his throat. 'I suppose this means, I could—'

'ABEL!' came a shriek from outside.

He stood up straight in an instant and Temperance leapt to her feet. 'Was that Gran?'

'I think so.'

'ABEL!' came another shout, Margie's voice breaking in between syllables. 'Where are you, love?'

Temperance and Abel raced to the front door and down the steps. Abel took long, urgent strides to reach his Gran.

'What's happened, are you OK?'

Huge sparkling tears ran down Margie's face, leaving track marks in her generous blusher.

'OK? I'm not OK! I'm bloody marvellous! Your dad just called. *Your dad.* He wants to see you. Soon! He gave me his number so you can call him back, come on.' She grabbed one of Abel's hands and yanked him back towards the pub.

He looked back over his shoulder at Temperance as his gran hurried him along. His smile was almost wide enough to reach each ear, a haze of disbelief in his eyes. 'You were right!' he laughed. 'Whatever you did really worked!'

Temperance watched them go, her heart feeling twice its size and full of bright white light. 'Right. Definitely time for another drink.' With a quick pit stop at home to dry her hair and throw on a bra and a jumper, she retraced Abel and Margie's steps to the pub.

Temperance wanted to first find Susie when she entered The Witch's Nose, but suddenly all she could see was fluffy white filling her vision and a bear grip around her ribs.

Diane was quietly sobbing into Temperance's shoulder. 'Thank you, thank you,' she whispered into her ear.

'Huh?'

'I don't know what you did, but it worked, clearly. Abel's getting his dad back! They talked for a little while and now Abel's having a walk to clear his head. A lot to take in, you know. Plans to make.'

'Of course. I can't even imagine. But you know,' Temperance studied the tops of her slippers as if a convincing get-out was embroidered on them along with the bunny face and ears, 'I didn't do anything, did I? Just one of those random things.'

Diane's glittering eyes narrowed. 'Three women go and chant around a fire and suddenly something miraculous happens.' Temperance opened her mouth to suggest the hog roast had been spiked and they'd just spent two hours in a mass hallucination, but Diane held up a silencing hand. 'I don't need the details. To be honest, I'm not sure I can handle them. Just take my thanks and blessings. If that's what you're into. You won't combust near a cross, will you? No, no, I don't want to know. We're doubly back into party mode now so park your beautiful bum down and I'll get you a stiff one.'

Diane skipped off to the bar before Temperance could tell her what she'd like in her glass. But Temperance was feeling altogether too zen to think twice about it. The *doom* was gone. The party was still in force. Susie and Stevie were safe. She could just enjoy herself.

A flash of red caught her attention and Temperance saw Susie's Converse poking out of the snug.

Temperance slid around the corner, through the narrow doorway, her arms reaching into a showbiz wave, and started belting out, '*I put a spell on youuu—*' At Susie's snort of laughter, she stopped herself short. 'Oh, hey Mark. Didn't know you were coming.'

Mark had a massive grin across his face, one leg resting on the opposite knee. 'Please don't stop! I felt like I was at a Vegas cabaret. It was awesome.'

'Ha! Um, a family inside-joke.'

'And then some.' Susie nodded. 'Mark wanted to come earlier but couldn't take his rig out because of the *freak weather blip* that we had.' Her eyes drilled into her big sister's.

'Yeah, wasn't that insane? I've been sailing here since I was about eight or nine and I've never seen anything like it. This intense pocket of low pressure, a proper thunder storm, all been and gone in half an hour. Bonkers.'

'Bonkers,' the Molland women said in unison.

Susie pointed at the stack of printouts spread out on the table before them. 'Mark wanted to show us how far he is with the process. He's filing it – himself – tomorrow.' She rubbed his arm. 'Plus, he realised he *forgot* his leather jacket last time when he was here. Don't suppose you've seen it have you, Tee?' If Susie had ever toyed with the idea of a career in panto, now was the time for her to apply for her equity card.

'Erm, yes, you know. I have. I . . . found it . . . somewhere. And took it back to the shop for safekeeping. Shall I go and grab it now?'

'I don't want to put you out, Temperance. Sit down and have a drink first.'

'It's no bother. It'll feel good to have one more thing ticked off my list today. Back in a sec.'

Temperance was just switching off the shop lights ten minutes later, Mark's jacket under her chin, when she saw Abel coming out of the back door of the pub.

Maybe he's finished his walk and he's ready to talk some more?

But he was carrying a holdall and striding away from the shop now. Towards his van.

Temperance watched, her breath trapped in her lungs, as he started the engine and drove away.

At least one thing was certain now: this wasn't a curse controlling Abel Gulliver. He was leaving East Prawle again, of his own free will.

26

Chapter 26

Susie slipped a twenty-pound note in the Try Again till.

'This is me, officially buying the 'ladette' T-shirt. I love it too much as a look and I want to keep it forever as a memento of what we achieved yesterday. I mean, you were the hero, Tee, but I had a sort of Robin charm alongside your broody Batman.'

Temperance nodded from the office doorway. 'Don't suppose in all your gratitude that you want to invisibly mend the gingham dress for me so I can get it out on the rack?'

'You're not keeping it?' Stevie sounded crestfallen.

Temperance shook her head. 'It's a beauty – a rare beauty. But I won't have another dressy occasion to wear it to for . . . a million years. It's a bit fancy for your average speed-dating night. And who knows what kind of chaotic energy it's clinging on to? It might inspire me to start more random fires in woodland.' She gave a hollow kind of laugh. 'Suse can do a cleaning ritual, then I'll mend it and it can go out on the shelf and find a new, merry little life.'

'If you say so.' Stevie turned back to the display she working on: a chunky woven tapestry of vintage belts, using a peg board and a lot of imagination.

Checking her phone for the hundredth time that hour, Susie huffed and put it face-down on the cash desk. 'Why won't he text me?!'

Her big sister let out a low whistle. 'You. Are. Smitten.'

'I am not! I'm just on edge about how it went at the council office. He could so easily just drop me a little message to say it's all done.'

'Or maybe he's still in there right now, and being respectful to their workplace by staying off his phone? I'm sure he'll be in touch when he can. Mark doesn't seem like the gameplaying type.'

Susie puffed out her cheeks. 'It's not . . . not about games, or *us* . . . it's about the preservation order, and the next steps of the campaign.'

'OK,' Stevie sing-songed with a sarky edge. Her British sense of humour was sharpening by the day.

Temperance noticed from the way her little sister hugged her own shoulders that she was feeling exposed. 'Sorry, we're just teasing. But in all seriousness, I love this laser focus you have for getting the preservation sorted. It's very cool.'

'Well, thanks,' Susie mumbled.

The shop doorbell chimed. 'It's done!' Mark appeared in the doorway, his hair tussled and his eyes slightly wide, as if he'd just seen a ghost. When in fact he was smack bang in front of a coven. 'The application is submitted and I told the family.'

'Oh my god.' Susie rushed over to hug him and he lifted her off her feet, spinning her around.

As he put Susie down, Mark kept one arm around her waist and put her other hand to his cheek. 'I feel . . . liberated!'

Susie searched his face. 'Are you sure? How did they take it?'

'My dad barked out "bloody hell" and my mum said "goodness", which is pretty colourful for repressed rich people. They didn't chuck me out on my arse or anything. They also didn't exactly fight me when I handed in my resignation. But . . .' he frowned, 'I knew I didn't belong there anymore. In some ways, it was like I'd already left. You know, in my heart. And I want to be the kind of person that takes risks, follows their instincts.' His looked straight at Susie and his smile picked up again, all the way to his ears. 'But now the preservation process has kicked off, and we're going to see it through! No one is coming for East Prawle while I have breath in my body. Step one: we celebrate.'

'Celebrate? I was hoping we could go over some ideas for the campaign? I think we can squeeze in a charity surf competition in early September, if we get going quick enough. An old mate of mine in Woolacombe will lend me loads of boards, I'm sure Margie would love setting up a beach bar for the day and we could call the papers, maybe get a few local celebs down . . .' Susie was ticking ideas after ideas off her fingers.

'How about we plan *while* we celebrate?' Mark suggested smoothly. 'Afternoon tea at The Harbour Hotel over in Salcombe. On me. Well, to be accurate: on the Beston portfolio account there before my parents take me off the signature list. We'll toast and plan and brainstorm and eat scones.'

'Scones!' Stevie squeaked from the back wall.

'Everyone is invited, of course!' Mark added. 'I've got enough lifejackets for all of us in the rig, we can be there in twenty minutes, sinking our teeth into clotted cream.'

Stevie blushed, 'I didn't mean . . . you don't have to . . .'

'A quintessential afternoon tea must be on your English adventure bingo sheet, Stevie,' Temperance nudged. 'Why not? The Harbour is mega fancy. I bet their cucumber sandwiches will be unforgettable. You deserve this experience! Besides, we could all do with a little treat after the last few days, don't you think? The, er, weird storm and everything.'

Susie squeezed Mark's arm. 'What if we bumped into someone from your old office? Or your family?'

He shrugged. 'I'm not running and hiding. I haven't done anything wrong. Besides, someone very wise once told me that if my family can turn against me over something like this, they're not all that great a family to have.' Mark leant forward and kissed her briefly. 'And the little chocolate gateaux slices they do at the hotel are,' he made a throaty growl, 'so good.'

Temperance scribbled on a piece of paper on the cash desk. 'Let's go then!'

They grabbed their bags and headed out the door, Temperance locking it behind her and sticking up her hasty sign: *Shut for afternoon tea. Cream then jam xxx*

27

Chapter 27

.

Temperance decided that twenty-nine was no age to mope over a boy.

She'd spent the last three days either keeping to the house or the store, letting the loss of her powers plus her first big love wash over her, but enough was enough. She'd avoided the pub for the longest stretch in her life – she didn't need any gentle but needling questions about what had gone on with her and Abel, why she'd desperately yelled his name over the green in front of the entire community, why she walked back from the cliff with him that day soggy and bedraggled – not while it still felt so raw. She had needed time to heal and think of a plausible lie. In her sleepless hours last night, Temperance came up with the earth-shattering, 'He'd left his phone on the bar and then I fell on some wet leaves. OK?!'.

But now was the time to get going again. If Temperance avoided The Witch's Nose any longer, Margie was bound to strut over and demand answers about what the chuff was going on with her. Susie had been spending all of her time either doing shifts or drawing up poster designs for her surf competition, now she had sponsorship from a local holiday rental company. She was either working or in her room 'planning' with Mark behind a closed door and Temperance didn't really want to be around to accidentally overhear all those muffled giggles.

She'd face the music. Over some scampi and chips, and maybe a few bourbons.

She decided, as she was approaching thirty, that she'd level up her drinks choices from now on. Anyway, it's not like she could accidentally get off her face and cast another doom-laden spell, not now her powers had gone.

As Temperance stepped into her trainers by the front door, she put her hand out for stability and her fingers grabbed hold of Susie's denim jacket hanging on the wall. A week ago, Temperance would have been able to shut her eyes and see Susie laughing so much at the pub that she temporarily ran out of breath. Or swearing at the campers who'd left a carrier bag of rubbish out in the elements so now the seagulls had spread it over three counties. She would have been able to read the good memories and the bad. Now she just felt the thick cotton under her hand. And nothing else.

Temperance closed the front door behind her, immediately turning and pressing her forehead against the peeling paintwork. 'He'd left his phone, I was just returning it. Then I slipped on some soggy leaves. That was it. Phone. Leaves. Done. Next subject.' She whispered into the wood.

As stepped down from her doorstep, the sight before her made her wobble on one ankle and shove a hand into the ivy for support.

'Abel?'

He was pacing up and down the road outside her garden gate,

a battered brown leather briefcase swinging in his hand as he did so. Flinching at the sound of her voice, he stopped dead in his tracks.

'Hi.'

'Um, hi. I thought you'd . . . gone back to Bath?'

Abel put the briefcase down between his feet and stuffed his hands into his pockets. 'Oh, yes. Well, after the airport.'

'Airport?'

He cleared his throat. 'Temperance . . . actually,' he looked over both shoulders, 'could we go inside? For some privacy.'

'Susie and Mark are pretty *together* in there,' she said. 'Pub?'

'Do you think we'd get much privacy under Margie's nose?'

She nodded. 'Fair point. There's always . . . the bus stop, I suppose.'

He seemed to weigh this up, his head tipping left to right. 'That seems right. Shall we?'

The sun had almost set into the sea as they walked at an awkward distance next to each other, to the old shelter. The sky was inky, with only tiny slivers of gold still stretched across it, while the swallows were noisily telling each other goodnight in the hedgerows.

Temperance perched on the wooden bench, swinging her legs back and forth for perhaps the millionth time in her life on this very spot. She pointed at the briefcase. 'Did you pick that up at the airport?'

'No, just my dad.'

'Your dad?!'

'Yup.' Abel smiled. 'Turns out when he said he wanted to see me, that night of the fire, he was already heading to a check-in desk. He and I had a chat. Have to admit I wasn't sure at first whether I wanted to see him right away, but I figured he was as powerless in all of this as any of us. So when he messaged me the flight details, I hopped in the van and drove off to London so I could meet him when he landed.'

A shiver of happiness shot through Temperance's heart. 'Abel, I'm so happy for you! That's . . . so brilliant.'

'I've got you to thank.' He nodded solemnly. 'Dad and I . . . we've spent the last few days talking, letting go of some stuff, making plans. He's not going back to live there again – he's going to find some work nearby eventually, slowly get back into East Prawle life. I think he's feeling pretty sheepish about suddenly turning up in the pub after all this time, having left us like that. If only we could tell everyone that it was down to a centuries' old curse, not to him being a total div.'

'That's the thing about magic: it doesn't make for the easiest small talk. But who cares what anyone else round here thinks – you've got him back, and that's awesome. I hope I can meet him, when he does brave the pub again.'

Abel's eyes locked onto hers. 'I hope so too. The thing is, one of the reasons I was on the fence about going to pick him up was that I'd already decided to head back to Bath. Because when I went for that walk it took me all of five whole minutes to know what I wanted.'

Her heart went leaden behind her ribs. Was she really going to have to listen to how thrilled Abel was to have a clear, unjinxed heart at last so he could live an uncomplicated life in Bath, far away from magical complications and wedding dresses floating into enchanted fires?

Temperance concentrated on keeping her voice steady. 'That's good. Good for you.'

He sat down next to her, his body angled her way, their knees almost touching. Something about him seemed younger, somehow. His shoulders weren't so rigid, his jaw wasn't locked in a scowl. It was like the clock had gone back, all the way back.

'I hope it will be. I got three paces out of the door when I knew it was you, Temperance Molland. I have always loved you. I love you so much that I kept far, far away from you because I thought it would save you pain.' Abel ran his tongue over his lips. 'It was you when we used to share salami sandwiches and complain about Mr Edgars in RE, right here.' Abel rapped the wood with his knuckles. 'It was *certainly* you on the floor of the cellar the other day.' His eyebrows raised, and she blushed right up to her ponytail. 'I had to keep you at arm's length this whole time when all I could think about was a million memories from growing up with you, and I wanted to ask what you've been doing, and if you were OK and who that smooth git on the dating app is – so I can go and let the air out of his tyres. I was planning to get in my van that day, head to my flat, pack up all of my stuff and bring it back here, because I'm done with Bath.' He finally paused for a breath. 'God, I'm absolutely bricking it. But, Tee, I want what I've been denying myself for twelve years: I want a shot at taking you out, buying you dinner, maybe sneaking a kiss at the end of the night.'

The blood was pumping in her veins like an illegal rave. 'I think we might have skipped that part, back in the cellar.'

'No, no, no. We'll do this properly. Aftershave, best shirt, arguing about how we split the bill. Would you do that, Tee?' His hand reached for hers now, gripping her fingers, his thumb rubbing against the centre of her palm.

'Yes. Now?' her voice squeaked hopefully.

'I wasn't thinking of *right now*,' he murmured, leaning slowly down, his lips pressing firmly against hers, his tongue following.

Temperance kept a hold of his hand in hers as they kissed, and moved her other to the back of his head, where Abel's hair went soft. She didn't want there to be any chance this could slip away from her again, or that it could all be a magical illusion: she was holding on tight.

He reached his free arm around her middle and pulled her in closer along the bench, effortlessly, without breaking contact.

A heat raced along her fingertips, through her hips and filled her head. It was like the sensations she used to feel when reading magic, but not one she'd ever felt during a kiss. It went deeper. Into her bones. It felt stronger.

Abel moved so he was kissing the side of her mouth, along her chin, down her neck. 'I can't stop,' he breathed.

Temperance gasped, the throaty sound echoing around the stone walls. Unlike in her dreams, there was nothing handy for them to hide behind while they got closer, and a very real chance of being discovered. 'Maybe . . . we should . . . find somewhere more private?'

He leant back just a few inches, a rugged smile moving across almost the whole width of his face. 'I'm really going to enjoy getting to know the beyond-PG you.'

Temperance ran her finger over his stubble, noticing the flecks of gold amongst the darker brown. 'The adult-rated Temperance has had a *lot* of thoughts about this. Well, dreams. And some of them took place in this bus shelter.'

His eyes went wide and a jolt of electricity hit her again. 'Tell me.'

Heat sunk low down through her body, ending up at the top of her thighs. 'It started innocent enough,' she said between light kisses. 'But then,' her fingers skimmed over his crotch and the hard shape there, 'I went looking for trouble.'

'Holy shit.' Abel laughed from deep in his throat and rested his forehead against hers.

'Susie will still be home,' Temperance said. 'We could . . . *talk more* at the shop.'

Abel yanked her so roughly that she thought her shoulder might come out of its socket. 'Oh – wait!' He turned on the spot.

'If there's some Bath-based curse you've fallen under where you turn into loofah at midnight, I can't help you anymore.'

'No: your present. Here.' He snatched up the well-used briefcase from the ground and laid it gently on the bench.

'Do you need me to witness some documents or something?! This doesn't really feel like the time,' she teased.

Abel pushed back the two brass lock plates and opened the lid.

It wasn't what Temperance was expecting from a 1960s-looking briefcase: Doritos, homemade sandwiches and cartons of Ribena. 'I thought we could pick up where we left off – a picnic, like old times?' He smiled cheesily.

'Oh.' She pressed her hands over her thumping heart. 'But why a . . .' Her eyes lit up with realisation. 'It's not the same briefcase, is it?' She was equally horrified and impressed.

The tips of Abel's ears turned red. 'When we had to return it to your mum after that drinking session, I'd done my best to clean it out but it was . . . permanently damaged.'

'So was my stomach chemistry.'

He laughed. 'She suggested I could help her change the lining over, as a sort of life lesson, I think. I actually really enjoyed it. It was, um,' he swallowed, 'supposed to be your seventeenth birthday present. Stashed it in Gran's attic when

I left, not sure why. I put your initials there.' He pointed at the edging of leather than ran in a thin strip around the inside, and the letters *TEM* that had been branded in place. 'Seeing as the gift was the same, I thought I'd keep the snacks from back in the day. But if you don't eat these anymore . . .' He picked up the crisps and Temperance snatched them back like a wild puma.

'You *will not* part me from my Doritos.'

'I got that right, at least. Sorry it's twelve years overdue.'

Temperance ran her hands over the Liberty lawn that Abel had replaced the original with. It was Betsy, her favourite print – Lee must have steered him towards it. She could see where his stitches were – he'd picked a pretty obvious red thread colour and it ran haywire all over the place. But it was perfect.

'Thank you. Abel, it's . . . it's the best present, ever. I love it. It's so . . . *me*. A bit of our past. I mean, it's such a good present that you've now unlocked a whole new area of certificate-18 Temperance content. Get your arse to the shop. Right now.'

The 'undressing each other like it was the last ten seconds of life on Earth' was not difficult. Abel pressing Temperance up against the cool office wall in just her bra and knickers was not difficult: it was incredibly hot. She had no idea how her legs were keeping her upright when her entire body was now made of molten lava, and especially when he grabbed one thigh and pulled it up around his hip. The tricky bit came when they went to lie down. Very few vintage stores come with a bed.

'Wait,' he gasped, his breath jagged, 'I've got an idea. And if we ruin it, I'll just give you all my money. I don't care.' He dashed to the front door, in just his boxers, and for one heart-lurching moment Temperance thought he was going again, out the door and out of her life.

But he stopped just shy of the door and used both hands to lift out the huge orange fake fur.

'This thing's so thick it's like a camp bed.' His smile was filthy and infectious.

'OK,' Temperance breathed.

He came back to her in the office, laying the jacket down and then shutting the door firmly behind him. They knelt down together, then lay down, on their sides, face to face. The inner lining of the coat was purple satin and it was like an iceberg butting up against a volcano: Temperance felt sure the heat of her body would melt it into nothing.

Abel ran his hand from the back of her neck, over her shoulders, down to her hip, and let it rest behind her knees. His eyes stayed locked on hers, as if wanting to read the tiniest indications of where she liked to be touched. Temperance felt like she was caught in the headlights of his gaze and all of a sudden it was almost too intense, too much.

She followed the line of his tattoo with her index finger, three neat peaks of waves in the sea.

'It must have been hard, leaving the beach behind when you left. I know how much you love it.'

His grey eyes were still looking deep down into hers. 'That wasn't the hard bit, Temperance. And the tattoo – it's not just about the sea.' He put his fingers over hers, pressing her touch into his skin. 'Three waves. You, me and Suse. How I feel about the village my home, is all wrapped up in you guys. I had to pretend that I didn't care, Tee, but a part of me never left. You and Suse were my world. Are my world.'

She blinked. 'You're not planning on doing *this* with her, are you? Because Doritos will get you a lot but they won't get you that.'

'Temperance Molland, you're talking way too much,' he murmured, closing the few inches between them.

His kisses changed tempo from inviting to exploring to owning, and he held her head with both hands, as if to fix her in place – now underneath him – forever.

Every joint, every muscle in Temperance melted away and then snapped back into life. She was used to reading a multitude of emotions with her powers and sifting carefully through each one but never had she been hit with a hundred intense bursts of feeling like this, all at once: the hardness of his knee as it pushed between her thighs, the scratch of his stubble against her collarbone, how his hands were soft but urgent, how ready she was for him, how hungry for this moment so many years in the making.

'God, Temperance,' he muttered against the skin at the top of her breasts. 'Can I?' He slid the bra straps from each of her shoulders and reached for the clasp around her back.

The noise she made didn't quite form a word but her frantic nodding got the message across. As she leant up, she reached her arms around him, behind his back, pulling him in and keeping the contact between them complete and unbroken. Her head was spinning and her pulse was racing but all she knew was that she had to put her skin on his skin, there was no other feeling like this. She kissed his shoulders, his neck.

'Fuck,' Abel whispered. Now her bra had been flung onto Susie's desk, his hands were free to skim over her tits, cupping the weight of them, his thumbs grazing her nipples, making her shiver with delight. 'I've thought about this for so long,' he breathed, as his head moved lower.

Temperance could only gasp in response when his tongue

ran over her most sensitive skin, her back arching up to meet him. '*Yes.*'

'What have you thought about?' he whispered, his mouth moving to her other breast.

Temperance could feel a rich curl of pleasure unfurl between her legs. 'Your . . ugh . . . hands, and your arms. Your mouth. What you could do to me. Oh god.' His teeth held her nipple for one ecstatic moment.

Abel's breath was suddenly hot against her stomach as he slid his hands under her knickers and pulled them down and off. His hands took hold of the top of her thighs, moving them apart gently. 'There's so much I want to do to you, Temperance.'

She felt his tongue moving slowly, pushing deep into her, setting her on fire. Temperance's fingers wove themselves into his hair as her hips started to sway and stir. His hands snaked back up her body while his mouth was busy, and he found her tits again squeezing and kneading them relent-lessly.

'Abel, Abel. *Please.*'

She couldn't bear any distance between them: she needed to see him over her, now. Abel was up on his arms, his biceps working, coming back to her, stopping only to tug off his boxers. Temperance could feel how hard and hot he was, against her stomach. The surge of almost egotistical pleasure rang through her whole being, as if at last she could truly believe that he wanted her as much as she wanted him.

His voice was only just there, broken and gravelly. 'I'm not sure I can wait any longer.'

'I can't either.' And somehow she knew he didn't just mean today: he meant all the lonely years that were behind them now, put to rest.

As Abel pushed inside her, in one certain, easy movement, Temperance felt herself open up like never before. A burst of warmth began in her hips but quickly filled her entire body, pulsing right down into her tingling fingertips and behind her eyes, her vision filled with a wash of royal blue that changed into bright white, like the very centre of a flame. 'Holy shit,' she gasped. She could feel him *everywhere*.

Abel didn't move for a moment, his weight on his elbows, his thumb along her cheekbone, his voice in her ear. 'Is that . . . Tee? What – I've never felt – fuck.'

'Me too,' she whispered back.

And if she didn't know better – if she didn't know she'd given up her powers in a trade off with a much bigger force – she would have said the feeling was pure magic.

Epilogue

Two weeks later

'Oh my god, you are too cute.' Susie watched Temperance run through the quickest closing-up routine of her life, shoving all the papers and receipts on the cash desk in a rough, teetering pile and shutting down the till in a flash.

'What?'

'You can't wait to see your *boyfriend*,' Susie teased.

Temperance rolled her eyes. 'We're just going for a meal and I need a bit of time to . . . get ready first.'

'Meaning you haven't shaved your legs for a couple of days.'

'It's actually scary how well you know me.' But even as she laughed, she felt the thrill of anticipation for tonight: her and Abel, having dinner at a pub three villages over, totally alone. No local gossips eyeing them when they can't keep their hands to themselves over a basket of bread rolls. Then back to hers. Hopefully nice and early, ready to exhaust each other. There were still some scenarios from those wedding dress dreams that Temperance hadn't gotten around to showing Abel yet . . .

A jiggling noise came from the front door. Temperance could see a colourful silhouette behind the glass. 'Sorry! We're closed now! Come back tomorrow if you like.' Her voice dropped so just that Susie would hear. 'These bloody grockles expect everything to be open seven days a week. Why can't

311

they just chill out?'

The door handle rattled again, more vigorously. And then the silhouette stepped away.

'Yeah, thanks,' Temperance muttered, catching the stapler as it tried to dive-bomb off her mountain of stuff.

But a loud bang had her whipping around, as the shop door flew open and clattered against the wall.

'Oopsie! Sorry about that.'

'That was *locked*,' Susie whispered, the hackles rising on the back of her neck.

As the woman walked confidently across the shopfloor towards them, Temperance knew she was a stranger. A stranger that had her mum's face, save for one extra beauty mark by the corner of her mouth and that her grey hair was cut into an asymmetric bob. She wore a creamy-gold coloured linen suit that was impossibly wrinkle free. And over her shoulder she seemed to be carrying . . . a quilt. Complex, multicoloured, beautifully stitched.

'In the very flesh! My *girls*,' the woman crooned.

'Um, can we help you?' Susie asked gently, but from the way her eyes were blinking on repeat, Temperance could tell she was just as freaked out by the similarity to Lee.

The woman lowered one tastefully plucked eyebrow. 'Temperance, Susie: is a hug too much to ask? Or should we be very British,' she wrinkled her nose, 'and just shake hands for now?'

Susie blinked again. 'I'm sorry – who are you?!'

With a tsk, the woman pulled a crisp, white hanky from the breast pocket of her jacket. As she whipped it open they could see a large embroidered letter F.

'It's me,' her eyes sparkled, 'Auntie Fiona!'

The three Molland women swapped looks, but only Fiona grinned madly.

The front door of Try Again squeaked on its hinges, a lightening-shaped crack running right through the glass.

'Well, run and pop the kettle on then,' Fiona said. 'We've *so much* to talk about.'

Acknowledgements

This book came to me, like a thunder bolt, while I was stood one of those bars-on-a-boat along the Thames in the summer of 2023. I was catching up with a group of lovely friends and, as we watched, this huge purple-black cloud roll up the river with purpose, as if it was headed just for us. It broke the hot afternoon, dumped a thick shower of rain on our heads and then – poof – it was gone again. Like magic. After that the characters and the location for *Weave Your Magic* came to me thick and fast – I was scribbling down ideas on the train home in a fever. Aside from books, my big love is sewing and fabric so I wanted my characters to feel that kind of connection, albeit it in a witchy way. I wrote the first draft in about two months around work and childcare: I had never had so much fun writing before and I just couldn't stay away.

My brilliant agent Hannah Todd did excellent and vital work in shaping this story with me, over several drafts and with superhuman levels of patience and insight. It just wouldn't exist without her. I want to thank her for being such a champion over the long, bumpy, long, unpredictable, long (did I mention long?) road to get here. Thanks also to Elinor Davies at the Madeleine Milburn Agency for all her brilliant edits and tireless help.

Thanks to JB for the nudge in the right direction.

There have been some dramatic downs on the path to

publishing this book, since that stormy night in 2023, but the one thing that always keeps me feeling 'up' is my gorgeous group of author friends. To Pernille Hughes I owe the hugest thanks for bringing me into the Love & Chocolate writers' group and for listening to every *single* excruciating twist in the tale along the way, all while remaining the fiercest cheerleader in the entire Romance world. To Andi, Nina, Lucy, Ru, Jules and Donna: thank you for always being in my corner, for really understanding the struggles and for celebrating each small win. You don't know how many times you've saved me from chucking in the towel. Here's to many more cake-based lunches for years to come.

For Kirsty Greenwood for always being funny as fuck, wise beyond her years and a true icon. Thank you for steering me onto the right path with my indie publishing. Again. Thank god you're still making room for me on your coattails.

To my OG besties Emma and Vanessa. There aren't words, really. You are my coven.

Thanks to my mum for being the best mum there ever has been and also sorry for the sex scenes in this book. And that I asked you to proofread it for me without factoring those bits in.

I'm hugely grateful for the talents of Rebecca Roy for her meticulous and sensitive copyedit and to Alexandra Allden for my *beautiful* cover. In both cases, I worried I would be an annoying client as an editor-turned-author but they bowled me over with their respective expertise. They are among the best in the whole business and they made the process as stress-free as could be.

I've set this novel (and its sequel) in an area of Devon that I love: East Prawle. I've been staying in nearby East

Portlemouth each summer for something like 16 years now but as they don't have a pub for me to centre my witchy world, I had to hop to the next lovely village over. My pub The Witch's Nose is a loving homage to The Pig's Nose and the many glorious afternoons and evenings I've spent there. If you ever get the chance to go to East Prawle *please* do – it's a rare beauty (and they really do have a basket of communal knitting in the pub, plus the NYE parties are legendary). I have taken some liberties with the layout of the village and its proximity to the sea but I've also written about curses and purple lightning so a little massaging of the truth is OK, to my mind.

To the whole Devon crew who are a massive part of why I love the place so much and why I wanted to set a whole fictional world there: we've gone from crab sandwiches and drunken nights to watching our next generation take up the dam-building mantle and that is my kind of wealth, right there. You know who you are. I love you all.

I have a really lovely husband. He doesn't get involved with the bookish side to me per se but he does roast a chicken like nobody's business, he makes me laugh every day and he will often point out the sensible thing amongst the publishing mess when I'm in a flap. He will never read this bit, unless I show him. And I'm not going to.

To Ella and Bill: if there is a deeper, mystical magic to the universe, then I think it probably sounds like the two of you laughing at some nonsense.

Finally (have you hung in this long? Good on you), the biggest of all the thanks to *you*, wonderful reader, who gave this author a chance. You've made my dreams come true by diving into these pages. Thank you, thank you.

CRAVING MORE MOLLAND MAGIC?!

Head over to www.carolinehoggauthor.co.uk to sign up for Caroline's newsletter and receive a FREE and EXCLUSIVE short story all about Temperance's early dating years . . .

Plus, you'll be the first to get sneak peeks of Book 2 in the series, cover reveals, competitions and more!

To make sure you get Book 2 the very second it's available, you can preorder it right here!

Also by

Caroline has also written five books under the penname of Poppy Dolan. Check out her (non-magical) romcoms in ebook:
The Bad Boyfriends Bootcamp
There's More to Life Than Cupcakes
The Bluebell Bunting Society
The Woolly Hat Knitting Club
Confessions of a First-Time Mum

Printed in Dunstable, United Kingdom

70578105R00183